THE HUSBAND'S SECRET

A PSYCHOLOGICAL THRILLER

FRANKLIN CHRISTOPHER

UNSTEREOTYPICAL PUBLISHING

ALSO BY FRANKLIN CHRISTOPHER

Psychological Thrillers

The Husband's Revenge

The Reflection

The Perfect Vow

TRIGGER WARNINGS

Dear readers,

After reading reviews and hearing back from some of you personally, I've decided to provide a list of potential triggers in this book:

Abortion
Miscarriage
Rape

I've done my best to handle these topics without being overly graphic. However, this book does contain some dark themes, so please read at your own risk. While I generally don't favor trigger warnings as they can sometimes spoil the plot, I've made an exception in this case to address readers' concerns.

I hope you enjoy the book.

SYNOPSIS

"He has a dark secret, but so does she.

Pamela Whitherspoon seemingly has it all—a stunning adopted daughter, a beautiful oceanfront home, and a wealthy, doting husband. But one void remains: a biological child of her own.

After multiple heartbreaking miscarriages, Pamela's dream of motherhood lies in tatters. With each pregnancy, her once-adoring husband Kyle grows increasingly cold and distant, inexplicably repelled by the prospect of fatherhood. His transformation from loving partner to virtual stranger leaves Pamela bewildered and devastated.

Their picture-perfect facade crumbles during a vicious argument about having children. In the aftermath, their housekeeper Chloe abruptly quits, cryptically alluding to something deeply disturbing she witnessed while cleaning the attic—something involving Kyle that she dares not speak aloud.

Driven by a mix of dread and curiosity, Pamela investigates. Hidden beneath a loose floorboard, she unearths a box of old VHS tapes. As she watches, Kyle's darkest secret unfolds before her eyes, shattering her world and filling her with a perverse relief that she never bore his child.

Now, Pamela faces an impossible choice: flee and bury the truth, or confront the monster she married and ensure he pays for his deception. In this chilling psychological thriller, she must navigate a labyrinth of lies to protect herself and her daughter from a danger closer than she ever imagined.

This Psychological thriller is perfect for fans of Freida McFadden, John Marrs, Lucinda Berry and Kiersten Modglin.

SIGN UP TO MY EMAIL LIST

SIGN up to my email list to get free stories and information on upcoming releases.

My Website

CHAPTER 1
KYLE

SOMEONE IS TRYING to kill my beautiful wife. The culprit? Her damn womb. To be honest, I don't care about her womb. I'm pretty happy she can't carry a child to term because I don't want—and never have wanted—children. It's just painful watching Pamela go through miscarriage after miscarriage, seeing the hope in her eyes die a little more each time—it's almost enough to make a man believe in curses.

Almost.

Our kitchen is a rainbow nightmare of streamers and tiny booties. Pamela bustles about, preparing for her friend Sheila's baby shower. The only problem is Sheila's not a real friend. She's one of those women who wishes she could have Pamela's life and hangs around just for the perks—like this shower that we were paying for–excuse me, that *I* am paying for. This is the third baby shower Pamela has planned this year, and frankly, I'm tired of footing the bill.

Most of these women are mothers at Marissa's school, and they are big supporters of her organic baby food business. A business that my wife doesn't need to own because, as a man, I take care of everything. She doesn't have to work because we come from money.

I watch my wife. There's a tension in her shoulders, a brittleness to her smile.

I spy her from the doorway, admiring how she moves with practiced efficiency. My wife is an average mocha-complected woman with beautiful skin. You'd think she would have acne with all the sugar she consumes, but her skin remains flawless. She has a certain grace about her, although she has gained weight over the years—about 31.7 pounds since our wedding day, to be exact. That's quite a bit of weight for someone 5'6. I secretly monitor her weight strictly for health reasons—of course. Pamela is not supermodel pretty, but attractive enough that I don't have to worry about too much competition. I hate competition. I'd rate her a 5.5/10 without makeup and a solid 8 with it—maybe a nine if she dropped the weight.

"Need any help, darling?" I ask, knowing full well she'll refuse. Pamela likes to do these things to prove she can handle everything.

She turns, startled by my presence. "Oh! No, I'm fine. Just finishing up the decorations."

I nod, moving closer to inspect her handiwork. The kitchen island is covered in multicolored miniature food items like candies, cakes, and everything sweet. It's all so... feminine. So maternal. So caloric.

It makes my skin crawl.

"It looks lovely," I lie because that's what good husbands do. "Sheila will be thrilled."

Pamela's smile wavers momentarily, and I can see the pain she's trying to hide. "I hope so," she says softly. "I want everything to be perfect."

Perfect. It's a word we use often in this house, a standard we both strive for. But perfection, as I've learned, is a moving target.

I watch as Pamela fusses with a bouquet of balloons, her movements becoming more agitated with each passing moment. I know what's coming–I've seen this dance before.

"I just feel so...damaged," she finally whispers, her voice cracking. "All of my friends are having babies and shopping for maternity clothes, and I'm still...barren. Despite all the steps we've taken." *She means the steps she's taken.* I don't want kids, and I've told her that, but if I tell her that now, the waterworks will start, and I just can't deal with my wife crying. It hurts me to see her cry.

I bite back the words that threaten to spill out. I want to tell her that maybe this is a sign, that perhaps we're not meant to be parents, that I'm content with just her, that she should be content with just me. But I'm not stupid. I know better than to voice these thoughts.

Instead, I move behind her, wrapping my arms around her softening waist and pudgy belly that I act like I love, even though it repulses me. I shrink stomachs for a living. I'm a personal trainer and nutritionist, but if I even mention her weight gain, it's no pussy for me, and I love her pussy. To be honest, it's been a while since we had sex. "Remember, all things work together for the good of those who love the Lord," I murmur, nuzzling her neck. "If it's in his will. It will happen." Bible verses make her feel better. My wife claims she's a Christian, but we're the type of Christians that show up to church on Easter and Christmas.

The lie tastes bitter on my tongue, but I swallow it down. It's what she needs to hear, after all. *Would it be wrong to get a vasectomy and not tell her? That would solve one problem but create another.*

Pamela leans back into me, seeking comfort. "I don't know what I'd do without you," she says. "What did I do to deserve such a fantastic and wonderful husband?"

You didn't do anything. I chose you Pamela.

I smile against her skin, breathing in the scent of her floral shampoo mixed with the sugary sweetness of the cupcakes she's been frosting. "I could say the same thing, darling," I reply, the lie smooth as silk on my tongue. She takes a bite of the cupcake, and I kindly smack her hand. "That is your third cupcake, Pamela, and you haven't even had dinner." She shot me a look that was a mixture of both sadness and hostility. "I digress."

As a man, it's my job to provide Pamela with shelter, an allowance for household things, and shopping money so she can keep herself nice and pretty for when we go out and mingle with other couples. It's a role I've perfected over the years—the caring and supportive husband.

But lately, it's been getting harder to maintain the facade.

Every time she talks about babies, I see our freedom slipping away. The quiet evenings, the spontaneous trips, the uninterrupted nights—all sacrificed on the altar of parenthood that includes Disney movies and microwave popcorn. I've tried to steer her away from that idea, suggesting we travel more and focus on our careers. But it's like she's possessed by this need to procreate. I've even bent my rule and allowed *her* to adopt Marissa, thinking that would quench her thirst for a child, but it only amplified it.

I'm seriously thinking about how much longer I can

keep up this charade. I chose Pamela because she was the type of woman who would never leave, the kind of woman I could mold to fit my ideal life. But now, her desperation for a child is threatening to destroy everything I've carefully built.

Pamela pulls away from me, returning to her task of arranging tiny cakes into the shape of diapers. I watch her, my mind drifting to darker places.

She's been adamant about building her business lately, even though we are rich. I'm talking about Will Smith and Jada Pinkett rich. Old money is what my mother calls it. She's supposed to submit to me and shouldn't have a say in the finances. But because her small baby food business is starting to turn a profit, she wants to start telling me how to invest and wants to know more about our accounts. That's my area to handle.

If she would just do her job and be content with the life I've given her, we wouldn't be in this mess. But she's stubborn, set in her ways. If she doesn't change course, I'll have to take drastic measures. She has no idea what I'm capable of.

My thoughts are interrupted by the sound of the doorbell. I roll my eyes. Here are the other two women helping make my life a living hell. Her reinforcements—my sister, Donna, the nanny Chloe, and Marissa, the daughter I never wanted.

"Hey, brother," Donna says, kissing me on the cheek. "I'm so proud of you," she whispers in my ear and rushes into the house with a handful of bags. She knows I don't want kids. Everybody knows, but my internally flawed wife doesn't care.

Chloe comes in behind her with Marissa. I don't get why she has to hold a six-year-old's hand. She smiles at me as if she's flirting but shouldn't because if Pamela ever catches her flirting with me, she'll kill her. She tried to get me to hire a male nanny, but I didn't want another man in my house, gay or straight. I needed to be the only masculine authority under this roof. As I watch them bustling about preparing for a baby shower and spending my money, I become annoyed.

Women were made to be men's helpmates and tend to their every need. It's their function and why they were created. God made woman from man and for man. Her entire existence is an extension of me. Wo-man. Female. The words that describe her have the male identity wrapped in them. *So why can't they accept their identity and fall into line? Why can't Pamela just obey me?*

A wise person once told me to find a woman who loves me more than I love her and that she would never leave. I followed their advice and did just that. I found a good southern girl who loved me and could keep a good house. I chose Pamela because she was the type of woman I could control. At least, that's what I thought.

But if I don't do something soon, I'm going to find myself in a desireless marriage with a 300lb wife. I fight so hard for us, for this perfect, childless life we've built.

"Kyle?" Pamela's voice pulls me from my thoughts. "Could you help me hang this banner?"

I paste on my most charming smile, which used to make her weak in the knees. "Of course, anything for you."

As I help her stretch the "Congratulations, Mommy-to-Be!" banner across the archway, I can't help but notice the way Pamela's eyes linger on the words. The longing in her gaze is palpable, a hunger I'm beginning to resent.

"It's going to be a lovely party," I say, trying to distract her. "Sheila's lucky to have a friend like you."

Pamela nods, but I can see the tears threatening to spill over. "I just...I wish it were me," she whispers. Now, the waterworks begin. Donna and Chloe quickly run over to Pamela and become her emotional anchors. "Is that terrible of me? To be jealous of my friend?"

"No. These are normal feelings. I get jealous of my friends all the time," Donna says.

"Mommy, can I pray for you?" Marissa asks.

"Yes," Pamela says, with a look of hope in her eyes. Marissa puts her hand on Pamela's stomach.

"Dear God, please bless Mommy with a baby in her tummy so I can have a little sister. Amen."

"That is so sweet, darling. Thank you for that. It makes Mommy feel so much better."

I loathe this child. She might be a perfect addition to another family, but she gives my wife hope for a child I don't want. I hold in my true feelings and walk toward my wife.

I pull her into an embrace, stroking her hair as she fights back sobs. "Donna is right. It's natural to feel that way. Your time will come."

The words taste like shit in my mouth. I don't want her time to come.

If Pamela can't let go of this obsession with having a baby, perhaps I need to take control.

The thought should shock me, should fill me with guilt. But instead, I feel a sense of calm wash over me.

"Why don't you freshen up? Everything is perfect for the party tomorrow. I'll get started on dinner," Chloe says.

Pamela nods, wiping at her eyes. "You're right. What would I do without you all."

As she heads upstairs, I survey the room. Everything is perfect, just as Pamela wanted. But it comes at a price.

And I'm wondering how much I will pay to maintain this childless paradise I've created. How far am I willing to go to keep Pamela focused solely on me and to keep our life exactly as I want it?

As I hear the shower start upstairs, I make a decision. It's time to take charge of this situation once and for all. After all, isn't that what a good husband does? It's either me or the baby, and I'm not going anywhere.

CHAPTER 2
KYLE

THE GYM IS PULSING with energy as the rhythmic clanging of weights, and the low hum of treadmills create a familiar backdrop. I stand by the weight rack, shirtless, sweat glistening on my well-defined abs. This is my domain, the kingdom I've chosen.

"Damn, Kyle," Jake, one of my personal training buddies, whistled. "You're looking ripped, man."

I grin, flexing slightly. "Just clean eating and hard work, brother. No shortcuts, no magic pills. That's the real path to health."

A group of women on their way to a spin class walks by as if on cue. Their eyes linger on my torso, and a petite redhead who looks like a mix between Beyonce and JLo reaches out to brush her hand against my arm until she caresses my chest.

"Nice tattoo," she purrs, her fingers tracing the cross inked on my biceps. "I love a melanated man with a spiritual side."

I give her a polite nod, maintaining my carefully crafted image. "Thank you. I chose the cross because I'm a Christian," I reply. Inside my mind, I have bent her over and have already given her all the dick she craves, but in real life, I cannot flirt with her.

As the women giggle and move on, my co-worker, Mike, nudges me.

"Dude, she had her hands all over you. You should hit that."

I frown, shaking my head. "Come on, man. You know I'm married."

"So? What Pamela doesn't know won't hurt her," Mike presses. "Live a little, Kyle. You're too hot to be tied down to one chick."

"What about that big booty goddess over there that's eyeing you?" Jake asks.

"That's not who I am anymore," I say, injecting just the right amount of indignation into my voice. "I made a vow before God and my wife. I intend to honor it."

Jake rolls his eyes. "Whatever, Saint Kyle. Your loss and my gain. Since you won't be taking that beautiful redhead up on her offer, I will."

Anger bubbles underneath my skin. I hate when my guy friends go after girls that want me. "Go right ahead. If you got the game to get her."

He pauses, eyeing me curiously. "I still can't believe you walked away from med school for this gig. Don't you ever regret it?"

I shake my head, launching into the explanation I'd rehearsed countless times. "Not for a second. In med school, all I saw were doctors pushing pills, treating symptoms instead of causes. Here, I can make a difference. I can help people take control of their health and their lives."

"Plus," Mike chimes in with a smirk, "the view's probably better here than in some hospital."

I laugh, playing along. "That's just a bonus, brother. I'm all about the holistic approach to wellness."

Jake wasn't letting it go, though. "But seriously, man. You were on track to be a doctor. That's a hell of a thing to walk away from."

I sigh, allowing a carefully measured amount of vulnerability to show. "Look, it wasn't an easy decision. But after I weighed the pros and the cons, I just couldn't be part of that system anymore. Besides, I don't need the money. I do this for the joy."

"I remember you talking about that," Jake nods sympathetically. "That must have been tough."

"It was," I agree. "But it opened my eyes. And then there was Dr. Harrison, my mentor. He showed me there was another way to help people, a better way."

"And Pamela?" Mike asks. "How'd she take it when you decided to quit?"

A genuine smile crosses my face at the memory. "Pamela's incredible. She encourages me to follow my dreams and believes in my vision of helping people through fitness and nutrition. Her support makes all the difference."

I don't tell them how Pamela's unwavering faith in me made it so easy to manipulate her, molding her into the perfect, supportive wife I need her to be. As I reach for my water bottle, I catch the time. Shit. The baby shower. I completely forgot about picking up my tux.

"Gotta run, boys," I say, grabbing my gym bag. "Forgot I have an errand to run before the shower."

"Shower?" Mike asks, confused.

"Baby shower," I clarify. "For Pamela's friend."

"You didn't invite us?" Mike asks.

"Married couples only, guys."

The guys exchange knowing looks. "Man, when are you two going to have a kid of your own?" Jake asks. "You're not getting any younger, you know."

I force a laugh, hiding the tension his words stir in me. "All in God's timing, brother. We're in no rush."

As I head for the door, I call back over my shoulder, "Are we still on for the game next week?"

"As long as it's at your place," Mike replies.

"My place it is," I say.

The gym door closes behind me, and I let out a long breath. Another reminder of the tightrope I walk every day.

But as I climb into my black-on-black Bentley Coupe, I push those thoughts aside. I have a tux to pick up and a baby shower to attend. The perfect husband routine never ends, it seems. For now, I must keep playing my part—the caring personal trainer and nutritionist, the devoted husband, the man who turns his back on a prestigious medical career to "help people." If they only knew the real reason, I couldn't stand the thought of bringing new life into this world.

CHAPTER 3
PAMELA

THE HOUSE IS PERFECTLY DECORATED, its grandeur befitting a luxurious San Diego estate. I attend to hosting duties, and Henry, my mother-in-law's butler, oversees the event, ensuring everything runs smoothly. The foyer welcomes guests with soaring ceilings and a magnificent globe crystal chandelier that casts psychedelic light across the Calacatta marble floors. As we walk deeper through the house, we are met with a sweeping staircase with an intricately carved mahogany banister, outlined in gold outlining, that curves gracefully to the second floor.

The room boasts floor-to-ceiling windows that frame breathtaking views of the Pacific Ocean. Plush cream-colored sofas and armchairs are artfully arranged around a statement fireplace adorned with hand-painted Mexican tiles, blending California's Spanish heritage with modern luxury. As guests continue to pour in, I wonder where Kyle is. He should be here by now.

The 24-karat gold-plated grandfather clock in our bedroom strikes 8:00 p.m., and its resonant chimes echo through our master suite. My heart races as I carefully tuck the pregnancy test underneath the trash bag inside the ornate crystal waste bin in our marble-tiled bathroom. This is the only place I can think to hide it until I have time to smuggle the telltale packaging out of our meticulously curated home. It has to be incinerated, obliterated —any trace of its existence can potentially shatter our nearly perfect marriage.

If Kyle stumbles upon a pregnancy test in this house, it will unravel all the painstaking progress we've made since my last devastating miscarriage. He'll spiral into thinking he isn't enough for me when, in reality, he is more than I ever dreamed of. Something fractured within me yesterday while planning this godforsaken baby shower. I found myself babbling about pregnancy in front of Kyle, fully aware of his aversion to the idea of children. I always become this way when I suspect I am pregnant or when surrounded by the pastel-hued, soft-edged world of baby paraphernalia.

My fingers tremble as I smooth my Hermès white dress, trying to quell the butterflies in my stomach—butterflies that are something more. I spray Kyle's cologne and deeply inhale his familiar scent. I often do this when I need to feel or sense his presence around me. Our life together is a masterpiece of calculated perfection, each brushstroke carefully applied over years of compromise and unspoken agreements. But now, with this new life growing inside me, I fear I might have accidentally thrown paint across our pristine canvas.

Kyle is my everything. My king. My knight in shining armor. He's my savior from a life previously riddled with mediocrity and poverty. I pinch my thigh hard. The sharp pain anchors me to the present but also serves as a reminder that this is my reality. I live in a 6,000 square-foot home in San Diego that overlooks the ocean; I have more money than I can spend and a gorgeous husband who absolutely adores me despite my average appearance that is enhanced by expensive makeup, clothing, and the best hairdressers our money can afford. I take a deep breath, give the bathroom one last glance to ensure I have left no trace of evidence, and prepare to go mingle with my house full of guests.

I stand at the top of my spiraled steps as my gaze sweeps over the multitude of guests, their laughter a melodious orchestra against the backdrop of my thoughts. I take a deep breath, appreciating the ocean breeze air freshener that sprays every fifteen minutes. This is the third baby shower I've hosted this year. Here I am in my overly expensive dress, draped in intrinsically flawless diamonds from head to toe.

I smile—all teeth and no warmth—as the servers refill crystal flutes with champagne I dare not drink. Sheila, my best friend—if such a term still holds meaning—sits in the place of honor. I've thrown myself into these celebrations, thinking if I surround myself with enough fertility, it might rub off on me—a modern-day rain dance in Louboutins.

The dress is formal, and everyone who is of any importance to Sheila is in attendance. I let her and her husband, Devon—a man I'm not fond of — invite whoever they desired. I had to plan this shower quickly because Devon is in the Navy and is going to be deployed the day after the shower. My only rule was married couples only. I don't want Kyle's mediocre and poverty-laden friends hitting on women who are completely out of their league and off the market.

This is Sheila and Devon's first child, and although I'm happy for her, jealousy devours me like a cancer. Most of the women in attendance are young, newly married women who are hoping to be mothers. I have the most attractive husband out of them all, the biggest house, and a husband who makes me orgasm every time we have sex, yet I still feel inferior—a sufferer of imposter syndrome in my own home.

It's why I need Kyle here. I'm a princess and the most beautiful woman in the world in his presence. Even with my mediocre appearance, he makes me feel beautiful. I despise solitude with pregnant couples. It makes me feel like a fraud masquerading as a mother. I love my adopted daughter, Marissa, but she doesn't have any part of me or Kyle in her DNA, and while I love her, it can't erase the longing I feel to experience pregnancy and see a child born with our features.

If Kyle and I separate, there will be nothing that ties me to him. Nothing that says this man was once mine. I want a child, but not just any child. I want Kyle's child. Giving birth to a man's baby is the one supreme act a woman can do for her husband, and my husband doesn't want that from me. Sometimes, I wonder if he wants children, but he just says he doesn't because we have trouble getting pregnant.

My husband is physically perfect, and in real life, a woman like me isn't supposed to be with a man like him.

A man who has never cheated on me, has green eyes, curly hair, and a body that would make Hollywood movie stars jealous. Now take all of that goodness and wrap it in extreme wealth and bundle it with an incredible sex life, and you have my husband. He is external and internal perfection, and if we ever divorce, my next man will be a step-down and pale in comparison. This is why I wonder where he is. It isn't because I don't trust him; it's because I don't trust women around him. I don't trust anyone around Kyle.

Ninety percent of the women at this baby shower are here to see him. Well, they are here to see him and to taste the one-of-a-kind homemade cuisine that Chloe assisted me in preparing. She and Marissa are at Sea World with one of Marissa's classmates and are having a Disney sleepover at a hotel so Kyle and I can host this adult and married-only baby shower.

I'm not the most attractive woman that Kyle has dated; I'm probably the least attractive if I'm being honest. But what I lack in physical attributes, I make up for in the kitchen. I know how to cook and be hospitable, all thanks to my pitiful excuse of a mother. She failed me in all areas except cooking for a man and keeping a home. Every dish in this house is made by me—from the fried lobster tails, sweet potato casserole, and truffle butter mashed potatoes to the creamed spinach and banana pudding cake with accompanying cupcakes. Cooking is my love language, and that's why my organic baby food business is slowly turning into an overnight success.

I check my watch. My husband, Kyle, should be here by now. But he isn't. My phone buzzes, and when I look at my text, I know He's with her—the redhead with haunting emerald eyes and a smile that conceals daggers. I despise women like her, these cheap whores posing as clients. She doesn't need to lose weight; she wants to climb on top of my husband's dick. I know her game because I've seen it played before. Hell, I've played it before in my slimmer, more youthful days. The investigator's photos are my daily dose of poison—glossy prints showcasing her desperate "accidental" touches, the way her eyes devour Kyle like he is her last meal. She wants to fuck him, and I can't blame her. Everyone wants to fuck my husband. Men and women.

She's lucky I'm a Christian because if I wasn't, let's just say I wouldn't be against meeting her in an alley one late night with a sock full of nickels. The whore claims she is trying to lose weight for her ten-year reunion, but there isn't one ounce of fat on her. I despise skinny bitches like her. He's married, and she knows this because he never—and I mean never—removes his wedding ring. I normally trust my husband, but it's starting to be hard to trust a man who's so good-looking like Kyle. Even when a man like him desires to stay faithful, the temptation from these hussies is strong for even the best men to fall. But after almost ten years of marriage, he has never cheated, and I know this because of a private investigator I have on retainer.

While I wait for him to arrive, my mother-in-law spots me from downstairs and makes her way toward me. Most times, mothers-in-law and daughters-in-law don't get along, but Beatrice is different. She sticks up for me, and to be honest, I think she likes me more than Kyle. When she reaches the top of the steps, she grabs my hand and holds it tightly. She is the mother that I wish I had.

"I don't know why you do this to yourself," she says. I shrug my shoulders.

"Some part of me believes that if I do kind things for pregnant women, that kindness will come back to me." I place my hand over my stomach, and a tear falls from my eye.

Beatrice grips my hand tighter. "Do you know?"

"Yes, I just took the test a few minutes ago."

Beatrice turns to me, her face a concoction of concern and empathy. "Pamela, I love you, but if I were you, I'd leave my son now and take my child with me. Do I need to remind you of the last time he found out you were pregnant?"

"Beatrice, that was over two years ago, and it was an accident."

"An accident that could have been avoided."

"Mama Witherspoon, he made a mistake."

"Tell yourself whatever you need to sleep at night on those Egyptian one-thousand-thread-count sheets. Our memories get fuzzy when money is involved. I know my son; either you need to accept the fact that he doesn't want children or leave him. We will make sure you are taken care of financially for life. You, Marissa, and the unborn child."

Just as I'm about to rebut her statement, my phone buzzes. The tracker placed in Kyle's car shows that he is only a few feet away. Some might call it invasive; I call it insurance.

The creak of the front door silences the room. Kyle steps in, his gym clothes a stark contrast to the black-tie atmosphere. A chorus of held breaths follows his entrance —he has that effect on people, on women. His gaze wanders across the room, and for a moment, I see a flicker of something in those green depths. Guilt? Annoyance? Before I can decipher it, his trademark smile blazes to life, dazzling our guests. I feel the stares boring into me. They all wonder the same thing: *How did someone like me end up with him?* Kyle is an Adonis carved from marble, and I am...well, I am the girl who knows how to make a mean pot roast.

He weaves through the crowd with the grace of a

lioness. I wonder why my beautiful, perfect husband fell for a homely girl like me. His eyes quickly dart up to me and his mother while my hand is still rubbing my stomach. I quickly remove it and watch as his beautiful, perfect smile melts from his face.

CHAPTER 4
KYLE

THIS BITCH IS PREGNANT. She's fucking pregnant again. That's all I can think about as I change into my tuxedo. I know I shouldn't have been so nice to her yesterday when she was preparing for this party. I should have spoken my mind. But that would have led to an argument, and it wouldn't have stopped the pregnancy from happening.

After I repeatedly tell her I don't want children, she defies me and gets herself pregnant. The rage boils inside me, a violent urge to push her down the stairs surging through my veins. Of course, I could never act on these impulses because I have a reputation and family image to uphold. Being a woman-beater isn't something any man can recover from, not even a guy as good-looking as me.

I gave Pamela numerous options: she could get her tubes tied, use birth control, take the morning-after pill, or get an abortion. She has a plethora of choices, but she refuses to obey the most crucial rule in our agreement—no fucking children. And now she's conspiring with my mother and sister on ways to soften me to the idea of a bouncing bundle of joy that I have no desire to have. I curse the day they all met. I hate that they're so close, and I'm the outcast. *Why am I the outcast in my home? Why is no one listening to what I want?* I take a deep breath and pop two pills in my mouth, followed by a few gulps of water to calm myself and bring myself back to a calm disposition.

Men only want a few things from a woman. First, we want to make sure she has good pussy. Pamela's pussy is top-tier. Her vagina molds to my dick, and we satisfy each other like no one else in this world could. She makes me feel better than any woman I've ever slept with, and I've slept with more than my fair share.

The second thing a man wants is for his woman and mother to get along. While Pamela and I were courting, I consistently asked myself, *Is this girl going to pass the mother test?* She surprised me and passed with flying colors. She and my mother get along *too* well. For most men, this would be enough, but there were two other critical factors that *I* needed to be met: she needed to love me more than she loved herself, and she had to be content with no children. Her being a good cook, keeping a clean house, and being mildly pretty were bonuses.

I never wanted a girl that was supermodel pretty. I had enough pretty for the both of us, and I didn't want men looking at my woman. I don't like competition. And now, I'll have to compete for my wife's attention with a child?

Motherhood ruins marriages. First, the body goes, then the sex, and next thing you know, your date nights are filled with juvenile activities. And let's not talk about the sleep deprivation and the lack of fellatio. I'm a personal trainer and amateur bodybuilder, and in order for me to look the way I do, I need my sleep, and I need my daily fellatio. Having children would change the trajectory of how I live my life, so I made a decision early on that I would not have them. I told Pamela when I met her that I would give her the world if she promised me three things:

Remain faithful.

Never get pregnant.

Never deny me sex unless she was physically ill or it was that time of the month.

I promised her that, in turn, I would provide her with a more than comfortable living. I keep up my end of the bargain, but she consistently fails to keep up hers. Despite not having to work, she is adamant about having a catering business where she only hosts baby showers. It's like she is purposely trying to force the idea of children down my throat. Now, she's had the idea to start an organic baby food line, and whenever I come home, she makes me taste all the flavors. The food is fantastic, but it feels like she's taunting me, purposely trying to warm me up to the idea of her being pregnant. If I ask any questions or tell her how I truly feel the waterworks start.

All she had to do was those three things, but she broke the agreement. She doesn't realize she's wrecking our marriage, and if she doesn't stop, we won't have anything left to hold on to. I rarely mention her over thirty-pound weight gain, and even though she'd been pregnant twice due to missed birth control pills, I didn't leave her for another woman even though I had every right to.

I forgave her.

I even agreed to adopt a child for her in our third year of marriage because she insisted she needed to be maternal. But every time I give her an inch, she goes a mile, and now I have to come home to the third baby shower this year and act like I love children and pregnant women when the whole thought of having a child and being around a pregnant Pamela repulses me.

I smile and shake hands with the guests while I watch my wife and mother talk and conspire against me. When my wife sees me, she quickly takes her hand off her stomach. Now I'm going to look like an insensitive bastard when I have to kindly and sternly remind her of our agreement.

Anger boils below my perfect smile. Just as I head up the stairs to talk to my wife, Sheila, the lady of the hour, grabs my hand and pulls me into a side room away from the party.

"Kyle, I'm glad you could make it. I thought you'd never arrive." She reaches down and grabs my cock as I push her hand away.

"I had a personal training session run over," I say, removing her hand from my forbidden area.

"Maybe you can help whip me back into shape after I have this child. A girl like me doesn't mind being worked out hard every now and then."

A sardonic chuckle escapes my lips as I level Sheila with a look of patronizing disbelief. "Sheila, sex between us is never happening again."

"We now share a child together, Kyle."

"I want nothing to do with you or that child, and if you don't back off, your husband will find an old video of you riding my dick and screaming my name. Rumor has it he beats his women." I unhook my arms from hers, allowing my eyes to rake over her overly made-up face and the Dolce & Gabbana hand-me-down she received from Pamela that clings to her pregnant body like a second skin.

"Kyle, you said you loved me. I did everything you wanted, and I didn't judge you for your weird proclivities. I'm better looking and have a better body than Pamela. I should be your wife. She can't even give you children."

I turn back toward her. "Now Sheila, you know we men throw around the word love amid an erotic moment. Every depraved man-whore within a five-block radius has no doubt entered and exited the temple between those legs. And need I remind you of the consequences awaiting any who dare trespass against my beloved Pamela's explicit boundaries?" I pause, smirking at her visible shudder. "So, for both our sakes, I suggest burying these depraved little fantasies, hmm? Lest the next hole both of us are in is a grave."

Sheila takes a few steps away from me, embarrassed that she attempted to flirt with me.

"If you keep ignoring me, I'll tell her the truth. I'll tell her everything." Sheila grabs a glass and a fork from one of the serving tables, strikes the side of it to get everyone's attention, and heads into the living room, where our guests are mingling. "Excuse me, everyone. Excuse me, everyone. I'd like to make a toast."

I lean in toward her and whisper, "Bitch, I will gut you and that child tonight if you even think about embarrassing me and my wife in my own home. It's fucking over. I love her in a way that I'll never love you."

I kindly grab a glass of champagne from the server's tray and gesture toward Pamela.

"Pamela, can you come down here and grace us with your beautiful presence?" Pamela seems surprised, and she should be because I only did this to stop Sheila from embarrassing us. I watch as my gorgeous wife walks down our spiraled steps. Her mocha skin glistens under the expansive chandelier lights. Makeup makes her capable of competing with every woman here.

"I'm amazed by this woman. Most of you are aware of our struggles with infertility, and despite that, this woman continues to host baby showers for her friends when we haven't even had a child of our own yet. Pamela, this is why I love you. I know you are the only woman for me. You put others' feelings before your own, and I know you are going to be a fabulous mother to our second child. I pray that God grants us the wish we so desire." I lean forward and place a kiss on her beautiful, full lips, watching as her once dry eyes now fill with tears.

Sheila looks like she is about to burst into tears and leaves the living room.

Pamela grabs my hand tightly before speaking. "My husband always knows just the right words to say at the appropriate time. It's why I love him. Never has he said an unkind word to me. Now, it looks like I have an announcement to make. This evening, I took a pregnancy test, and Kyle and I are expecting. I thought about holding the news, but I'm so excited I can't contain it. I'm six weeks pregnant. Kyle, God has answered our prayer." I stare at my wife for a few seconds, my mind racing. Her words echo in my head: *God has answered our prayer*. My prayer was never for a child. I force a smile, pulling her into an embrace and acting surprised and delighted about the news. Inside, I'm seething.

What kind of psycho did I marry, and how am I going to force her to get rid of this thing?

After the party, the guests filter out, leaving behind the remnants of their joy and laughter. Pamela is glowing, her smile radiant as she hugs her friends goodbye. I keep up appearances, shaking hands and thanking people for coming. Inside, my anger simmers, barely contained.

Once the last guest leaves, I turn to Pamela, my smile dropping. "We need to talk," I say, my voice low and controlled.

Pamela looks at me, confusion flickering across her face. "Kyle, what's wrong? I thought you'd be happy."

I lead Pamela into our bedroom, closing the door behind us. The silence in the room is heavy, pressing down on me.

"Happy? You thought I'd be happy? Pamela, we had an agreement."

Her eyes fill with tears, and she reaches for me, but I step back. "Kyle, please. I thought maybe you'd changed your mind. I thought—"

"You thought wrong." My voice is cold, cutting through her words. "I don't want children. I've never wanted children. And you went behind my back and got pregnant again."

Pamela's tears spill over, running down her cheeks.

"Went behind your back? Kyle, I love you. I want a family with you. I thought—"

"I don't care what you thought," I snap, the anger finally breaking through. "You broke our agreement. And now you're going to fix it."

Her eyes widen, and she shakes her head. "No, Kyle. I can't. I won't."

I step closer, my voice dropping to a dangerous whisper. "You will. You will get rid of this pregnancy, or there will be consequences."

Pamela's face crumples, and she collapses onto the bed, sobbing.

I stand there watching her. My heart a cold and unfeeling lump in my chest. I must maintain control. I must make her see reason. I leave our bedroom and head to the only place that can bring me back to equilibrium—my man cave, the attic.

CHAPTER 5
KYLE

THE ATTIC'S musty air clings to me like a second skin as I marinate here, my mind a maelstrom of conflicting emotions. Pamela's revelation echoes in my ears, a constant reminder of the betrayal gnaws at my core. I've been up for five hours. Sleep eludes me, my body restless with pent-up energy and simmering rage. I grab my pills out of my dresser drawer and swallow them with a big gulp of water.

As I lie on my sofa, staring at the ceiling, my second cell phone buzzes. Only a select group of people have this number, and Pamela isn't one of them. My heart rate quickens as I read the message: *"Meet me at the gym in an hour."* I slip the phone into my gym bag, setting it to silent.

The first hints of dawn creep across the sky as I slip out of the house, careful not to wake Pamela. The cool ocean morning air bites at my skin, a sharp contrast to the heat building inside me. I breathe it in deeply, savoring the familiar routine of my early gym sessions. It offers a semblance of control in a world that's spinning out of my grasp. I thought about going for my morning run along the boardwalk, but I need a different kind of workout this morning. A memory of my father pulls me toward the ocean. I make my way down the wooden steps to our private beach. The sea stretches before me, an endless canvas of blue-green possibility.

I take off my shoes and dig my toes into the cool sand, feeling the grains shift beneath my feet. The salty breeze whips around me, carrying the rhythmic sound of crashing waves. I close my eyes and breathe deeply, trying to center myself.

Unbidden memories of my father flood back. I can almost hear his hearty laugh, see his sun-weathered face crinkling with joy as we get on our boat with our family of animals—dogs and cats who never fight. That was the first thing she made me get rid of when he died all my beautiful animals. She said just looking at them made her sick. The ache of his loss hits me anew, a physical pain in my chest. He loved me unconditionally, but my mother...she only tolerated me.

Bitterness rises like bile in my throat as I think of my mother. Her stern face, her cold eyes as she told me I couldn't see him one last time. "You don't need to remember him like that," she'd said, her voice brooking no argument. I clench my fists, anger pulsing through me at the memory.

My thoughts drift to Aunt Eleanor, my father's sister. I rarely see her and when I do it's never without my mother present. Mom and Eleanor never got along; I could feel the tension even as a kid. After Dad died, Mom wasted no time cutting off that entire side of the family. Sometimes I wonder about my cousins, about the family gatherings I'm missing out on. But that bridge was burned long ago, leaving me stranded on this island of my mother's making.

As I stand there, letting the rhythmic crash of waves wash over me, I feel a sense of calm slowly seeping into my bones. The tension in my shoulders eases slightly. I make my decision. I'll go to the gym, work out this restless energy, and clear my head. Then I'll deal with... everything else. One problem at a time, I tell myself.

Just as I'm about to leave the ocean a seagull flies toward me. I reach in my pocket and pull out a bag of nuts that I always keep on me just in case I get hungry, and I watch as it eats out of my hand. As it eats out of my right hand, I look around to make sure I'm alone. When the coast is clear. I grab its neck with my left hand and then twist it with both hands until its dead. I watch as the noises it makes slowly decreases and the life slowly drains from its body.

Adrenaline surges through my body and a peace comes over me. I haven't done this since I was a child, and I can't believe how much I miss it. How much I need it. I remove my shirt and wrap up the dead bird with it and put it in the car. I walk to the ocean and clean the blood from my hands and then put on my spare tank top that I keep in the trunk. I feel calm; more in control. The drive to the gym is short, my mind churning with plans and possibilities the entire way. As I pull into the parking lot, I notice it's nearly empty, save for a single vehicle.

I sit in my car for a long moment, hand hovering over the door handle. I know I should turn around, go home, and face my problems head-on. But the pull is too strong. I've satisfied my need for blood now I need to satisfy my need for sex.

With a deep breath, I step out of the car. As I walk

towards the gym entrance, I feel a familiar mix of anticipation and guilt coursing through my veins. I'm about to lose myself in the only way I truly know how, consequences be damned. All this is Pamela's fault, her pregnancy was the trigger. It's awakening my inner demon.

The men's locker room lights buzz overhead as I strip naked, my movements deliberate. I pause and look at my beautiful physique in the mirror. I am visual perfection. I'm tall, masculine, hairy in all the right places, caked in defined muscle from head to toe and I have a big dick that gives women instant orgasms the moment it enters inside their sacred temple.

I watch as men ogle at me as they passed by. Some admiring me while others want me to fuck them. I can see it as they gaze into my green eyes. I've never fucked a dude, but the idea of making a grown man submit does turn me on. It's not really about attraction or being gay. It's about control. I always need to be in control. I look closer in the mirror and notice a grey hair and realize that I will immediately need to take care of that. It's important that I don't look my age. Youth is beauty in this world. The soft patter of water from the shower area reaches my ears. I can smell her perfume already—an intoxicating mix of lavender and something darker, more dangerous. It's a scent that lingers on my skin long after we part, a constant reminder of my betrayal.

Cindy's waiting for me.

Steam billows around me as I enter the shower stall, enveloping the lithe figure before me. Cindy's red hair clings to her shoulders, water droplets tracing paths down her pale skin that I ache to follow with my tongue. Our eyes meet, a silent understanding passing between us.

"You texted," I say.

"It's been over two weeks since our last session. I needed you," she replies.

I step closer; the heat of the water doesn't compare to the fire building inside me. "I've been working through some things," I admit. "I miss your body, baby."

"After you left me, I didn't think I'd see you again. You left me all alone, Kyle."

"I always planned on seeing you again, and I'm here now. We just have to be careful so that my wife and mother don't find out."

In one fluid motion, I lift Cindy, her legs wrapping around my waist. I enter her with a forceful thrust, eliciting a gasp that echoes off the tiled walls. Our bodies move in a frenzied rhythm, the hot water cascading over us, washing away the guilt and shame that cling to our skin. I bounce her up and down on my manhood for what seems like an hour as moans fall from her lips in elevated tones.

"You want to have my baby, don't you?" I growl, my voice low and dangerous as I carefully lick on her nipples and caress her breast.

Cindy's nails dig into my shoulders, her breath coming in short gasps. "Yes, Kyle. I want you, and yes, I want to have your babies. Please don't stop. I need you inside me."

A dark chuckle escapes my lips. "Call me Daddy, baby."

"Yes, Daddy Kyle," she moans, her body gliding against mine.

The shower stall becomes our own private universe,

the outside world fading away. I lose myself in the sensation, in the power I hold over Cindy. Here in this steamy sanctuary, I'm not the man struggling with his wife's unexpected pregnancy. I'm a god, worshiped and obeyed.

As our climax approaches, my thrusts become more erratic, more desperate. With a final, guttural groan, I spill myself inside her, our bodies shuddering with release. Cindy's hands travel over every inch of my body, mesmerized by my physique. I haven't been appreciated this way in a while, and the feeling is intoxicating. Her sex doesn't compare to Pamela's, but she's a very close second.

We stand there for a moment, panting, the water washing away the evidence of our transgression. As the fog of lust begins to clear, I notice a change in Cindy's demeanor. Her usual glow is replaced by a nervous energy, her eyes darting away from my gaze.

"What's wrong?" I ask, a note of concern creeping into my voice. Cindy bites her lip, hesitating. "Kyle, I have something to tell you. Please don't be mad."

A cold dread settles in the pit of my stomach. "What is it?"

"I'm pregnant."

The words hang in the air between us, heavy with implication. My mind races, images flashing before my eyes—Pamela's tearful announcement, the shocked faces of our party guests, and now this. *Two women pregnant? Allegedly?*

But instead of the panic I expect to feel, a strange calm washes over me. A smile spreads across my face as I pull Cindy close, pressing a kiss to her forehead.

"That's great news," I murmur, my voice thick with emotion. "My wife can't give me babies. That's why I'm leaving her for you. I can't wait to share my life with you."

Relief floods Cindy's features as my lips trail down her neck, across her collarbone, and finally to her breast. I lavish attention on her, my tongue tracing circles around her nipple as my hand caresses the slight swell of her belly.

Sinking to my knees, I press my face between Cindy's thighs, my tongue exploring her most intimate areas. Her intense and loud moans turn me on. My tongue develops a mind of its own as it explores the unending depths of her vagina. As I lose myself in the act, a part of my mind whispers that this is Pamela's fault. *If I had been enough for her, I wouldn't have had to seek satisfaction elsewhere.*

The water begins to run cold, jolting us back to reality. We dry off in silence, the weight of our secret hanging between us. As we dress, stolen glances and lingering touches speak of promises yet to be fulfilled.

In the locker room, I pull Cindy close for one last kiss. "I'll call you later," I whisper, my breath hot against her ear. "We have a lot to discuss, Mrs. Witherspoon." *Women love to be called by the last name of the men they are fucking.* Cindy looks at me with a hunger I haven't seen before. She stands on her tiptoes and kisses me again.

"You really mean that, Kyle?"

"Of course."

"Just don't leave me this time."

"I'll never leave you again," I assure her.

As I watch her get dressed, a mix of emotions swirls within me. And beneath it all, a darker current stir—a hunger that neither woman can fully satisfy.

My phone buzzes in my pocket.

A text from Pamela: "Where are you? I want to talk."

My jaw clenches as I read the message. Yes, we do need to talk, but not about what Pamela thinks. As I slide into my car, my mind races with possibilities and, more pressingly, how I will keep my urges in check long enough to navigate this delicate situation.

As I pull out of the parking lot, my reflection catches my eye in the rearview mirror. For a moment, I barely recognize the man staring back at me—eyes wild with a mixture of lust and panic, a predatory smile playing at the corners of my mouth.

The drive home feels interminable, each mile bringing me closer to a confrontation I both dread and crave. By the time I pull into the driveway, my hands are shaking with a potent cocktail of adrenaline and anticipation.

Pamela is waiting for me in the kitchen, her face a mask of worry and hurt. "Where have you been?" she asks, her voice trembling slightly. I force a smile, stepping forward to place a kiss on her cheek. Pamela's eyes search my face, looking for something—reassurance, perhaps, or a sign of the man she thought she had married. "Kyle, we need to talk about the baby. About our future."

For a moment, I consider coming clean, telling Pamela everything—about my relationships with Cindy and Sheila. But as I open my mouth to speak, I catch sight of my reflection in the kitchen window.

The man staring back at me isn't the Kyle that Pamela knows. It's someone else entirely—someone capable of juggling two lives and two women. Someone who can lie without flinching, who can play the part of the loving husband while harboring secrets that would destroy everything.

I'm excited about the pregnancy with Cindy, but dreading the pregnancy with Pamela, and for very good reasons. I have to make sure that Pamela never finds out about Cindy or Sheila because if she does, she won't see me the same way, and it's important that Pamela sees me as the only man she has ever wanted.

As I turn back to Pamela, I plaster on my most convincing smile. "There's nothing for us to talk about, sweetie. You know what needs to be done, so just do it so we can get back to being a happy couple. The game has changed, and I'm determined to be the one holding all the cards when the dust settles."

CHAPTER 6
PAMELA

THIS WASN'T GOING to end well. I knew that as soon as Kyle saw me touching my stomach, he would be furious. When he called me downstairs and started talking to the crowds of people. I didn't expect to say anything, but once I said the first word the others slipped from my lips like untrue words from a liar's tongue. I wanted to suck them back in, but I couldn't.

I felt like releasing our secret would allow me to keep this baby. We've always been so secretive about our other pregnancies, and I wanted to approach this one differently. Then Kyle made that beautiful monologue to our families and friends, and I thought maybe he was changing his mind about having children. But that was just hopeless wishing on my part. Kyle has barely spoken to me or touched me since I made that announcement last night. In fact, he slept in the damned attic. This is unlike him. I'm talking to him, and he's not talking back.

Kyle has never put his hands on me; he's rarely even raised his voice, but I can feel an anger oozing from him that I've never felt before, and it scares me. In our almost ten years of marriage, he's never not spoken to me for an entire night. He's never ignored my words. I take a deep breath and stand in the bathroom doorway, watching my husband put on his blazer as he gets ready for his weekly meeting with his financial planners—a meeting that I'm not allowed to attend.

His father, Kenneth, died when Kyle was a kid. He taught him about investing while he was alive, and they made a fortune in Google, Apple, and Coca-Cola when they were young companies—a fortune in the hundreds of millions of dollars. To avoid spoiling him, Kyle was forced to attend college and work for fifteen years before he could touch his multi-million-dollar inheritance. It was all documented in the will. His father wanted him to know the value of working and investing before he inherited his fortune because he didn't want him to squander it. He receives a monthly allowance from the trust, the amount I'm not privy to know, but he will not gain full access until the age of thirty-five. That's a little over a year from now. If we divorce, I won't get anything unless I've been married to him for ten years. I didn't find any of this out until our wedding day when his lawyer showed up and demanded I sign a prenup.

Before our marriage, I promised him I didn't want children. But seeing my friends and colleagues have babies over the years has made me yearn to experience pregnancy. I'm not trying to be difficult or break our vow. I'm just changing, and aren't people allowed to change?

When we first met at Edington University, I didn't have a desire to have children because of a traumatic incident that happened to me on campus. But, after being with Kyle and seeing how good a man he is to me and Marissa, he makes me want to change. He is more than enough. My wanting a child now doesn't mean that he's not enough. But he thinks he's not enough for me, and there's nothing I can say to prove otherwise.

"Are we going to talk about this, or are you going to continue to ignore me?" I say.

"What are you going to do about it?" he asks.

"Do about what?" I ask.

"Pamela, let's not embrace stupidity."

"I was hoping that maybe we could keep this child," I whisper. Kyle chuckles. I sound like a little child asking my mother for a puppy I found on the side of the road. Just hearing myself ask him for permission makes me sick to my stomach, but it's my fault. I've let him make all the important decisions in our marriage. Kyle rises from the bed.

"Keeping it is not an option. You know how I feel about pregnancy and having children. It's like you want me to be evil toward you, Pamela."

"Of course not," I say.

He doesn't say anything; he just goes to his dresser drawer and pulls out a thick stack of papers and a blue fountain pen, then throws them on the bed. I grab the papers and look at them. At the top, it says, 'Dissolution of Marriage'. He stops fiddling with his tie and turns his undivided attention to me. I look up at him as tears form around my eyelids.

"You're leaving me for that red-haired, green-eyed bitch you train at the gym!"

"Pamela, you're smarter than that. I care about my image too much for me to be branded as the pretty, light-skinned black man who cheated on his beautiful, mocha-skinned wife with a fertile young recent college grad while my wife is pregnant.

I'm leaving you because you care more about having a child than you care about me. You are willing to risk your marriage to be a mother to a child you have never met. So go be a mother, but I want absolutely nothing to do with that child that's brewing in your belly and take Marissa with you. As far as I'm concerned, neither of them are mine."

"But it's yours." Kyle chuckles.

"Of course it's mine; it's not like you have suitors lined up around the block to fuck you." Kyle walks toward me, grabs his cock, and rips open his shirt. He lifts my chin and puts his lips as close to mine as he can without touching them. "Don't you love me Pamela?"

"Yes, Kyle I really do."

"Then why do you insist on trying to anger me. I don't want fucking children Pamela." I watch in horror as he takes his arm and slides every item off my vanity until everything crashes against the floor. He then takes one of my perfume bottles and hurls it at the mirror until it has broken into a plethora of uneven glass pieces. "I love you so much. I promise I love you so much but you and your insistence on having a child is causing the monster in me to awaken and I'm trying so hard to keep him caged. Every mention of a child makes you less and less attractive. I tolerate Marissa because I love you, but ever since we adopted her, you've changed. We have less sex, you're gaining weight, and you attend to her needs before mine. She's your priority, and I'm just the daddy that pays for everything, the financier. I'm being used to fund a child's life that I had no desire to have. A child who will destroy us. All I want is a wife who would love me and only me, but that seems impossible to get from you these days."

I get on my knees in front of Kyle and take his hands

in mine. The only time Kyle talks to me like this is when I'm pregnant. It's like he's a different person, and I don't understand.

"Kyle, I thought that since we adopted Marissa, you had changed your views on children."

"I agreed to adopt Marissa because I wanted you to shut up about having a baby. I gave you Marissa, and now you are still pestering me about having kids."

"But Kyle why don't you want children. Maybe if we talked about it and went to therapy we could get to the bottom of this."

"Pamela, I don't want children because I'd be a horrible father! People like me shouldn't have kids!"

"Baby, I understand that parenthood is scary but together we can do it."

"You're not hearing me. All you care about is being a mom. You're pushing me away, and before you know it, I'll be in another woman's arms, and you can't even see it."

"But I know once we have our own child, it will be different." I grab his hand. "I'm scared too, Kyle, especially with our family histories, but I have faith."

"If you have this baby; I will not only divorce you. I will use every resource I have to ensure you will leave this divorce penniless. I want to live my life with you, Pamela, but it appears that as wonderful as I am, I'm not *fucking* enough for you."

"Why can't I want you and a child?"

"Because, I'm not willing to be a horrible father so that you can be a mother. If you want me to leave you for a younger woman who will be happy shopping all day and having sex with her hot husband, then have the fucking baby. But if you want to live in this life of opulence and luxury and continue having me as a faithful husband on your arm then you know what you must do."

"Please don't leave me alone and pregnant; I'll end up like my mother."

Kyle grabs his blazer and heads for the door, but before he leaves, he turns around and looks at me one last time.

"Keep studying your history, Pamela, and you will be sure to repeat it." He slams our bedroom door and leaves me alone to make the hardest decision of my life. It's either him or the baby, and I don't know who I'm going to choose. I rub my stomach as tears flow down my cheeks. "I promise he didn't mean it, Kayla," I whisper to the tiny life growing inside me.

CHAPTER 7
PAMELA

SHEILA WAS SO satisfied with how the shower turned out that she promised to treat me to lunch as a thank you, so I chose a popular spot called Brigantine Seafood and Lobster. It's a delicious spot in downtown San Diego where you can actually see the ocean from your table.

I sit across from Sheila, both of us cradling our swollen bellies—a visual reminder of our shared condition and the complex web of emotions it entangles. The hushed murmur of the restaurant envelops us and the cocoon of white noise does little to calm my frayed nerves. I can't get the image out of my mind of Sheila taking my husband into the side room. *What* do *they have to talk about that* I'm not *privy to?*

"I think I'll have the salmon en croûte," Sheila announces, closing her menu with a flourish that seems unnecessarily dramatic. "The omega-3s are so good for the baby's development and its very low in mercury. What about you?"

I hesitate, my eyes scanning the options. The words blur together, my mind too preoccupied with the fight that Kyle and I had last night to focus on something as trivial as lunch. "I'll have the chicken piccata," I decide, ignoring Sheila's raised eyebrow. I can almost hear her judgment–*shouldn't I be more concerned about nutrition?* As if she's not eating salmon sandwiched between a puff pastry. "I'm not eating any seafood I need this pregnancy to go smoothly."

"I didn't see Marissa at the shower. How is she?"

"She's fine. I had Chloe take her to SeaWorld and they had a sleepover. They will be back today."

"She's such a cutie," Sheila says.

"Yeah, she's my little angel."

As the waiter takes our orders and retreats, Sheila leans forward, her voice dropping to a conspiratorial whisper. "I must say, your pregnancy announcement at the shower was quite the bombshell. Kyle looked absolutely floored. I thought he didn't want anymore children?"

My fingers tighten around my water glass, the cool surface a stark contrast to the heat rising in my cheeks.

"He doesn't, but how do you know he doesn't want children," I reply, my voice barely audible?

A predatory glint flashes in Sheila's eyes so quickly I almost miss it.

"He told me."

"He told you?" I asked, shocked.

"I'm sorry, Pamela. I didn't know it was a secret. Don't worry I haven't told anyone."

"It's fine," I say. But I make a mental note that Kyle and I are going to have a conversation about this. Sheila leans forward as if she is waiting for me to divulge juicy gossip.

"Have you decided what you're going to do?" The question hangs in the air, heavy with implication. I feel my chest tighten, the weight of my situation pressing down on me. I wish Kyle hadn't shared that information with Sheila, but it's too late to take it back now.

"We're...still discussing our options," I manage, avoiding Sheila's piercing gaze. I can feel her eyes on me, probing, searching for weakness.

Suddenly, Sheila's hand shoots out, grabbing my wrist with surprising strength. Her touch sends an involuntary shiver down my spine. "Don't let him talk you into getting rid of your child. You keep that child Pamela. Do you hear me?"

I snatch my hand away from her. Surprised by her intensity.

Each word is like a dagger, precisely aimed to inflict maximum damage. I struggle to maintain my composure, my mind racing back to Kyle's reaction at the shower—the shock, the barely concealed panic in his eyes. His words saying one thing but his body language saying another.

"Sheila, what were you and Kyle discussing when you pulled him into our second living room, away from the party with all the other guests?" I take a sip of my sparkling grape juice and watch her for signs of lying.

"It's complicated," she says, her voice sounding hollow even to my ears.

"Complicated?"

"He told me not to tell you because he figured you would be mad."

I sit up straight, a mixture of anger and suspicion on my face.

A cruel smile plays at the corners of Sheila's mouth. "Oh, now you're upset. I guess I should just tell you. Kyle offered to help set up my nursery next week."

I freeze, my fork clattering against my plate. The

sound seems to echo through the restaurant, drawing curious glances from nearby diners. "He...what?"

Sheila's smile widens, shark-like. "He was so insistent. He said he wanted to get some 'hands-on experience.' Isn't that thoughtful of him?"

The room begins to spin. I grip the edge of the table. I can feel the eyes of the other diners on me, their gazes burning into my skin. The chatter of the restaurant fades to a dull roar, drowned out by the pounding of my heart.

"I don't understand," I murmur, more to myself than to Sheila. "He was so adamant about not wanting children, and now..."

Sheila leans back, a look of smug satisfaction on her face. "Well, perhaps he's had a change of heart. Or perhaps..." She trails off, her implication hanging in the air like a noxious cloud.

My eyes snap up, meeting Sheila's gaze. I can feel something dangerous stirring inside me, a mix of anger and fear that threatens to boil over. "Perhaps what, Sheila?"

Sheila shrugs, a picture of innocence that doesn't reach her eyes. "Maybe Kyle just doesn't want kids with you, Pamela."

"What exactly are you implying?" I ask, my voice low and dangerous. I can hear the tremor in it, betraying my inner turmoil.

Sheila's eyes widen in mock surprise. "Well, the streets have been talking, and I didn't want to tell you, but the rumor is that Kyle has been sleeping around with other women and that he's gotten someone pregnant."

My blood runs cold. Kyle does disappear early in the morning, but I've never heard anything about him cheating from my private investigator, and I know where his car goes—to the gym and back. "You're lying," I hiss, even as doubt begins to creep into my mind. The words taste bitter on my tongue, more a desperate plea than an accusation.

"I knew I should have kept this to myself. Now you're mad at me. I should have just shut up—it's not my business. Wives always side with their husbands in this type of situation. Next time, I'll just keep my business to myself." The arrival of our food provides a momentary reprieve from the tension. I stare at my chicken piccata, my appetite gone. The once-appetizing dish now turns my stomach. Across the table, Sheila digs into her salmon with relish, a self-satisfied smirk playing at the corners of her mouth.

As we eat in strained silence, my mind races. Kyle's adamant stance against children, his shocked reaction to my pregnancy announcement, his sudden interest in helping with Sheila's nursery—none of it makes sense. And now Sheila's confession that he's cheating.

As we finish our meal, Sheila dabs at her mouth with her napkin, the picture of refined elegance. "Well, this has been lovely. Do keep me updated on your...situation. And remember, if you need any advice or support, I'm always here."

I nod mechanically, my mind still whirling. A chill runs down my spine. *What game is Kyle playing? And what is Sheila's role in all of this?* The questions swirl in my mind.

Just as Sheila is about to pull out her credit card to pay for dinner, I gently grab her hand.

"I got this. I'm sorry for blowing up on you. It's not your fault. You were just being a good friend."

Sheila places her hand on her stomach, resting protectively on her baby bump. A steely resolve settles over me. "It's okay, Pamela. I'd be a nervous wreck too if I thought I was on the verge of losing a man like Kyle," she says.

I smile nervously and place a protective hand over my own belly, a fierce determination burning in my chest. I will protect my child and confront Kyle and this mistress head-on. The game they're playing, whatever it may be, ends now.

"Well, look at the bright side. At least you have Marissa. She's a doll and I hope she will adopt my future daughter Naomi as her little sister."

Before yesterday that thought would have pleased me. Who doesn't want their friends' kids to be like siblings as they grow older? But after hearing Sheila's confessions at this brunch, I'm not sure how much longer I want to be friends.

As I signal for the check, I can feel my heart racing, adrenaline coursing through my veins. The path ahead is unclear, fraught with danger and uncertainty. But one thing is certain—I will not be a pawn in their game. It's time to take control, to fight for my family and my future.

I step out of the restaurant into the bright sun, squinting against its glare. The world seems different now, shadows lurking in every corner. But I am no longer afraid. I am angry, determined, and ready for whatever comes next.

Watch out, Kyle. The hunt is on, and I won't stop until I uncover the truth—no matter how ugly it might be.

CHAPTER 8
KYLE

I SIT in my personal sanctuary, my eyes glued to the flickering screen before me. The familiar images play out, a secret indulgence that both thrills and shames me. My heart races as a mixture of excitement and fear courses through my veins. This is my escape, my hidden world that no one else can touch. I grab a couple pills from my desk drawer and swallow them with my freshly squeezed grapefruit juice.

Suddenly, a sharp ping cuts through the air, startling me. It's my phone. I grab it, my fingers trembling slightly as I swipe to unlock the screen. A message from Jake, my gym buddy. Shit. I've completely forgotten that I invited him and Mike over for the game.

Panic surges through me as I scramble to shut down the video. My movements are frantic, almost manic, as I stash everything away in my hiding spot. The secret compartment clicks shut, and I take a deep breath, trying to calm my racing heart.

The doorbell chimes, echoing through the house. I freeze for a moment, then force myself into action. I descend from the attic, each step feeling like I'm moving through molasses. At the bottom, I turn the lock, sealing away my secrets once more.

I make my way to the living room; I can hear Pamela's voice, cheerful and welcoming. The thought sends a pang of guilt through me, but I push it aside. I paste on a smile as I enter the room, just in time to see Jake and Mike step inside.

"Damn, bro!" Jake exclaims, his eyes wide as he takes in our home. "Your crib is fire! I had no idea you were living like this."

I force a laugh, trying to sound casual. "Yeah, we're doing alright." But inside, I'm tense. I try to keep my wealth low-key at the gym, preferring to blend in, but I needed to drive a Bentley to attract the type of women I want—the type of women I need.

They move through the house like they're in a museum, oohing and aahing over everything. The marble floors gleam under their feet, reflecting the light that streams in through the floor-to-ceiling windows. Outside, the ocean stretches to the horizon, a view that never fails to take my breath away.

"This is really dope, man," one of the guys says, running his hand along the back of an Italian leather sofa.

We settle into the living room, the massive TV already on, prepped for the game, thanks to Pamela. She never forgets anything. That's when Chloe appears, and I feel my stomach drop. She's wearing one of her typical outfits—short shorts and a tight tank top that leaves little to the imagination.

I see the way Jake's eyes light up, the way he looks her up and down. "Who's this?" he asks, his voice dripping with interest.

"The nanny and housekeeper," I say quickly, my tone sharper than I intend. "She helps us around the house."

Chloe's eyes narrow slightly at my words, but she doesn't contradict me. Instead, she turns to Pamela, who's just entered the room.

"Can you get some snacks for our guests?" Pamela asks her, and I see the flash of anger in Chloe's eyes. Lately, she doesn't like being ordered around, especially by Pamela. But she nods stiffly and heads to the kitchen.

As Pamela moves further into the room, I notice Jake's gaze shift to her. His eyebrows raise slightly, and I feel a surge of protective anger.

"Wow," he says, not even trying to be subtle. "Are you two expecting?"

I see Pamela flinch, her hand instinctively moving to her stomach. "Yes, we're six weeks."

An awkward silence falls over the room. Jake shifts uncomfortably, but then he smiles at Pamela. "Well, you look beautiful. Pregnancy really suits you."

Pamela's cheeks flush slightly. "Thank you," she says. "I appreciate that." Then, to my surprise, she adds, "You're looking pretty good yourself, Jake. Those workouts are clearly paying off."

I feel a surge of jealousy at her words. My hands clench into fists at my sides, and I must force myself to take a deep breath.

Jake grins, clearly pleased with the compliment. "Thanks, Pamela. Kyle and I have been hitting the gym hard lately." Pamela smiles and then heads upstairs to the bathroom. Once she's out of sight, something inside me snaps. The exchange, innocent as it may be, feels like a violation. My vision blurs red at the edges as I turn to

Jake. "That's my wife," I spit out, my voice low and dangerous. "Don't disrespect her like that."

Jake's eyes widen in surprise. "Whoa, bro, chill. We're just exchanging compliments. No disrespect meant."

But I can't stop. The anger, the frustration, the guilt—it all comes pouring out. "Get out," I say, my voice shaking with rage. "Both of you, get out of my house."

"Kyle, what the hell?" Jake stands up, confusion and anger warring on his face. "We're supposed to be watching the game. Why are you tripping?"

"I said get out!" I'm shouting now, my fists clenched at my sides. "You don't get to come into my house and hit on my wife!"

Jake throws his hands up in exasperation. "Bro, I just said she looked good! It's a compliment! What, I can't say nice things to your girl?"

"She's not my girl, she's my wife!" The words explode out of me, filled with a possessiveness I didn't know I had. "Now get the fuck out before I throw you out!"

The guys leave, muttering and shooting me dirty looks. As the door slams behind them, I'm left standing in the suddenly quiet living room, my chest heaving.

Pamela comes down the stairs, her eyes wide with concern and confusion. "Kyle? What happened? Where did everyone go?" What's all the commotion?"

I turn to her, still seething. "They left. I made them leave."

Her brow furrows. "Why? What happened?"

"He was hitting on you," I spit out. "Talking about your body, how you look. And you were flirting right back! I won't stand for that disrespect in my own home."

Pamela's expression shifts from confusion to frustration. "Kyle, he was just being nice. It was a compliment.

And I was just being polite in return. Why are you so upset about this?"

"Because you're *mine*! You belong to me." The words come out harsher than I intend, but I can't stop myself. "How would you feel if women were always complimenting me, talking about my body?"

Pamela lets out a short, humorless laugh. "First of all, I don't belong to anyone. Secondly, are you kidding me? Women compliment you all the time, and I don't freak out about it because I trust you. That should mean something. When people compliment me, you should be proud, not jealous. But lately... I don't know who you are anymore."

The truth of her words stings. I don't recognize myself either. "What do you mean?"

"A little birdie told me that you've gotten someone pregnant. Is it true?" Her words hit me like a slap. I open my mouth to respond, but nothing comes out. The anger drains away, leaving me feeling hollow and ashamed. *How does she know?*

Pamela shakes her head, disappointment evident in her eyes. "I'm your wife, Kyle. How could you?"

I mean to lie, but something inside me won't let me. "Wow, you don't trust me," I mutter, already heading for the door.

"Kyle, wait—" Pamela calls after me, but I'm already gone, slamming the door behind me.

As I drive away from our beautiful house, my mind is in chaos. I find myself heading toward the gym, toward the one person who doesn't know me as Kyle, the successful businessman or Kyle, the devoted husband—the redhead with the knowing smile and the sinful curves.

I know it's wrong. I know I'm making everything worse. But right now, I don't care. I just need to escape, to forget who I am for a while. As I pull into the gym parking lot, I see her coming out, gym bag slung over her shoulder. Our eyes meet, and she smiles that smile that promises so much and asks for so little.

I get out of the car, my decision made. "Hey," I call out to her. "Want to grab a drink?"

"You know I can't drink, but I'll watch you drink."

I pull out a ring from my pocket and place it on her finger. "Will you wear it and never take it off?"

She looks at me for a long moment, then nods. A few tears fall from her eyes. "Yes, Kyle."

As we walk to my car, I feel a mix of excitement and self-loathing. This is who I am now, I realize. A man of secrets, of lies, of stolen moments. A man running from himself.

I place my hand on her stomach. "I can't wait to meet Kyle Jr."

"I can't wait to meet him either," Cindy says as she kisses me, and I return the kiss.

But as I open the car door for her, as I breathe in her perfume and feel the warmth of her body next to mine, I push those thoughts away. For now, I'll just be someone else. Someone without responsibilities, without guilt. Someone free.

CHAPTER 9
KYLE

AFTER MY EVENING WITH CINDY, I retreat to my sanctuary in the attic. Pamela's car wasn't in the driveway and I was thankful because I didn't want to talk to her. I needed to be alone. This space—my man cave—is where I can be my true self, away from prying eyes and questions. The attic door creaks as I unlock it, a sound that always soothes me, signaling my escape. Once inside, I lock the door behind me, ensuring my solitude.

I sink into my worn leather chair and watch as the images on the screen calm me. I pull open the side drawer and pop a few pills. These tapes and pills are my medicine, my cure. They keep me normal. Once I've calmed myself, I turn off the computer and my thoughts drift to the kind of women I find irresistible—beautiful, petite, and curvy. That's what attracts me, and it's one of the many reasons I don't want children. I've seen it too many times—women from high school and college transforming from tens to fives after having kids. I don't want that for my life.

The first time Pamela miscarried, I felt relief. I know it sounds horrible, but I didn't want children. Yet seeing Pamela's pain tears at my heart. When she hurts, I hurt. She never understands the emotional toll pregnancy takes on me. It's not something most women consider. They never ask, "How is this affecting my husband?" No one asks me how the miscarriage affects me, if I need counseling, or if we should try again. The baby showers, the pregnancies, the wedding—everything is about her. I'm just the sperm donor, the investor, and the chauffeur to doctor appointments.

The second miscarriage which technically was a still birth was my fault. I stare at the rain pattering against my office window, the sound bringing back memories I try to suppress. I close my eyes, and suddenly I'm back in that car five years ago...

I grip the steering wheel tightly, as I navigate through the rain-slicked streets. Pamela sat in the passenger seat, the silence between us heavy with unspoken words.

Finally, Pamela broke the silence. "Kyle, we need to talk about this."

My jaw tightened "What's there to talk about?"

"You've been distant for weeks," Pamela said, her voice quiet but firm. "We haven't been connecting. I feel like you're pulling away."

I sigh; my eyes on the road. "I'm not pulling away. I just... I need some time."

"Time for what?" Pamela's frustration was evident. "We're married, Kyle. We're supposed to face things together, not shut each other out."

"I'm not shutting you out," I snap, immediately regretting my tone. I take a deep breath. "I'm just processing how this happened. I told you I didn't want kids."

Pamela turns to face me. "I forgot to take my birth control. It happens Kyle."

"But we agreed to no kids."

"So, what exactly are you saying Kyle."

"I'm saying we should get rid of it."

"You want me to abort my baby?"

I opened my mouth to respond, but a flash of red caught my eye—taillights much closer than they should be. I slam on the brake, but the car hydroplanes, spinning wildly.

The world blurred into a cacophony of screeching tires and shattering glass. A sickening crunch of metal fills our ears as airbags explode around us.

When the chaos subsided, I blinked, disoriented. The acrid smell of deployed airbags filled my nostrils. I turn my head, wincing at a sharp pain in my neck.

"Pamela?" I call out, panic rising in my throat.

"I'm here," she responds, her voice shaky. "Are you okay?"

As the gravity of the situation sinks in, I reached for Pamela's hand. "I'm so sorry," I whisper, the weight of our argument suddenly insignificant in the face of what could have been lost. We found out later she lost the baby, and I haven't forgiven myself for that yet.

I now realize I haven't fully healed from that traumatic moment. Deep down, I know I'm not capable of being a good father. I tell Pamela it's about her weight gain and all the superficial bullshit, and while there's some truth to that, I can't be trusted. Pregnancy isn't beautiful. It's one of the most traumatic and life-altering experiences a couple can go through outside of sickness or death. I left the room when Pamela delivered a still born child that night because I can't handle the emotions that accompany it.

The hardest part about Pamela being pregnant is seeing her excitement. Even though she's crying, I can see her aching for my approval, hoping I will change my mind. It's as if she forgets that one of the deciding factors for me marrying her was her initial lack of desire for children. Both of our childhoods were riddled with trauma, and we vowed never to have children. We wanted to enjoy a life of wealth and luxury without passing on our trauma to another generation. We had long, intense conversations about this, agreeing that having children was selfish and arrogant.

People have kids because they want to leave a legacy, to be remembered, sprinkling their seeds throughout the world in hopes their lineage lives on.

Now her views are changing, and it's breaking my heart. I want to tell her the real reasons I don't want children, but how do you have that conversation with the woman you love more than anything in the world, especially when you see how happy she is to have a child growing inside her?

As I think about the harsh words I said to my wife, I feel like shit. There's only one person who can give me advice on this situation without judging me: my sister, Donna. I can always count on her to hear my side of the story.

I could book an appointment with my therapist, but it

would be a week before I could get in. So I swallow my pride and phone my sister. As the phone starts ringing, I want to hang up, knowing I will sound like an ass.

"Hey Donna," I say when she answers.

"What's bothering you, Kyle? You don't sound like your usual chipper self."

I check again to see if the door to the attic is closed, deciding how to explain my situation without sounding like a complete asshole.

"Pamela is pregnant..."

"I know, brother. I was there when you gave that beautiful speech. I'm very proud of you for how you handled it because I know you don't want kids."

"Donna, I have concerns."

"I know you do. You always have concerns," she laughs.

"This isn't funny. She broke our vow. We agreed not to have children before we married, and now she's not thinking about what I want. It's all about her desires with no emphasis on my needs."

"Brother, it takes two to tango. Why haven't you gotten snipped?"

"I considered it, but Pamela said I shouldn't do it. She's concerned I might change my mind about having a child and then be unable to."

"You know those can be reversed, right?"

"Yes, but the success rate is only between 40% and 90%."

"So, did you two talk about it?"

"Yeah, I told her she needed to choose me or the baby." A lengthy pause follows my statement. "Hello?" I speak.

"Kyle, please tell me you didn't tell your newly pregnant wife what you just told me." I stay quiet, not having the courage to admit to my sister that I had given Pamela that ultimatum. "Oh my God, you gave your wife of almost ten years, the woman pregnant with your child, a choice between you or her baby? You're a selfish and inconsiderate prick. Do you know what women go through while being pregnant?"

"I called you because you're normally a voice of reason, but you're judging me like my feelings don't matter."

"Kyle, I'm sorry, but your feelings don't fucking matter at this moment."

"Donna, what's wrong with you? Do you even hear yourself? This is a marriage where both of our feelings should matter."

"You are not the one with a life growing inside of you. You don't have to deal with weight gain, morning sickness, or emotional shifts. We do."

"But Pamela chose this. This isn't what I wanted."

"Did you outline it in the prenuptial agreement?"

"No, it was a verbal agreement."

"Then my advice is to either divorce her now, pay her a fat settlement, and exit her and the child's life, or shut up and smile like the other millions of men in the world and accept that you are about to be a father because you are the one who put your raw dick in her."

"See, this isn't right, Donna. Women always tell us to express ourselves, but when we do, we get demonized and judged. Meanwhile, they can spew any venom they want, and we just take it. I haven't even mentioned the other things I have to deal with, like her weight gain and lack of sex."

"Normally, I don't judge you, brother. I let you be

your rich, selfish, and spoiled self. But you're hitting a sensitive area. Trust me, calling you a prick was the best I could do, and that message was filtered. This woman you pledged to live with forever wants to give birth to your children, and you're concerned about sex and her body's appearance? I knew you were shallow based on the number of women that enter and leave your life, but this is a new low. I thought you had finally matured when this relationship didn't end after the 1.5-year mark, but I guess I was wrong."

"Donna, you're not listening! It's not just about her physical appearance. I don't want kids. I compromised and adopted a baby girl, which brought Pamela so much joy. But now I'm going from no kids to two children. Women change when they have kids. They love their husbands less, they have less sex, they date less, and the romance dies. I don't want that. That's why Clay cheated on you. Women, as amazing as they are, can't fuck their husbands and raise children simultaneously. One suffers, and it's usually the husband."

"How did you know that? I didn't share it with anyone but Mom." Just as I'm about to counter her argument, I hear a dial tone. I quickly text Mom and Clay, letting them know I had accidentally spilled some information, then turn off my phone because I don't want a scolding. Women tell us to communicate, but when I finally express myself, I'm crucified for my thoughts or concerns. This is why we cheat—because women don't know how to handle the truth, and the side piece will be happy with a Chanel bag, good dick, and will listen to our problems.

I know this sounds horrible, but I'm seriously contemplating leaving Pamela. I don't want to end up being worse than I already am. I compromised by adopting a baby girl, bringing my wife so much joy. But the thought of Pamela being pregnant and having a child is something I didn't sign up for. It's something that will destroy us, but how can I let her know that without being an asshole?

CHAPTER 10
PAMELA

AFTER KYLE LEAVES the house without naming the other woman or providing details, I go out for some air. When I return, I want answers. Who is this woman, and why did he offer to decorate Sheila's nursery? I can't understand why he would help her during her pregnancy but would vehemently oppose doing it for our child. My heels echo like gunshots throughout the cavernous foyer.

"Kyle, are you here?" The unnatural silence presses against my eardrums, a stark contrast to the baby shower's orchestra of voices. A familiar and expensive scent lingers in the air—my perfume, but overpowering, almost suffocating.

My fingers tense around my Hermes Birkin bag—a seventh-anniversary gift from Kyle—as I call out, "Chloe?" The name dies in the oppressive quiet.

An icy tendril of unease coils in my gut as I ascend the grand staircase. A thought plagues my mind. *Does Kyle have another woman here? Would he be that stupid as to cheat in our home?* I pull out my gun from my bag. I've always kept one in my purse after that incident in college. I won't be caught helpless and vulnerable again. I know it's against the law in California, but I don't care. If this motherfucker is cheating in my house while I'm pregnant with his child, I'm going to kill her and make sure he's wounded enough to never do it again. Each step feels heavier than the last as if the air thickens around me. At the landing, a faint clink of glass on marble slices through the silence.

My heart pounds against my rib cage as I approach our master bedroom. The door stands slightly ajar, a sliver of light spilling onto the dark hallway floor. The scent of perfume grows overpowering, almost nauseating. I pull out my gun and push the door open, the hinges groaning like a dying animal. The scene before me sends a jolt of adrenaline coursing through my veins.

Chloe stands frozen at the vanity. My prized Clive Christian No. 1 in her trembling hands. Our eyes meet in the mirror, and the color drains from Chloe's face.

"Mrs. Witherspoon!" The bottle wobbles precariously in Chloe's grip. "I... I didn't..."

My voice comes out low and dangerous. "What are you doing in here, Chloe?" Chloe's eyes dart around like a cornered animal. "I'm so sorry, I just...it smelled so lovely..." she stutters.

My gaze rakes over the chaos of the vanity—opened compacts, uncapped lipsticks, smears of color everywhere. My carefully curated sanctuary violated. I let out a long sigh and collect my nerves before I speak.

I pick up a used tube of Chanel limited edition. The violation feels almost physical. "Chloe, come have a seat here." Chloe drops her head and comes over to sit on the bed.

"If you want to use my things, just ask me. I have

more than enough to share. You don't have to steal. You do a good job here, and I want you to feel comfortable around me."

"I'm so sorry, Mrs. Witherspoon."

"It's okay, but please call me Pamela. You make me feel like an old woman when you call me by my last name. How about we go shopping later this week and pick out some really nice things for you?"

"You are so kind, Mrs. Witherspoon... I mean Pamela. Thank you for not firing me."

"Have you seen Kyle?" I ask.

"The last time I talked to him, he said he had some business to take care of in the attic."

"He's always in that damned attic. I'm going to demand a key. There shouldn't be a room in my house I can't go into," I say.

CHAPTER 11
PAMELA

I KNOCK on the attic door, but either Kyle is ignoring me, or he's not upstairs. Since his Bentley isn't in the driveway, I assume the latter. Over the last couple of days, it's like he's avoiding me. I'm starting to notice a pattern. Whenever I'm pregnant, he stays far away from me. It's as if I repulse him. Part of me wants to get a hammer and beat the deadbolt off the door to ensure he's not up there. I linger at the top of the steps and contemplate an abortion. I don't want to go through with it but I have no other option if I want to keep my marriage.

Tears fall from my eyes so hard that they block my vision as I walk down the steps. I can't believe I must choose between my husband and my child. It doesn't seem fair. As I make the lengthy descent down the stairs, I release a scream when something sharp pricks the flesh of my barefoot. Electricity surges through my body.

I've stepped on sharp objects before but not while walking down spiral steps. My hands dance in the air, trying to grab hold of something, anything that could break my fall. I trip over the next step, and my life flashes before my eyes. I grab my stomach to protect it and brace my fragile body as I prepare my mind for the twenty-plus-step tumble down our marble stairs.

All I can think about is my baby. Is *she going to be, okay*? My thoughts then turn to Kyle. He's not the kind of man who takes bad news kindly, and I know all his anger will be funneled at Marissa. Visions of him punching a wall or throwing pieces of my finest China on the floor plague my mind. When he finds out about how one of her toys could have killed me, he will be furious. This would just further his argument about not having children. Maybe this fall will end in death, and I won't have to suffer anymore. I'll finally be free of him and the responsibilities of being his wife because I don't know how our marriage will recover from this. We barely recovered from the first two miscarriages.

As I lay at the bottom of the stairs, I attempt to move but can only move my head slightly. My heart races through my chest as I think about everything that could be wrong with me. *Am I paralyzed? Have I broken bones?* I try to wiggle my legs first, then my arms, then my feet and fingers to no avail. I lift my head off the ground and stare at my six-year-old daughter at the top of the steps. Then I hear her scream so loud I think she'll blow out my eardrums. I feel a piercing pain in the lower region of my body. I watch her run away, no doubt fearful of the consequences her actions caused.

In that instant, I know everything I need to know. I open my mouth to call her name, or anyone's, but I can't produce a sound.

My head throbs like someone pounding on a solid oak door. My body aches all over, and out of the corner of my eye, streams of blood roam across the floor, coloring everything they touch. *Is she gone?* My little baby Kayla, the baby I fought so hard to keep, might never make her debut on Earth, and Kyle will blame Marissa—not for the loss of pregnancy but for hurting his wife. *What if I die and Kyle punishes Marissa?* My eyes close, my breathing slows, and my body shuts down. I can't die today because I don't know what Kyle would do to our daughter. I have to fight for the baby because I don't know how she would survive without me.

CHAPTER 12
KYLE

I SIT at my desk and watch my screen: my heart races, anticipation, and guilt warring within me as I wait for the familiar signal.

Three soft knocks echo in the stillness, barely audible but deafening to my heightened senses. I turn off the volume on my computer and move to the hidden panel in the wall, my fingers trembling slightly as I activate the mechanism. The door swings open silently, revealing Chloe silhouetted against the darkness of the passageway. My father constructed this passageway when he built this house. Not even my mother or Pamela know of its existence. He told me it was my job to keep it that way. It was a secret he carried to his death.

For a moment, we stand frozen, drinking in the sight of each other. Chloe's wide, conflicted eyes meet my intense gaze. The air between us crackles with unspoken tension.

"We shouldn't be doing this," Chloe whispers, even as she steps into the attic from the secret passageway. The door closes behind her with a soft click, sealing us in our private world.

"Kyle, I feel bad about this. Your wife just pointed a gun at me, then offered to take me shopping after I was in her bathroom using her things. I feel bad and scared of what might happen if she finds out the truth about us, about our past."

"Everything Pamela has, I bought. I gave you permission to go in her vanity, so you shouldn't feel bad. If it helps, I feel horrible as well, but I need you, Chloe. I need to feel your body against mine. You are saving my marriage. You are the glue that keeps this family together. Without you, all of this would fall apart."

"But what about the gun?"

"Trust me. She won't find out. Besides, Pamela has never shot that gun; I think it's more of an emotional support gun."

"This is wrong, but I want you so bad, Kyle."

I reach for her, my hands cupping her face with a gentleness that belies the storm of emotions raging within me. "I know," I murmur, my thumb tracing the curve of her cheekbone.

"But I can't stay away from you."

Our lips meet in a searing kiss, days of pent-up longing and forbidden desire pouring out in a single, breathless moment. Chloe's arms wrap around my neck, pulling me closer as if trying to meld our bodies into one. My hands roam her back, relearning the curves and planes I've memorized over countless clandestine meetings.

When we finally break apart, both of us are breathing heavily. Chloe rests her forehead against my chest, listening to the rapid beating of my heart. "This is insane," she says, her voice muffled against my shirt. "We're going to get caught."

I stroke her hair, the silky strands slipping through my fingers. "We've been careful," I assure her, but the words ring hollow even to my own ears.

Chloe pulls back, her eyes searching my face. "Have we? Pamela almost caught us in her room earlier. I'm just glad she didn't look under the bed and see you naked." I managed to come up with an excuse, but... Kyle, she's not stupid. She's going to figure it out eventually."

"I have Pamela wrapped around my little finger. You just let Daddy Kyle handle Pamela." I remove my shirt and watch Chloe's eyes navigate my body. This is why I work out. This is why I hit the gym hard because even the most moral woman can't tell me no once I get naked. My money gets their attention, my eyes draw them to me, and my voice and body get them out of their clothes and me inside them. I pull down my pants and watch Chloe's eyes bulge. I watch as she pulls down her panties and steps out of them.

I turn to the window, staring out at the moonlit ocean below. The calm ocean waves mock me with their orderliness, a stark contrast to the chaos of my personal life.

Chloe stands beside me, close enough that I can feel the warmth radiating from her body but not quite touching. "How much longer can we keep this up?" she asks, her voice barely above a whisper. "You promised me, Kyle. You said you'd leave her for me."

I close my eyes, pain etching lines across my face. "I know. I will. I just... I need more time."

"Time?" Chloe's laugh is bitter, edged with years of disappointment. "We've been doing this for three years, Kyle. How much more time do you need?"

I turn to face her, reaching to take her hands in mine. "It's complicated, Chloe. You know that. There's the business to consider, our reputations..."

"And Pamela," Chloe finishes for me, her eyes flashing with hurt and anger. "Always Pamela."

I cringe at the accusation in her voice. "That's not fair," I protest weakly.

"Isn't it?" Chloe pulls her hands from my grasp, pacing across the attic floor. "You say you love me, but you won't leave her. You sneak around with me in attics and hidden passageways, but you sleep in her bed every night. Tell me, Kyle, what part of that is fair?"

Her words hang between us, heavy with truth and recrimination. I feel as if I am being torn in two, caught between the life I've built with Pamela and the passionate, all-consuming desire I feel for Chloe. She is like a younger version of Pamela. Pamela before the pregnancies.

"I do love you," I say finally, my voice rough with emotion. "More than I've ever loved anyone. But it's not that simple."

Chloe stops pacing, turning to face me with tears glistening in her eyes." Then make it simple," she pleads. "Choose me, Kyle. Choose us."

The rawness in her voice breaks something inside me. I pull Chloe into my arms. Our lips meet in a desperate, hungry kiss, as if we could solve all our problems through sheer passion alone. I pick her up and slide her over my manhood, and she moans in satisfaction as our bodies become one.

We move together with practiced familiarity, hands roaming and bodies pressing close. I back Chloe up against the wall, pinning her there with my body as I trail kisses down her neck. She gasps, her fingers sliding through my hair, pulling me closer.

For a few blissful moments, the world falls away. There is no Pamela, no guilt, no half-truths. There is only Chloe and me, lost in each other, our bodies moving in perfect synchronization.

But reality has a way of intruding, even in the most private of moments. A loud noise from the floorboards below freezes us both in place, hearts pounding with sudden fear.

"Did you hear that?" Chloe whispers, her eyes wide with panic.

I nod slowly, disentangling myself from her embrace. We stand in tense silence, straining to hear any further sounds from the house below. After what feels like an eternity, I relax slightly. "It's probably just the house settling," I say, but my voice lacks conviction.

"It sounded like a scream," Chloe replies.

The spell is broken. We begin to put on our clothes, the air between us thick with unresolved tension and unspoken words. Chloe moves toward the hidden door, but I catch her arm, pulling her back to face me.

"I meant what I said," I tell her, my eyes intense and earnest. "I do love you, Chloe. And I will leave Pamela. I just need to figure out the right way to do it."

Chloe studies my face, wanting desperately to believe me. "When?" she asks simply. I hesitate, and in that moment of hesitation, Chloe sees the truth. Her shoulders slump in defeat.

"That's what I thought," she says quietly.

"Chloe, wait-" I start, but she cuts me off with a raised hand.

"No, Kyle. I'm done waiting. I'm done being your

dirty little secret." She takes a deep breath, squaring her shoulders. "Either you tell Pamela the truth—about us, about everything—or I will."

The ultimatum hangs in the air between us, heavy with finality. I feel as if the ground has dropped out from beneath my feet. "You wouldn't," I say.

Chloe's eyes are sad but determined. "I would. I have to. For both our sakes." She reaches up, cupping my face in her hands. "I love you, Kyle. But I can't keep living like this. It's killing me."

She presses a soft, lingering kiss to my lips—a kiss that feels too much like goodbye. Then, before I can react, she slips through the hidden door and is gone, leaving me alone in the attic with the weight of her ultimatum pressing down on me.

I sink to the floor, my back against the wall, mind reeling. How has it come to this? How have I let things spiral so far out of control? I think of Pamela downstairs, blissfully unaware of the storm about to break over our lives. I think of Chloe, probably crying in her room, torn between love and self-preservation.

And I think of myself—the lies I've told, the promises I've broken, the lives I've irreparably damaged in my selfish pursuit of having it all.

I make a decision. I can't go on like this, living a double life, hurting the people I care about most. Something has to give.

I jump when I hear a scream.

With heavy steps, I make my way downstairs. My blood runs cold as I stare at Pamela on the floor in a puddle of blood.

"Help! Someone help! My wife is dying!" I yell.

I drop to my knees beside Pamela, my hands shaking

as I reach for her. The sight of the blood pooling around her makes my stomach lurch. I frantically check for a pulse, relief washing over me when I feel a faint throb beneath my fingers.

"Chloe!" I shout, my voice cracking with panic. "Call 911! Now!"

I hear Chloe's footsteps thundering down the stairs, followed by her sharp intake of breath as she takes in the scene. She fumbles for her phone, her voice trembling as she speaks to the emergency operator.

As I wait for help to arrive, I cradle Pamela's head in my lap. My mind races, trying to make sense of what's happened. *Did she fall? Did she do this to herself?* The possibilities terrify me. *Did I cause her to do this?*

Pamela's eyelids flutter open, and she looks up at me with dazed, confused eyes. "Kyle... is the baby okay?" she whispers, her voice barely audible.

"Shh, it's okay, Pamela. Help is on the way. Just hang on," I tell her, my voice choked with emotion. Tears blur my vision as I hold her close, praying for the sound of sirens.

Chloe kneels beside me, her hand on my shoulder. "They're on their way," she says, her voice soft and shaky.

Minutes feel like hours as we sit there, the three of us bound by a silent, desperate hope. The sound of distant sirens finally breaks the tension, and I feel a glimmer of relief.

"Hold on, Pamela. Just a little longer," I whisper, squeezing her hand. The paramedics burst through the door, taking over with practiced efficiency. I step back, watching helplessly as they work to stabilize Pamela and prepare her for transport. Chloe stands beside me, her face pale and drawn.

As they wheel Pamela out on a stretcher, I follow, my heart heavy with dread and guilt. I glance back at Chloe, who gives me a small, supportive nod. I know our situation hasn't changed, but right now, all I can focus on is Pamela and getting her the help she needs.

In the harsh light of the ambulance, I take a deep breath, bracing myself for the consequences of my actions. No matter what happens next, I know that my life—and the lives of those I care about—will never be the same.

CHAPTER 13
PAMELA

BRIGHT LIGHTS SURROUND me as I open my eyes. Am *I dead?* I don't really want to die. Maybe I did at that moment when I fell down the steps, but I'm not done living. My thoughts immediately go to Marissa. This isn't her fault, I tell myself. *She's just a child, Pamela. She didn't do it on purpose.* I do my best to release the anger I'm harboring toward my daughter and silently pray that the child inside me is okay. That would be a horrible way to die. I can almost hear the headlines: *Wealthy pregnant woman plummets to her death, the culprit—her daughter's prickly toy.*

I blink rapidly to gain focus. When my eyes adjust, I see my mother-in-law, sister-in-law, and Kyle staring at me. Relief washes over me. I'm not dead. *Thank you, Jesus, for not answering that prayer.* I grab my stomach and wonder if the baby is okay.

"Where is my baby? Is my baby, okay?" I ask.

"Thank God; you are okay," Donna says.

"Pamela, are you okay? What happened? How did

this happen?" Kyle asks. Mama Witherspoon pushes her handsome son out of the way, grabs a chair, and sits next to me. She takes my hand in hers, massaging them as she motions for Kyle to move aside.

"Move, boy. The woman just fell down a flight of stairs, and you're asking too many questions." Mama Witherspoon pushes my overgrown bangs out of my face and tucks my hair behind my ears.

"We don't know about the baby yet. We're waiting for the doctor to come back with news. I tried to get information, but he stayed tight-lipped. Moral bastard." Kyle steps forward, trying to stand between me and his mother, but Mama Witherspoon squints her eyes, peering into his soul. It's the stare my mother used to give me when I did something she disapproved of. I call it the black mama stare down. Kyle rolls his eyes, grabs his coat, and heads toward the door.

"I could have lost a child and my wife, and out of nowhere, my mother and sister both step in like they're Jesus fucking Christ without any concern for my emotional well-being!" He marches out of the hospital room.

"And don't come back until you bring us some butter pecan ice cream—triple scoops!" *Why is Kyle upset about losing a baby he didn't want?* As much as I hate to admit it, I thought he'd be somewhat relieved or even hoping I had lost the child. I'll have to get to the bottom of this later.

"Pamela, do you mind if I go check on him and make sure he's okay?"

"No, Donna. Go right ahead. He probably needs you more than I do. Besides, I have my other mother here."

Donna kisses me on the cheek and leaves the room,

leaving me alone with Mama Witherspoon. Most of my girlfriends hate their mothers-in-law, but that's one area where I lucked out. My mother-in-law is fabulous. She keeps Kyle in line and always has my back when we fight. It's the relationship I wanted with my mother, but she's too busy telling me how to live my life while constantly reminding me how horrible a job I'm doing as a mother and wife.

"Don't be so hard on him, Mama Witherspoon. He's just concerned about me."

"That's the problem. He should be concerned about you and the baby," she says.

"To him, the baby and I are one."

"You're too easy on him. I don't know what you see in him." I sit up straight and fold my arms across my chest.

"The same thing you saw in his daddy: those green eyes, curly hair, and all the muscles."

"I call them the devil's eyes—damn recessive gene. That boy has never had to work hard for anything. He just blinks those damn long eyelashes, and when people see those rare green eyes on a black man, they're ready to do his bidding."

Mama Witherspoon sneers in disgust, then takes out a mint from her purse and pops it in her mouth. She hands the container to me, and I take one, even though I don't like mint. My mother told me that when someone offers you a mint, take it. It's their passive-aggressive way of saying your breath stinks. I cup my hand over my mouth, blow into it, and try to smell my breath.

"Your breath doesn't stink. I'm just being polite."

"Thank you."

"You're welcome."

"Mama Witherspoon, he does work hard. He goes to

work every day and makes a good living for us as a personal trainer and nutritionist."

"Don't give him a pass for the bare essentials. His father was a multimillionaire by his age. A man is supposed to work, my dear. And believe me, he's only working until the trust releases his inheritance. Do you really think you could live this life of opulence on a personal trainer's salary? He gets a thirty-thousand-dollar monthly allowance from his trust. That's how the bills are getting paid."

"Thirty thousand?" I almost spit out my Altoid.

"Yes, and there isn't a mortgage to pay because we own that house outright."

"I knew he got an allowance, but not thirty thousand?"

"Yes, and once he hits thirty-five and inherits millions, he'll quit that *good job* and whisk you and your small family to Los Angeles so he can pursue his nonexistent bodybuilding or acting career. But that's enough about Kyle. How are you?"

Mama Witherspoon reminds me of the way regal women dressed in those older movies from the '50s and '60s. Her jet-black hair hangs in loose waves over one shoulder. Her caramel skin is smooth as porcelain, and her lips are full and appear as if they've been painted with strawberries.

Mama Witherspoon savors the extravagant life but never forgets her humble beginnings. I admire her slim figure and the fact that she isn't one of those Hollywood mothers competing with their daughters twenty years her junior. She hasn't had a knife taken to her face, and if she has, you can't tell. She works out hard because Kyle is her trainer. Today she's wearing a yellow flowing skirt and an off-white blouse that matches her shoes perfectly. Everything else is accented in gold, including her diamond earrings, bracelet, and belt. The only thing that's not in gold is a new necklace she's wearing. It's a ruby encrusted seahorse pendant and its absolutely stunning.

"I'm fine, but I'm not sure about the baby."

"I didn't ask about the baby. I asked about you. We women do this all the time. When someone asks us a question, we talk about our kids, our husbands, or our pets. We are not extensions of the people we provide for, my dear. We are whole human beings. Now, let me ask you again. How are you?" I hold her hand tightly and fight back the urge to cry. She's right. I rarely check in with myself to see how I'm feeling. It's always about Marissa, the child I'm carrying, or Kyle. I take a few seconds to digest her question.

"Physically, I feel better than I did when I fell down the steps, and I'm definitely sore all over, but I'm a mess mentally. When I saw all that blood, my mind went to a dark place. If I lost this baby, I don't know what I'll do. I don't know what happened. I'm always careful when I walk down the steps. The next thing I knew, I stepped on something sharp and lost my balance. It's all my fault. If I had been more careful, I might have seen the sharp toy on the steps, and I might be giving birth to our first baby in a few months. I guess that could still be the case, but I'm expecting the worst. It doesn't help that Kyle told me that he doesn't want any more children. He basically told me to get rid of it."

Mama Witherspoon leans toward me. "My dear, you didn't purposely fall down the steps to lose the baby just to appease my asshole of a son, did you?" I pause and listen to her words fully. *Did she say what I think she said?*

"No, it was an accident. I mean, maybe I subconsciously wanted to lose the baby because I didn't want to lose Kyle, but I'd never consciously hurt myself."

"Fuck Kyle," she says. I open my mouth, gasp, and cover it with my hand. I can't believe she would say such harsh words about her son.

"Excuse my French. I know as a Christian woman I shouldn't say such words, especially about my son, but he's his father's son, and this situation hits a personal chord with me." She folds her hands in her lap and turns her face away, not wanting me to see the emotion welling up in her. I touch her arm, and she turns toward me. She pulls a tissue from her purse and dabs underneath her eyes, then uses the same tissue to wipe mine.

"Personal chord?"

"Before I had Kyle, I had a couple of miscarriages, and Kenneth, Kyle's father, was insensitive as well. I felt alone and unworthy because he didn't want children either. The Witherspoon men like to have their women to themselves. They're a bunch of selfish bastards. I'm glad the chauvinistic pig died early."

"Mama Witherspoon, I'm sure you don't mean that."

"Oh, I mean every damn word." Our conversation comes to an abrupt halt when Kyle comes back into the hospital room with two cups of butter pecan ice cream. I clap in excitement. I haven't had ice cream in months. He hands one to his mother and starts eating out of the other cup.

"I know you didn't walk in here with two cups of ice cream and one of them isn't for your wife."

"She doesn't need ice cream. She just had three cupcakes when preparing for the baby shower and God knows what she ate when she went to lunch with Sheila."

"He's right. I don't need any. I've gained quite a bit of weight." Mama Witherspoon hands me her ice cream.

"Eat every drop. And nobody needs ice cream. It's just a creamy, delicious treat." She then swings her hand back and smacks her son upside the head.

"Now you know good and well I taught you better than that. You don't tell a woman what she can put in her body. How would you feel if the shoe were on the other foot?" Kyle slams his ice cream down on the table.

"Okay, I've had enough reprimanding for the day." He picks up his mother and throws her over his shoulder in the kindest and gentlest way a son could, then walks toward the door. I watch as she kicks her legs and beats against his back. It's funny watching them interact. They're more like brother and sister than mother and son. If I'm honest, seeing him pick up his mother and carry her out of the room turns me on. I watch the veins in his arms and neck bulge as he carries her toward the door. When he reaches the door, he ducks down, careful not to bang her head against the door frame. It's just the laughter I need during this intense and uncertain time of pain.

Just as he's setting her down, our doctor steps toward the door. Kyle whispers to the doctor. I'm proficient at reading lips. It's a skill I picked up as a kid so I could figure out what my mother and stepfather were arguing about.

"Could you please make sure she doesn't come back here? My wife needs her rest, and she's disturbing her comfort." He flashes a smile, and the doctor nods and politely leads Mama Witherspoon down the hall. She looks into the room and motions for me to call her if I need her. I nod and blow her a kiss. She's feisty but sweet.

Kyle grabs the doctor and steps out of view for a few minutes, then returns to the room.

He knows I can read lips, which is why I believe he made sure I couldn't see what he was saying to Dr. Hemlock. *What does he not want me to hear?* When Kyle returns to the room, I'm reminded of how tall he is. Whenever he stands by me, I normally wear heels, so he doesn't seem much taller than me. But as I look up at him now, I have a new appreciation for his height. He rubs his hands through his curly hair, folds his arms across his chest, and leans against the door frame. He's wearing an olive V-neck sweater that hugs every muscle on his body. He looks like he could be a Calvin Klein model—a Black Superman. Think of a Black Henry Cavill.

"I think you love my mother more than you love me," he says.

"Just a tiny bit," I say, pinching my index finger and thumb together.

"That's why I decided to even the score."

"Please don't tell me you did what I think you did?"

"I bought your mother a plane ticket, and she's on her way here as we speak. She might even be here already. Mrs. Bianca likes me a little more than she likes you." He mimics my hand motion, pinching his index finger and thumb together.

"Kyle, please tell me you're joking. You know I can't stand my mother."

"If something happened to you, she'd want to know. It was the right thing to do."

A lengthy pause follows as I realize all the work I'll have to do when she arrives. I'll have to reorganize my whole linen closet and make sure I have white bath and washcloths and her favorite water, Voss, or I'll have to hear her nag. My mother came from poverty, but ever since we started taking care of her, she's acted as if she's richer than we are. It doesn't matter if I'm pregnant or have lost the baby—she'll speak her mind and tell me all the ways I'm incompetent or how I'm failing as a wife and mother. Kyle takes the ice cream out of my hand and throws it in the trash.

"This isn't good for you." I turn away from him. Things like this make me angry at him. He's acting like an angry big brother, treating me like his little sister instead of his wife. I really believe that my wanting children is the reason he's turning cold toward me.

"You know you can't stay mad at my sexy ass." He reaches from behind me and cups my breast, and a moan escapes my lips. Sometimes I hate that my body responds to him this way because it often leads to sex, so we never get to solve our problems. We just end up pacifying them with incredible sex.

"See? I've got the magic touch." He isn't wrong. All he has to do is touch my body, and it obeys him like a willing servant. I turn back to face him.

"Why did you offer to help Sheila with her nursery?"

"Her husband is deployed, and she's all alone. It was a blessing he even made it to the shower. I was just helping *your* friend out."

"Are you sleeping with her?"

"Sheila? No. She's not even my type, and you know that. You know I have a thing for dark chocolate. It's filled with antioxidants." Kyle nibbles on my ear. It takes everything in my power to move him from off me because his tongue feels so good on my ear lobe. I grab his face and look into his mesmerizing green eyes.

"Well, she said you had a baby by another woman. Are you the father of Sheila's child?"

"Hell no! She's hormonal and is mistaking my kindness for weakness. I'd never cheat on you, sexy. Sheila wants to be you. I told you she wasn't your friend. Can't you see she's trying to put a wedge between us? You're my everything. And I hate to say I told you so, but I told you Sheila was jealous of you, and you shouldn't have done that shower for her."

"But she's one of my only friends."

"I thought I was your best friend." Kyle leans forward and nibbles on my neck. "You like how my tongue makes you feel, don't you? I make you crazy, don't I?" I quickly stick my finger in his ice cream and put it in my mouth. He lightly smacks my hand as if I'm a toddler.

"No ice cream. It's not good for you."

"But it's good for you?" He lifts his sweater, showing me his lean, tight stomach.

"When you have abs of steel like these, then you can tell me what I can or cannot eat. Until then, you're on a no-dairy, no-sugar diet. It will keep you from gaining so much weight."

I know he's right, but I don't like how much control he has over everything concerning me. It's those damn green eyes. I'm a sucker for a pretty boy, and Kyle is the poster boy for pretty.

I hate to admit it, but deep down, I don't think I can do better than Kyle, so I follow his commands in fear of losing him. There are times I wonder if this is really love. *Does he really love me, and* do *I really love him, or* are *we just comfortable together*? He could have any woman he wanted, and he chose me despite my many flaws. And trust me, I have many. He married me after that awful event in college, and I vowed never to leave him because he stood by me at my darkest hour.

I don't think I'd ever find another man who looks like him, smells like him, and makes love to me like he does. He's a ten, and now that I've been with a ten, no other man could measure up. I'm damaged goods, yet he protects me. I'm broken, and he stands by me, so if he can put up with me at my worst, the least I can do is deal with some harsh words now and then.

"Whatever you say, Kyle," I say as I sink down into my small, uncomfortable hospital bed. He rubs his index fingers up and down the inside of my arm. Whenever he does this, it comforts me.

"Are you okay?" he asks.

"I'm fine. A little sore, but I'll manage."

"We'll manage," he says as he lifts my chin and places his full lips against mine. I can taste the remnants of his butter pecan ice cream on my tongue.

"Your lips taste like butter pecan."

"That's not the only thing of mine that tastes like butter pecan."

"You're such a nasty boy."

"Do I need to remind you there's nothing about me that resembles a boy?" He unbuckles his belt and unzips his zipper.

"Kyle, you better not pull it out in here. Your mom is in the hallway, and a doctor or nurse could walk in at any minute."

"Everybody in this hospital has seen a dick before. If they haven't, their first one would be the surprise of their life." Kyle and I pause when we hear the hospital door open and someone clears their throat. Kyle quickly zips up his pants and buckles his belt.

"Are you decent?" Dr. Hemlock asks.

"Yes, sir. How is the baby?" I ask.

Dr. Hemlock steps forward and bows his head slightly. My heart sinks as I immediately understand what that means.

"I'm sorry, Kyle and Pamela. The baby didn't make it." I burst into tears while Kyle sat there and said nothing.

CHAPTER 14
KYLE

THE IMAGE of Pamela at the bottom of the stairs flashes in my mind, making my breath catch. She could have died. The realization strikes me, leaving me dizzy. If I lose her...

The thought of raising Marissa alone chills me. I can't do it. If the unthinkable happens, I'll give her up for adoption without hesitation. I'll start fresh, find a new wife, one who agrees to a strict "no children" policy.

My gaze drifts to Marissa sitting with Chloe. Chloe looks peeved, probably because she knows I won't leave Pamela. Marissa's small face is tight with worry, her legs swinging as she clutches her favorite stuffed animal. For a moment, I feel resentment toward the child. If she had just picked up her toys like I told her a hundred times, none of this would have happened.

When Dr. Hemlock says, we lost the baby, I feel relief, mixed with annoyance. This will put Pamela in another depression, and when she's depressed, we don't have sex, and when we don't have sex, I seek satisfaction elsewhere. My phone buzzes—my second phone. I pull it out and see a text from Cindy.

Cindy: So, when can I see you again?

Me: Tomorrow morning. Same time, same place.

Cindy: I can't wait.

My cheating and lying are all Pamela's fault. If she were content with just me, I wouldn't have to cheat. But since she's obsessed with having a baby, I have to find someone else to give me attention. Chloe, and Cindy are perfect for satisfying my appetite. Chloe works for me, so we can fuck anytime, and Pamela will never find out.

Cindy's only twenty-five. As long as I pay her car note, she's happy being my side piece. She'll be mad that I'm not leaving Pamela now that she lost the baby, but she doesn't know where I live or who my family is.

Sheila's a problem. She knows too much about us and has purposely inserted herself into our lives after I told her I wasn't interested. I need to find a way to get her out. A big check might solve that problem.

My eyes linger on Chloe, taking in her slender figure and the way her dark ponytail swings as she moves. Desire stirs, quickly followed by self-loathing. I shouldn't be thinking about the nanny—not now, not ever. But the way those jeans hug her hips...

Shaking my head, I stand, my legs unsteady. I walk over to Marissa, kneeling to meet her eyes. The urge to discipline her, to make her understand the consequences of her actions, is overwhelming. But I'm aware of the judgmental eyes on me. If I spank her here...

I force my voice to stay calm, though I can't keep the edge out. "Marissa, didn't I tell you to pick up your toys? Because you didn't listen, Mommy's in the hospital.

You're not going to have a little brother or sister because she lost the baby, and it's your fault."

The words hang in the air, sharp and cutting. Marissa's lower lip trembles, tears welling in her green eyes. Part of me feels satisfied seeing the impact of my words. Another part—a part I try to ignore—feels a twinge of guilt.

Chloe reacts swiftly, fiercely. She covers Marissa's ears and shoots me a look of disgust. "What is wrong with you, Mr. Witherspoon?" she hisses. "She's just a child. Would you say that to *our child*?"

"What do you mean our child?" I whisper.

Chloe cups Marissa's ears tighter. "I took a pregnancy test. I'm pregnant."

"How many weeks?"

"Eight."

"I can't wait until you have my baby," I whisper. A flash of anger at Chloe's insubordination is quickly overshadowed by joy. She's pregnant with my baby. I had three women pregnant, and now, with the miscarriage, there are only two. My life is finally back on track.

It's strange, but I don't want Pamela to have children, yet the thought of other women carrying my babies excites me. These women let me do things to their bodies that I'd never do to precious Pamela.

Chloe removes her hands from Marissa's ears.

Marissa's small voice breaks through my thoughts. "I promise, Daddy. I did put all my toys away. Please don't spank me, Daddy. I'll do better." She throws her arms around me, her tiny body shaking with sobs.

I'm not moved by her tears. She's a manipulator. To others, she's cute and innocent, but I know better. I'm the master manipulator. I pride myself on being the perfect husband and father, but I've just shattered that illusion in front of a room full of strangers.

Forcing a smile, I reach into my pocket for a handkerchief. I gently wipe Marissa's tears away, my voice softening. "Daddy's sorry, baby girl. I know it's not your fault. Daddy's just a little sad."

As Chloe leads Marissa to the vending machines, I watch them go. I can't help but appreciate the sway of Chloe's hips, the way her jeans hug her curves. When she bends down to help Marissa, it sends a jolt of desire through me. I'll enjoy watching her body change as she carries my child.

I quickly avert my eyes, shame and arousal battling within me. I hired Chloe for her looks. I can admit that to myself. She's eye candy in the monotony of domestic life. I promised I'd never cross the line, but I did. There's no point in stepping back now.

Movement across the room catches my attention. It's my mother, her face a mask of concern. I brace myself for another lecture, another reminder of my failings as a husband and father.

To my surprise, my mother has a seat next to me and rests her hand on my back, rubbing soothing circles. For a moment, I allow myself to relax under her touch. Then she leans in close, her lips brushing my ear. "The next time you put your hands on me, I'll cut them off, you ungrateful piece of shit. And if I find out you're fucking the nanny, I'll make sure your dick is severed clean off. Your infidelity is costing me millions. The only woman you're allowed to fuck is Pamela. Do you fucking understand?"

I remain silent, shock rendering me speechless. My mother's nails dig into my arm, drawing blood. "Do you fucking understand me, boy?" she repeats, her voice low and dangerous.

"Yes, Mother," I manage to grit out, my teeth clenched against the pain. Beatrice straightens, smoothing her skirt as if nothing happened.

"I also took care of your Sheila problem. She won't be causing you anymore trouble."

"What do you mean you took care of the Sheila problem? What happened to the baby mom? Did she have the abortion?" My mother doesn't answer my question. With a final warning glance, she walks out of the hospital, her heels clicking on the linoleum.

I sit there, my mind reeling. At almost thirty-five, I'm still under my mother's thumb, still dancing to her tune. The realization fills me with rage and determination. It's time to take back control, to reclaim my manhood.

As I watch Chloe and Marissa return from the vending machines, a plan forms in my mind. I'll show them all—my mother, Pamela, the world—that I'm in charge of my destiny. I'll do whatever it takes to make that happen, no matter the cost.

My resolve hardens. The perfect husband, the doting father—those roles have been mine for too long. It's time for the real Kyle Witherspoon to emerge, consequences be damned.

CHAPTER 15
KYLE

15 YEARS ***earlier***

The crisp autumn air carries the scent of fallen leaves as I stride across Edington University's immaculate quad. My Italian leather shoes crunch over the multicolored leaves, each step a reminder of the vast differences between myself and the average student.

I am Kyle Ashton Witherspoon, scion of the late business tycoon whose name adorns the imposing School of Economics building looming to my left. Years of meticulous grooming have honed my ability to exude normalcy effortlessly. A casual smile here, a subtle flex of my quarterback's physique there—all carefully choreographed moves in an elaborate performance I've been rehearsing since childhood under my parent's guidance.

As I approach my luxurious off-campus apartment, a familiar dread coils in the pit of my stomach. The sight of the cream-colored envelope protruding from my mailbox sends a jolt of anxiety through me—another tuition bill. Despite our family's vast wealth, these reminders of financial obligation always trigger a visceral response, a deeply ingrained fear of losing it all.

With trembling fingers, I retrieve my phone and hit the speed dial for my mother before I even close the heavy oak door behind me. The extravagant interior of my apartment—all sleek modern furniture and abstract art pieces chosen by my mother's decorator—suddenly feels suffocating.

"Mom," I say, my voice betraying more tension than I intend. "There's another bill; it's Twenty-five thousand."

"I'll handle it, Kyle. But you need to visit financial aid and update our mailing address. Use San Diego, not Hawaii. We've discussed this."

"Yes, ma'am." The words feel automatic, remnants of childhood conditioning drilled into me since before I can remember.

"Now," her tone shifts, all business, "are you following the regimen?"

I clench my jaw, feeling the familiar resentment bubble up. As a junior in college, these constant check-ins grate against my desire for independence. But I know the stakes all too well.

"Yes, Mom. Medication daily. Watching the tapes. Everything's locked up tight in the safe."

"Kyle," her voice softens, almost imperceptibly, "I know you resent this, but one mistake could ruin everything—your future, your sister's, mine. Ever since your father—"

"I know, Mom," I cut her off, not wanting to rehash old wounds. The weight of unspoken family secrets presses down on me. "I'm handling it. I promise."

A beat of silence hangs between us, heavy with

unspoken tensions. Then: "What about that cheerleader? Vanessa?"

My free hand curls into a fist, nails biting into my palm. "What about her?"

"She's not suitable, Kyle. Her background, her aspirations—they don't align with our family's needs. You know this."

Anger flares, quickly tamped down by years of ingrained obedience. "Mom, I—"

"End it," she says, her tone brooking no argument. "And, Kyle? It's time you stepped away from football. We have bigger plans for you than the NFL."

"But Coach says I have a real shot at—"

"Kyle." Her voice turns to ice. "We've discussed this. Medical school, then a professorship. That's your path. Football is a distraction and, frankly, beneath someone of your station."

"Yes, Mother."

"Now check your text messages. I have an assignment for you. I've pulled some strings and got you a job."

"A job? I don't need a job. We have plenty of money."

"Oh dear Kyle, it's not a job where we trade our time for money. It's volunteer work. You start tomorrow, and I don't want to hear a word." I look at my text and frown—it's an abortion clinic.

"But Mom, why an abortion clinic?"

"Because it's the perfect place for you to meet your wife. A broken woman for my broken Kyle."

The call ends abruptly, leaving me in suffocating silence. I catch my reflection in the floor-to-ceiling windows—green eyes that my mother always said could charm anyone, perfectly tousled hair, the picture of privileged perfection. But beneath that carefully crafted exterior churns a whirlwind of conflicting impulses and guarded secrets.

To the world, I have it all—looks, wealth, athletic prowess, and a future brighter than the sun. But in the privacy of my thoughts, a darker truth lurks: I am broken, a carefully controlled monster playing at humanity.

My gaze drifts to the locked safe in the corner of my bedroom. Inside lie the medication that keeps me balanced, the tapes that reinforce my mother's lessons, and the mementos of past indiscretions that could never see the light of day.

Despite all my advantages—the money, the opportunities, the adoring gazes of countless women and men on campus—I've never felt more trapped. I am a puppet dancing on strings woven from family expectations and the ever-present fear of my own nature.

As night falls over the campus, I stand at the window, watching the carefree students below. They laugh, they love, they live with a freedom I can never know. For them, college is freedom. For me, it is just another gilded cage.

I press my forehead against the cool glass, closing my eyes. In that moment of vulnerability, a single thought echoes through my mind: How long can I keep up this charade before the monster within breaks free? It is at times like these I want to commit suicide. My life isn't my own, and because of my disorder, I have to navigate life differently than my friends. I am the best-looking guy on campus, my family has more money than 1,000 individual families, I go to the finest schools, wear the finest clothes, and fuck the prettiest girls, but despite all my privilege, I am broken inside and can't live life on my own terms. Privilege doesn't matter when you're a monster.

CHAPTER 16
PAMELA

THE STERILE HOSPITAL room feels suffocating as I watch Chloe step inside, my heart skipping a beat when I realize Marissa isn't with her.

"Where's Marissa?" I ask, panic edging into my voice.

Chloe's reassuring smile does little to ease the knot in my stomach. "She's with your sister-in-law, Donna."

"I went back to the house and packed you a few things. I didn't know how long you would be here."

"Thanks, Chloe, that was very thoughtful. I appreciate it."

Relief washes over me, but it's short-lived as I notice the tension in Chloe's shoulders, the way her fingers twist nervously at the hem of her shirt.

"Can we talk, Mrs. Witherspoon?" Chloe's voice is barely above a whisper.

I nod, steeling myself for whatever is coming. "Of course. What's on your mind?"

Chloe takes a deep breath, her eyes darting around the room as if checking for eavesdroppers. "I hate to bring this up at such a painful time for you, but... I'm putting in my letter of resignation tonight."

The words hit me like a physical blow. I lean forward, wincing at the pain that shoots through my abdomen—a stark reminder of the child I just lost.

"Oh no, Chloe, please don't leave us now," I plead, my mind racing. "Is it the money? We can pay you more if that's the issue. I know the cost of living has skyrocketed lately."

Chloe shakes her head, her expression a mixture of fear and resolve. "It's not the money, Mrs. Witherspoon. It's... it's your husband." I shake my head and lean forward in curiosity.

"What about Kyle?"

"Well, when I went back to grab you some clothes, I went into the attic and saw something on his computer screen that disturbed me, and I don't feel safe."

A chill runs down my spine. "What was it, Chloe? And why were you in the attic?"

Chloe's voice drops even lower, forcing me to strain to hear her. My heart pounds in my chest.

"I'm sorry, Mrs. Witherspoon. I just can't stay in your house anymore."

"What did you see, Chloe? What was so bad that it's making you want to quit?"

Chloe steps closer, her eyes wide with what looks like genuine fear. "I'm afraid to say. I think... I think you should check out the attic yourself." She hesitates, then adds, "Kyle also blamed Marissa for your fall. That's not something a father should say to his six-year-old daughter."

I feel as if the room is spinning. *Kyle blaming our daughter? And what could possibly be in the attic that would frighten Chloe so much?* "And if I were you..." She leans in close, her breath warm against my ear. "I'd take my daughter and leave."

"Chloe, you never answered my other question. Why were you in the attic?" Chloe pauses before speaking.

"I was cleaning."

"But how did you even get in the attic, Chloe? The only person who has a key is Kyle. I don't even have a key."

"I'm sorry, Mrs. Witherspoon? It just happened. I didn't mean to."

When the realization hits me about what Chloe is alluding to, I can barely breathe. I begin taking long, deep breaths to calm myself.

"Oh my God, you're the fucking whore that Sheila told me about. You're the bitch that is pregnant by my husband." The words send a shiver down my spine. Before I can respond, Chloe is at the door. She places her hand on her stomach. "Get out, Pamela. Before it's too late."

My mind races, conjuring up increasingly disturbing scenarios. *How long has he been having an affair? How long has she been pregnant?* And *if he did, why was he mean to me and kind to her? What could Kyle possibly be watching in the attic? Porn? Gay porn? But surely that wouldn't be enough to scare Chloe away. Was it something illegal?* My mind wonders to a thought that I just can't fathom but I quickly push it out. *But if that were the case, wouldn't Chloe have told me to go to the police? Has he hurt Marissa?* Is this why he doesn't want kids. Is Kyle a ...?

The not knowing is maddening. I know I have to find a way into that attic, have to see for myself what Kyle is hiding. But first, there are other fires to put out. I make a mental list:

1. Talk to Marissa, reassure her that the miscarriage wasn't her fault and find out if Kyle has ever hurt her.
2. Confront Kyle about his conversation with our daughter and the cheating.
3. Finally, uncover the secret in the attic.

CHAPTER 17
BEATRICE

TWENTY-SIX YEARS Earlier

I recline on the cushioned lounge chair, feeling the warmth of the afternoon sun seep into my skin. The glossy pages of a fashion magazine rustle between my fingers as I flip through them, desperately trying to savor this rare moment of tranquility. All around me, the air vibrates with the sounds of summer—the rhythmic splash of water, the high-pitched squeals of delight, and the constant hum of happy chatter as kids frolic in the community pool.

It was supposed to be a perfect day, a much-needed respite for both of us. But then I saw him—Kyle—sprinting towards me, his face a deep crimson, eyes wide and brimming with hurt. My heart clenches at the sight. I immediately know what this is about.

I drop the magazine. Its pages flutter, forgotten to the concrete. I sit up straight. "Kyle, honey, what's wrong?"

Before he could utter a word, he collapses into my arms, his body collides with mine with such force that I nearly toppled backward. He buries his face against my chest, his frame shaking with heart-wrenching sobs that seem to emanate from somewhere deep within him.

"They... they said I have girl boobs, mom!" His voice cracks, each syllable laced with a pain that no child should have to endure.

My heart shatters seeing him like this—so vulnerable, so confused, so hurt. I hold him tighter, wishing I could cocoon him from the world and its casual cruelties. But I know I can't, and this wasn't the first time I grappled with this particular worry.

I stroke his damp long hair, still cool from the pool water, trying to find the right words, even though I knew they would bring their own kind of pain. "Kyle, sweetie," I began softly, gently pulling back just enough to look into his tear-filled green eyes. "I've been meaning to talk to you about this."

He sniffles, wiping at his nose with the back of his hand, leaving a glistening trail across his sun-kissed skin. "Talk to me about what?"

I take a deep breath, the scent of chlorine and sunscreen filling my lungs. "You're... you're different, Kyle. A little different than some of the other kids. And I think... maybe it's time you start wearing a shirt when you go into the pool."

His face falls, and my heart plummets along with it. I could see the confusion and hurt swirling in his eyes like storm clouds gathering on the horizon. "Why? Why do I have to wear a shirt?"

I hesitated, hating every word that was about to come out of my mouth. "Because, sweetie, you're a bit chubby, and... your chest, it's a little different. It does make you look like you have man boobs. I just don't want people to make fun of you, like they did today. I don't want you to keep getting hurt."

His lower lip trembles, and I could see the tears well up again, threatening to spill over like a dam about to burst.

"Stop crying. You're a boy and boys don't cry." Kyle wipes his eyes then speaks.

"But... why can't I just be like them? Why do I have to hide?"

I sigh, feeling the weight of this conversation pressing down on me like a physical force. I wish I had the power to make it all go away for him, to reshape the world into a kinder place.

"Kyle, I know it doesn't feel fair. And it's not. But you're not like them. And that's okay. Everyone's body is different, and that's what makes us unique. But sometimes being different... it makes things harder."

He looks at me with so much sadness in his eyes, I could almost see his innocence cracking like thin ice. I could tell he was struggling to understand, to reconcile this harsh reality with the carefree world he'd known until now. "A shirt might help, honey. It'll stop people from focusing on your body, and you can just enjoy yourself without worrying about what they say."

"What do you mean I'm different?"

"Kyle, you're fat. When you are a kid it's cute, but this world isn't kind to fat people. If you want people to be nicer to you. You should cut back on the sugar and start working out with me. People will do anything for beautiful people. You're my handsome little boy and if you cut that girl hair and start working out. You will be the best-looking boy in the entire school."

"You really think I would be the best-looking boy in the entire school?"

"You're already the best looking but if you started lifting weights, you'd not only be the best looking but the most attractive and when you are attractive people ignore your other flaws."

"What other flaws?"

"Oh, darling you know about the other flaws; don't you."

He nodded, but it wasn't with the kind of acceptance I'd hoped for. It was a defeated nod, like he was surrendering to a battle he never asked to fight. I hate that look. I hate I couldn't protect him from the world and its judgments.

"But, Kyle," I added, my voice softer now, almost a whisper against the backdrop of continued pool noises," a shirt doesn't change who you are. You're still my strong, wonderful boy. It's just something to help you feel better... to keep you from getting hurt like this again."

He wipes his tears with the heels of his palms, but the weight of what I said lingered in the air between us, as tangible as the humidity. I could see him trying to process it, his young mind grappling with concepts no child should have to face. And I knew he would. Eventually. But for now, I just held him close, the sun warming our entwined figures, knowing no matter what I said, some things would always be hard for him. For both of us.

As we sit there, the sounds of laughter and splashing continues around us, a stark reminder of the carefree summer day this was supposed to be. But for Kyle and me, something had shifted. A small piece of childhood innocence had been chipped away, replaced by a harsh lesson about the world and its sometimes-cruel expectations.

I press a kiss to the top of his head, breathing in the mingled scents of chlorine and the strawberry shampoo he loved. "I love you, Kyle," I murmur, "No matter what. Always remember that.

He nods against my chest, his breathing slowly steadying. "I'm going to have you start meeting with my therapist, Dr. Lawson. She is a licensed therapist. She will be able to help you navigate this troubled time." I then reached over and grab two white pills from my purse. "Take these they will help with your urges and the anxiety you are feeling." I hand Kyle my bottle of water and watch him swallow the medicine.

"Thank you, mother," he replies. And as we sit there, inside our own little bubble amidst the chaos of the pool, I silently vow to do whatever it takes to help him navigate this world—a world that isn't always kind to those who don't fit the mold.

CHAPTER 18
PAMELA

THIS DAY IS PROVING TOO much. I've just lost a child, discovered my husband's affair with the nanny, and now I have to deal with the fact that my husband could be a monster. The antiseptic smell of the hospital burns my nostrils, a constant reminder of where I am and why. I should have known Kyle would blame Marissa—he always does. A nagging thought gnaws at me: *Is this why I've never been able to carry a child past twelve weeks? Is the universe trying to tell me I'm not fit to be a mother? That Kyle and I are not meant to be parents?*

I push these thoughts aside, feeling the cold sweat on my brow. I can't deal with this right now—one crisis at a time. When the doctor finally discharges me, I make my way to the waiting room on shaky legs, my mind reeling from the revelation of Kyle's betrayal. The fluorescent lights overhead seem harsh and unforgiving, matching my mood. I spot Marissa with Donna, my heart clenching at the sight of my daughter's worried face. Her green eyes are wide with concern.

"I'm sorry you lost the baby, mommy" Marissa says,

her lower lip trembling. "But I promise I put away all my Legos."

I kneel, ignoring the sharp pain that shoots through my body. I need to look my daughter in the eye, to make sure she understands this isn't her fault and to make sure Kyle hasn't harmed her. The linoleum floor is cold against my knees, grounding me in this moment.

"This is not your fault, sweetheart," I say firmly, fighting back tears of frustration and betrayal. "This is Mommy's fault. Mommy was clumsy. You did nothing wrong." I watch as the guilt and shame melt away from Marissa's face, replaced by relief. In that moment, I realize the immense power parents hold—the power to empower their children or burden them with trauma. I silently vow, as I have so many times before, to be nothing like my own mother. And unlike Kyle, I won't betray my family's trust.

I reach into my purse, feeling the cool plastic wrapper as I pull out a lollipop. I hand it to Marissa with a forced smile, the muscles in my face aching with the effort. My daughter's face lights up, revealing a gap-toothed grin that makes my heart swell with love, momentarily overshadowing my pain. "Marissa, I have a very important question to ask you about Daddy. Can you promise to be honest?"

"Of course, mommy; you taught me to never lie." I took a deep breath before I formulated my question. Just as I am about to ask. Kyle is there, his grip tight on my arm as he pulls me aside. His cologne, once comforting, now turns my stomach. "We shouldn't be rewarding her with sugar after what she just caused," he hisses, his breath hot against my ear.

Rage flares in my chest, fueled by the knowledge of

his infidelity. I yank my arm free, fixing Kyle with a glare that would have withered a lesser man. "We just lost a child, Kyle," I say, my voice low and dangerous, barely above a whisper. "Correction: I just lost a baby I was carrying in my body for six weeks. A couple of scoops of ice cream or a lollipop isn't going to kill us. Unlike your lies and betrayal."

Kyle's face pales, then darkens, but I press on, months —no, years—of frustration finally boiling over. "I'm taking an Uber home. Maybe you should drive home alone and think about the things you've said and done today. And while you're at it, think about how you're going to explain to our daughter why Chloe can no longer work for us."

"What happened with Chloe?" Donna asks, her voice laced with concern. She covers Marissa's ears, her maternal instincts kicking in.

"He's fucking her, and she's fucking pregnant!" I yell, my voice echoing off the sterile hospital walls. I see heads turn, but I'm beyond caring. Donna's eyes widen in shock, then narrow as she turns toward Kyle.

"Kyle, are you fucking serious? Your wife has trouble having children, and you fuck and get the nanny pregnant?" Donna's voice is a mix of disbelief and disgust.

Kyle turns his glare on Donna, but she just laughs—a harsh, bitter sound. "Now you know I don't care about you giving me a stare-down. You're wrong, brother, and you need some serious help."

"I'm doing my fucking best!" Kyle spits, his face contorted with rage. "One day, everyone will know! You all make me out to be the bad guy, and I'm just trying to survive here!" Tears well in his eyes, but he quickly turns away so we don't see him cry. For a moment, I feel a pang of sympathy, quickly squashed by my anger. *What did he mean he's trying to survive and one day we will know?* I'm the one dealing with a cheating husband with a baby on the way, a miscarriage, and a husband who has a deep dark secret I have yet to uncover.

Before anyone can respond, Kyle storms off, pausing only to hurl a chair across the waiting room with a guttural scream that makes everyone flinch. The crash of metal against tile echoes through the room, a physical manifestation of the chaos in our lives.

"I've never seen him like this," Donna says, her voice tinged with worry.

I take a deep breath, pushing down the fear, confusion, and heartbreak that threaten to overwhelm me. I turn to Marissa, forcing a smile. "Let's go get pizza, sweetie. We can have a mommy-daughter day."

As we walk out of the hospital, Marissa's small hand clutched tightly in mine, my mind whirls with unanswered questions. *What is Kyle hiding in the attic? What do Donna and my mother-in-law know that I don't? And how much longer can I ignore the growing darkness in my husband?*

One thing is certain—something must change. And as I step outside the hospital, I make a silent vow to uncover the truth, no matter the cost.

As Marissa and I settle into the Uber, the leather seats cool against my skin, my phone buzzes with a text from an unknown number: **"Pamela get out before it's too late."** My blood runs cold as I stare at the screen, the words seeming to pulse with an ominous energy. *Who could have sent this? And what awaits me in that attic?*

With a shaky breath, I delete the message and turn to Marissa, forcing a smile. "How about we get some ice cream after pizza?"

But even as my daughter cheers, her excitement a stark contrast to the dread settling in my stomach, I can't shake the feeling that my life is teetering on the edge of a cliff. The world outside the car window blurs as we drive, mirroring the chaos in my mind. One wrong move could send us all tumbling into the abyss.

As the Uber pulls away from the hospital, I make a silent promise to myself and to Marissa that whatever truths lie waiting in the attic, I will face them. The time for ignorance and complacency is over. Now it's time for answers.

CHAPTER 19
KYLE

I STAND BY THE WINDOW, peering through the gap in the curtains. My jaw clenches as I watch car after car cruise down the street, none of them carrying Pamela. The ticking of the clock in the corner seems to mock me, each second a reminder of my wife's defiance.

I run a hand through my hair, my mind racing. Pamela has never talked back to me before, let alone gone to dinner without my permission. The loss of control gnaws at me, a festering wound to my ego.

"I'm not some average Joe," I mutter, my reflection in the window glass staring back at me with cold, green eyes. "She should be worshipping the ground I fucking walk on."

My hand instinctively reaches for my phone, muscle memory dialing Chloe's number before I catch myself. The device feels heavy in my palm, a tangible reminder of temptation. *I'll deal with her later.*

To my surprise there is a text:

Cindy: *You didn't show up. Are you okay?"*

I can't deal with this now. I ignore the text and put my phone back in my pocket.

The house creaks around me; the silence is oppressive. She should have been home with me, but instead, she's out with Marissa—the demon child. My lip curls at the thought of my adopted daughter. The little bitch is probably responsible for Pamela's fall. I overheard her complaining about not wanting a sibling, and it wouldn't surprise me if the spawn of Satan had pushed her mother down the stairs and Pamela is covering for her.

My fists clench. Though I didn't want another baby, seeing Pamela in pain twists something inside me. If there was any way to give Marissa back, to return to the life of just me and Pamela, I'd do it in a heartbeat.

With heavy steps, I climb the narrow staircase to the attic, the wood groaning under my weight. The converted office space feels more like a cage than a sanctuary, the slanted ceiling pressing down on me. I slump into the leather chair behind my desk, the material creaking in protest.

The blank computer screen stares back at me, a dark mirror reflecting my turmoil. My foot taps an erratic rhythm against the floorboards as I fight the urge to watch the tape—the forbidden recording that offers a twisted sort of comfort. "I am stronger now," I whisper, a mantra that sounds hollow even to my own ears. "I can resist this."

Minutes stretch into hours, the shadows lengthening as night falls. My eyes keep darting to my phone, willing it to light up with a message from Pamela. But the screen remains stubbornly dark, each passing moment stoking the fire of my rage.

The absence of an invitation cuts deeper than any

blade. She hasn't even considered asking if I wanted to attend dinner. White-hot fury surges through my veins, demanding release. I rise to my feet with a loud roar, causing the rafters to shake. In one swift and forceful movement, I sweep everything off my desk.

Papers flutter to the ground like wounded birds. Pens clatter across the hardwood. I release a primal scream.

The guttural sound reverberates off the walls, but instead of purging my anger, it only seems to fan the flames. Desperate for relief, I slam my fist into the nearest wall. The impact sends shockwaves up my arm, pain blossoming across my knuckles.

For a moment, blessed clarity cuts through the haze of my fury. Physical agony as an antidote to emotional torment—it's a crutch I've leaned on for years. Anything to dull the ache that threatens to consume me. I stare at the fresh dent in the drywall, then down at my bloodied, already-bruising hand. A familiar calm washes over me, my breathing slowing. With trembling fingers, I reach for my phone, scrolling to Chloe's number.

The call goes straight to voicemail, her cheery greeting a stark contrast to the darkness swirling inside me. With a snarl of frustration, I hurl the phone against the wall. It shatters into a constellation of broken glass and circuitry.

"What's all the commotion up there?"

The unexpected voice jolts me out of my spiral. I freeze, straining to identify the intruder. After a moment, recognition dawns—Pamela's mother, Bianca. *How long has she been in the house?*

Quickly composing myself, I descend the attic stairs, closing the door firmly behind me. I step into the living room, coming face to face with my mother-in-law.

Bianca's eyes widen as she takes in my disheveled appearance, gaze lingering on my injured hand. "What have you done to your hand, handsome?" she asks, her voice a mix of concern and something else - something that makes my pulse quicken.

Before I can respond, Bianca has taken my hand in hers, leading me to the bathroom. Her touch is soft, almost reverent, as she tends to my wounds.

"Now you know you're too handsome to be doing harm to this beautiful body," she murmurs, her breath warm against my skin as she leans in close to examine my knuckles.

The sting of alcohol on my cuts is a welcome distraction from the inappropriate thoughts beginning to form. Bianca's hands are so different from Pamela's - smaller, softer.

"Thank you," I manage, my voice rougher than I intend. "My temper just got the best of me. I try not to show my anger around others. I thought I was here alone."

Bianca's lips curve into a knowing smile. "My flight got in early," she explains, fingers lingering on mine as she finishes wrapping the bandage. "What made you so angry you had to punch a wall?"

The concern in her voice is genuine, and I find myself opening up. "It's your daughter," I admit. "We just lost a child, and she's out here going on play dates with Marissa."

Bianca's expression hardens, a flash of something unreadable crossing her features. "Say no more," she says, her tone shifting. "That daughter of mine has always been hard to handle. You must be firm with her, Kyle. She takes your kindness, your generosity for granted. She doesn't fully appreciate all you have to offer."

As she speaks, Bianca's eyes meet mine, filled with an admiration that makes my breath catch. Her gaze roams over me, lingering on the muscles visible beneath my shirt.

"Well, thanks, Ms. Thompson," I say, suddenly aware of how close we're standing. "It feels good to be appreciated."

Bianca laughs, a rich, throaty sound that sends a shiver down my spine. "I told you to call me Bianca," she admonishes playfully. "Think of me more as Pamela's older but better-looking sister. We're only fourteen years apart, after all."

Before I can process the implications of her words, Bianca has taken my hand again, leading me to the kitchen. She gestures for me to sit, then moves behind me, her hands coming to rest on my shoulders.

"Where did you learn to do this, Ms.- I mean, Bianca?" I ask as she begins to knead the tension from my muscles.

"I've been studying to be a masseuse," Bianca explains, her fingers working magic on my knotted shoulders. "It's proving to be quite lucrative."

I let out a low groan of appreciation. "I'd pay you whatever you want if I got this kind of treatment every day."

Bianca's hands still for a moment. She moves around to face me, her expression a mix of surprise and something darker. "Pamela isn't giving you massages every day?"

"Massages?" I scoff. "She barely gives me sex. It's like once a week now."

"I'll have a talk with her," Bianca promises, her tone serious.

"Thanks, but please don't let her know I told you, I say quickly. "It will just make me seem weak and make her disrespect me more."

Bianca's smile turns conspiratorial. "This will be our little secret," she assures me. "I know how to bring things up without involving you. Have you eaten yet, Kyle?"

When I shake my head, Bianca's eyes light up. "Stay here," she instructs. "I'm going to whip you up some fresh fried chicken, yams, mac and cheese, cornbread, collard greens, and some of my favorite sherbet punch."

"That sounds like a lot of work, Ms..."

"It's Bianca," she interrupts, "and it's nothing. I love cooking... especially for young, handsome men like yourself."

The air between us crackles with tension. I know I'm treading dangerous ground, but I can't help the smile that spreads across my face. "Thanks, Bianca."

I watch as she sashays away, my eyes trace the curves of her body. Pamela's mother has kept herself in incredible shape, looking far younger than her forty-seven years.

I shift uncomfortably, acutely aware of my body's response to Bianca's flirtations. I quickly stand, heading for the living room to put some distance between us. The last thing I need is more complications in my already troubled marriage.

But as I settle onto the couch, my mind wanders. If Pamela ever divorced me, the thought of exacting revenge with her mother is darkly appealing. The image of Bianca bent over, screaming my name, flashes through my mind.

The sound of approaching footsteps and voices outside snaps me back to reality. They're home. In a flash,

I'm on my feet, dragging a chair to position it directly in front of the door. My heart pounds as I sit down, legs spread wide in a posture of dominance.

The door swings open, and all conversation stops as Pamela and Marissa spot me. Tension fills the silence.

"Why are you sitting right by the door, Kyle?" Pamela asks, her voice tight. "It's weird and stalkerish."

I narrow my eyes. "Waiting to confront you."

"Confront me about what? If anyone should be doing the confronting, I should be confronting you."

"About leaving me while I'm grieving our child."

Marissa's small voice cuts through, confused. "Daddy, Mommy said she could get pregnant again."

Something snaps inside me. "Marissa, Mommy wouldn't need to get pregnant again if you picked up your damn toys. It's your fault."

Tears fill Marissa's eyes. "Mommy, did I really make you lose the baby?"

Pamela kneels, pulling Marissa close. "No, baby. Mommy was just clumsy."

"I promise I picked up all my Legos. I really did, Daddy," Marissa sobs, covering her eyes as she runs from the room.

Donna, standing quietly to the side, steps forward. "I'm taking Marissa to my house while you two sort this out. I'm going to talk to Devon about postponing our mission trip because Marissa shouldn't be in the middle of this." She gives me a disapproving look before following the distraught child.

Pamela turns to me, fury etched in her face. "What is wrong with you?"

"I'm grieving, Pamela."

"Grieving?" Pamela's voice rises. "Grieving your

mistress? Because you didn't even want this baby. I thought you'd be happy I lost it."

My composure cracks. "I'm grieving for the loss of my wife," I spit. "Every time you get pregnant, I lose a piece of you. A part of you dies with the child, and that's another part of you I can't have. And it's your fault I was fucking Chloe."

The words hang between us, heavy with accusation. Pamela recoils as if slapped. "If you had kept fucking me, as we agreed, and stopped trying to have a baby I didn't want, I wouldn't have fucked the nanny," I continue, my voice rising.

"I'm not your personal Barbie doll. It's not my job to cater to your every need."

"But you used to, Pamela," I counter, desperation creeping into my voice. "You used to want me and only me. You used to be okay with just us, but now you're obsessed with having a baby. Don't you see how it's tearing us apart?"

Before Pamela can respond, Bianca's voice cuts through the tension. "You're going to lose a good man trying to keep having babies when he says he doesn't want any," she says, matter-of-factly. "Get those tubes tied and give that man what he needs before you lose him and he finds someone prettier and willing to do what he wants. You hear me, Pamela?"

Pamela's eyes narrow as she turns to face her mother. Without a word, she grabs my hand, gripping it tight. "Kyle, can I speak to you in the bedroom?"

"Listen to your mother. You could learn something."

Pamela's control snaps. "This bitch doesn't even know who my damn father is, and you want me to listen to her?

She's a jealous good for nothing hag who let my stepfather repeatedly rape me."

The crack of Bianca's hand across Pamela's cheek echoes through the room. "I'm your mother first," she hisses, "and don't you ever call me out of my damn name and Stanley was a good man. I don't know why you make up such awful things."

"Get your shit and get out! Both of you!"

I scoff, crossing my arms. "You can't put me out of my own house."

Without another word, Pamela strides out of the living room. When she returns moments later, my blood runs cold. In her hand is a gun, its metal gleaming in the low light.

"Get your shit and get out!" Pamela repeats, her voice steady despite the trembling in her hand.

My bravado falters. "You wouldn't dare."

The gunshot is deafening in the confined space of the living room. Plaster dust rains down from the new hole in the ceiling as the acrid scent of gunpowder fills the air. I stumble backward, my face pale. "So this is how you treat me, Pamela? After all I've done for you?"

Pamela advances, the gun still raised. "You mean after you cheated on me with the nanny? Called me fat? Offered to help other pregnant women but ignored me?"

"Look at this lifestyle you have," I retort, gesturing wildly around the room. "Do you know how many women would love to have a man like me, Pamela? I'm a fucking multi-millionaire. I work out hard to keep this body in shape for you. I've never hit you or forced myself on you, and I make your pussy purr and your body shake every time we have sex. I'm a fucking god amongst men."

My voice breaks as I continue, raw emotion bleeding

through. "I even married you after that guy raped you in college. I stood by your side, and when you got pregnant, I told you I would take care of the baby even though it wasn't mine. If you wanted to abort it, I wouldn't judge you. I've done things for you that you don't even know about. Things I'm ashamed of. All I've ever asked is that you put me first and just love me."

Pamela's resolve wavers; she lowers the gun slightly. "Kyle, you did support me through one of the worst times of my life, and it's one of the reasons I fell in love with you, but you're also the reason we don't have children," she whispers, her voice barely audible.

"What did you say?"

Pamela's grip on the gun tightens. "I said it's your fault I don't have a child. The last time I was pregnant, we were in an accident, Kyle. I lost the baby because you made an illegal turn."

The accusation hangs in the air, heavy and suffocating. My face drains of color as my mind races back to that day. The screeching tires, the crunch of metal, Pamela's agonized scream—it all comes flooding back in a rush.

"Pamela, are you still holding that against me?" My voice cracks, a mix of disbelief and hurt. "It was an accident."

Pamela's eyes narrow, a dangerous glint in them. "Was it really though, Kyle? I'm starting to think you did it on purpose, just because you wanted me to yourself."

The words hit me like a blow. I stagger back, my legs bumping against the coffee table.

"You think I would endanger our lives and another person's just to get rid of a child?" My voice rises with each word, pain and anger intertwining. "You really think

I'd hurt the woman I love more than anything? That hurts, Pamela. That cuts deep."

"At this point Kyle, I won't put anything past you."

Unable to bear the weight of her accusation, I turn and stride to the bedroom. I emerge moments later with my jacket slung over my arm, brushing past Pamela without a glance.

"Kyle, I'm sorry. I didn't mean it," Pamela calls out, her voice breaking as tears stream down her face. But her words fall on deaf ears as I wrench open the front door and step into the cool night air.

CHAPTER 20
PAMELA

BIANCA'S VOICE cuts through the silence, dripping with disapproval. "Now look at what you've done. You drove a good-looking, rich man away."

I whirl to face my mother, fury reigniting in my eyes. The gun in my hand suddenly feels heavier, a cold reminder of how quickly things have spiraled out of control. "How dare you?" I spit, my voice trembling with rage. "You have no idea what I've been through, what we've been through."

The living room, once a symbol of our perfect life, feels like a battlefield. The scent of gunpowder still lingers in the air, mixing with the cloying smell of my mother's perfume.

Bianca crosses her arms, unmoved by my outburst. Her face, so similar to mine yet harder, colder, is a mask of judgment. "All I see is a foolish girl throwing away a good thing. You think men like Kyle grow on trees?"

"You just found out I was raped in college for the first time and your first statement to me is about driving away a good man?'

"You think you are the only woman to get raped Pamela? It happens to women all the time. Get over yourself."

"Is that what you told yourself when I told you what Stanley did to me?"

"Stanley was a good stepfather to you. He was a good man. I don't know why you like to make up stories about him."

"Get out," I whisper, my voice dangerously low. When Bianca does not move, I raise the gun once more, pointing it at her. The action feels surreal, like I'm watching someone else control my body. "I said, get out!"

Bianca's eyes widen in shock, but she quickly composes herself. "You will not dare," she says, echoing Kyle's earlier words. The parallel is not lost on me, and it sends a chill down my spine. I step forward and push the gun into the middle of her forehead.

For a moment, mother and daughter, we stand locked in a silent battle of wills. Then, without another word, Bianca grabs her purse and heads for the door. She pauses on the threshold, turning back to fix me with a cold stare.

"You'll regret this," she warns, her voice laced with venom. "Mark my words, Pamela. You'll come crawling back, begging for forgiveness. But it might be too late."

Her words cut deep, reopening old wounds I thought has long since healed. The weight of her disappointment, a familiar burden, settles on my shoulders once more.

The door closes behind Bianca with a hard and loud click, leaving me in the eerily empty house. The gun slips from my fingers, clattering to the floor as I sink to my knees. The cool hardwood against my skin grounds me, a stark contrast to the emotional turmoil raging within.

Sobs wrack my body as the events of the day crash

over me. The loss of my baby, the betrayal of my husband, the harsh words of my mother—it's all too much. I curl in on myself, my cries echoing off the walls of the empty house. Each sob feels like it's tearing me apart from the inside.

Through my tears, I catch a glimpse of movement outside the window. Kyle's car, still parked at the end of the driveway. My heart leaps for a moment, hope warring with anger and hurt. But then the engine roars to life, and I watch as he pulls away, disappearing into the night.

I'm left alone with the aftermath of our confrontation.

My perfect life is falling apart, and I can't shake the feeling that this is just the beginning.

I drag myself to my feet, my body heavy. The gun lies on the floor, a stark reminder of how close we came to tragedy tonight. With shaking hands, I pick it up, securing it back in its lockbox.

I make my way to our bedroom—my bedroom now, I suppose. The bed, with its rumpled sheets, seems to mock me.

I curl up on Kyle's side of the bed, burying my face in his pillow. His scent surrounds me, and for a moment, I'm torn between the urge to find comfort in it and the desire to scrub it away completely.

CHAPTER 21
PAMELA

THE HOUSE SETTLES AROUND ME, creaking and sighing like a living thing. In the wake of my confrontation with Kyle and my mother, a heavy silence has descended, broken only by the steady tick of the grandfather clock in the hallway. Each second seems to mock me, a reminder of how quickly my world has unraveled.

I wander from room to room, a ghost in my own home. The spaces feel cavernous, empty of the warmth and life they once held. In the kitchen, a half-empty glass of wine stands on the counter—my mother's, abandoned in her hasty departure. I grab it and throw it against the wall. I watch as the glass shatters. My white walls now speckled with crimson. I feel 1% better. I grab a bottle from the wine rack and throw it at the wall and this time I let out a guttural scream hoping to feel 2% better. But I don't feel better. My feeling is unchanged and now I have a wall that looks like it was painted by a preschooler.

The living room still bears the invisible scars of my argument with Kyle, the air heavy with unspoken words and shattered trust.

Marissa's room, usually a sanctuary of childhood innocence, feels like a reproach. Stuffed animals stare at me with glassy eyes, silent witnesses to my failure as a mother, a wife, a daughter. I close the door softly, unable to bear their mute judgment.

As night deepens, I find myself drawn inexorably towards the one part of the house I have always avoided—Kyle's attic sanctuary. With him gone and my mother banished, this is the perfect opportunity to investigate what had frightened Chloe so badly. When me and my daughter were having pizza, I questioned her to see if Kyle had harmed her in any way, but she insisted that the only thing Kyle had done was say some mean words and spank her on the hand a couple of times.

I scheduled her an appointment with a child psychologist to see if they could find out more information. The mystery tugs at me, offering a focus for my swirling emotions, a purpose amid chaos. I go to the garage, grab a sledgehammer, and swing it at the lock with all my might, swing after swing until I have busted the lock and the door swings open.

Heart pounding, I climb over the debris and head up the attic steps. Each step feels like a decision, a choice between blissful ignorance and potentially devastating truth. As I reach the top, I flick on the light, illuminating what appears to be a combination of an office and a man cave.

The attic looms before me. My heart hammers against my ribcage. The wooden stairs creak beneath my feet.

The air hangs heavy, thick with the scent of old books and leather, undercut by a faint metallic tang that makes my skin crawl. My eyes dart around the room. The leather couch, once a symbol of luxury, now seems to leer at me. Everything is a chaotic mess. Papers and pens are all over the floor along with staplers, markers, and post-it notes. It looks like someone had a tantrum and threw everything off the desk. The neat freak in me wants to clean it up, but I don't have the time to clean up my downstairs mess, let alone Kyles. I step over the items on the floor and peruse the space.

Bookshelves line the walls, an intellectual fortress. My gaze skims over the titles—of business tomes, historical accounts, and... medical texts? My brow furrows. *Had Kyle rekindled his interest in medicine*? I reach out, fingers trailing along the spines, half-expecting to trigger some hidden mechanism. But the books remain stubbornly static, guarding their secrets.

The normalcy of the scene is almost maddening. *What could have possibly frightened Chloe so badly?* I go toward the computer, but it's locked. I try a few passwords, but after so many tries and no correct attempts, I lock myself out. My mind races, conjuring increasingly horrific scenarios. Each heartbeat seems to whisper, "Deeper, deeper," urging me further into the attic's depths. I get up from Kyle's desk and continue exploring.

Suddenly, the world tilts. My foot catches on something, sending me sprawling across the rough wooden floor. Pain blooms in my knee, a sharp counterpoint to the dull ache of fear in my chest. "Ouch!" The cry escapes my lips before I can stifle it, echoing in the stillness of the attic.

As I push myself up, wincing at the sting of abraded skin, my gaze falls on the cause of my fall. A floorboard, slightly raised, as if inviting investigation. Curiosity overrides caution, and I find myself prying at the wood, my heart racing as it gives way beneath my fingers.

The hidden compartment gapes before me. Nestled within, incongruous and somehow sinister, sits a black gym bag. My hands tremble as I reach for it, the nylon material cool and slick against my skin.

I hold my breath, half-expecting alarms to blare or Kyle to materialize, catching me in the act. But there is only the quiet rustle of fabric as the bag's contents are revealed.

VHS tapes and pill bottles with different color tops. Dozens of them, dusty with age. For a fleeting moment, relief washes over me. Is this merely Kyle's hidden cache of pornography? A secret, perhaps, but a mundane one? I examine the pill bottles, but they have no information on them but the name Dr. Lawson. *Who the fuck is Dr. Lawson and why and what is he prescribing my husband? Is Kyle sick and hiding it from me?*

But as I examine the tapes more closely, that fragile hope shatters. Each is meticulously labeled with a woman's name and a date. *Are these sex tapes?* I continue looking at the names hoping that one of them will provide a clue to what is on them. I freeze when I see my best friends name on one of the tapes:

Sheila Carruthers

The implications hit me like a physical blow, stealing the air from my lungs. My mind reels, grasping for explanations, each more horrifying than the last. *What atrocities are recorded on these tapes? Why has Kyle gone to such lengths to conceal them? And why is Sheila's name on one?* I count the tapes. There are over twenty tapes in this gym bag. This was too much to take in. Just as I was about to close the bag, I saw a tape with the date that I'd never forget. It was the date of my horrific college incident.

I sit back on my heels, the weight of the gym bag

suddenly unbearable in my lap. The attic seems to close in around me, the walls pulsing with unspoken horrors. I am drowning in possibilities, each more nightmarish than the last.

For a moment, I consider retreating. I could replace everything, creep back downstairs, and pretend this night has never happened. Kyle and I could continue our life, imperfect but known. Marissa will grow up in a home untainted by whatever dark secrets these tapes hold.

But even as the thought forms, I know it's impossible. The seed of doubt has been planted, and it will grow, poisoning every interaction, every tender moment. I will forever see Kyle through the lens of suspicion, searching for glimpses of the monster that might lurk beneath his careful façade. Not to mention, I have beat the door down so he will eventually find out.

Decision crystallizes within me. With quick, decisive movements, I grab the gym bag. The need to know, to see, burns within me, an all-consuming fire that drowns out reason and caution.

As I hurry from the house, my mind whirls with possibilities. Where can I go? Who can I trust with this terrible burden of knowledge? The pawn shop downtown materializes in my thoughts—old Mr. Johnson, with his endless supply of outdated technology and his penchant for minding his own business.

I jump in my car with my husband's gym bag as I head to uncover the secrets that my husband has so carefully hidden from me in the attic.

CHAPTER 22
PAMELA

AFTER I REALIZE the Mr. Johnson's pawn shop is closed for the evening, I continue searching Google to find one that is open. I spend hours on the phone, my desperation growing with each dead end, until finally, I found one that has what I needed. A VCR–a relic from a bygone era. The neon signs of the pawn shop flickered like dying fireflies.

As I pull into the crumbling parking lot, the realization of where I am hit me like a punch to the gut. This isn't the manicured suburbia we call home. Graffiti-covered walls loom around me, and shadowy figures lurk in nearby alleys. I clutch my purse.

The bell above the door jangle discordantly as I enter. I brace myself for musty air, but instead, a wave of sweetness envelop me. Cherry incense masks whatever secrets this place holds. My eyes adjust to the dim interior, taking in the jumbled shelves of castoff treasures and broken dreams. Musical instruments with missing strings hang like forgotten laundry. Tarnished jewelry glint under flickering lights. And there, behind the counter, stands a man who seems to fill the entire space. He is a mountain made flesh—easily six and a half feet tall, with arms thick as tree trunks. His blonde hair hangs in greasy strands around a face hidden beneath an unkempt beard. But it is the tattoo that draws my eye—a heart on his right bicep with 'Lola' scrawled in flowing script. Who is she? A lost love? A daughter?

He looks up from his phone, and the transformation is startling. His blue eyes crinkles at the corners, and a smile split his beard like sunshine breaking through storm clouds.

"You the lady here about the VCR?" His voice is surprisingly gentle. I nod, relief washing over me.

"Yes, I'm so glad you have one. No one carries them anymore. He chuckles, a sound like gravel in a tumbler.

"They've become little collectors' items. Funny how things come full circle, ain't it?"

My fingers fumbled with my purse. "What do I owe you?"

"Fifty dollars ought to do it."

I pull out a crisp hundred-dollar bill. "Keep the change as a tip."

His eyebrows shoot up, disappearing into his shaggy hairline. He studies me for a moment, curiosity replacing surprise. "If you don't mind me asking, why do you need a VCR at 8:00 p.m. at night? What's so pressing you cannot wait for a few days to have it delivered?"

I freeze, my mind racing. The truth hovers on my lips —about the mysterious package, the unlabeled tape, the gnawing fear that has driven me here. Instead, I force a smile.

"Just want to watch some old family movies. The

pawnshop owner's eyes glare at me, something unreadable passing across his features.

As the man wrapped up the VCR, I cannot shake the feeling that I am balancing on a knife's edge. Whatever is on these tapes, it threatens to shatter everything I know to be real. And yet, I know with bone-deep certainty that I have to watch it. The bell jangles again as I leave, the cherry-scented air giving way to the acrid smell of the city. I clutched the VCR to my chest like a lifeline as I hurry and lock myself in my car.

CHAPTER 23
PAMELA

THE HILTON BAYFRONT HOTEL emerges before me, its exterior a stark contrast to the turmoil within. I drive and let valet park my car because I refuse to hunt for one in the parking garage. This place has become my sanctuary, a haven where I escape the suffocating reality of my life at home. The promise of a hot stone massage, room service, ocean front view and a fully equipped bar offers temporary respite from the storm of my emotions, but at the moment, my mind is only on one thing—what is on Kyle's tapes.

As I walk into the expansive foyer, the bellhop takes my overnight bag, but I make sure to keep Kyle's gym bag and my purse with me. They know me here and I keep the suite booked in case I need a mini vacation, or if someone comes in town and I don't want them staying at our home. My phone buzzes insistently. Kyle's name flashes on the screen. My finger hovers over the button, but I do not answer. Either he is trying to draw me back—Kyle always knows exactly what to say, the right words to pull me back into his orbit—or he has been home and discovered that I found the tapes.

I close my eyes, memories flooding back in a torrent of pain and anger. Kyle's voice, sharp with disdain, calling me fat in front of Marissa. The look of confusion and hurt on our daughter's face. His callous disregard for my feelings when he invited my mother over, knowing full well the tension it would create. The constant pressure for intimacy even as I struggle to heal from the miscarriage that left me physically and emotionally raw.

But it is his last transgression that finally shatters the fragile peace between us. In a moment of cruel manipulation, he dredged up my most traumatic experience, wielding it like a weapon to guilt me into feeling sorry for him. The memory of it makes me want to vomit. No, I will not respond. Not this time. I head over to the bar. Since I'm not pregnant. I plan to drown myself in fruity alcoholic beverages.

"Can I get a strawberry daquiri?" I ask the bartender. I place my credit card on the counter. The bartender nods and commences to making my drink.

As if on cue, my phone rings again. This time it is Mama Witherspoon's name that lights up the screen. I hesitate, then answer on the third ring. I take a deep breath, forcing cheer into my voice.

"Hey, Mama Witherspoon," I say, praying my voice does not betray the tears I am desperately holding back.

"Where are you, dear?" The older woman's voice is warm with concern. "I stopped by the house with some food, and no one was there. I figured you went to a hotel because you didn't want to see your mother."

I feel a rush of affection for my mother-in-law. "You know me so well," I admit, my façade cracking slightly.

"I'm at The Hilton Bayfront Hotel. I just needed to be alone."

"I know the feeling. Nothing like a night at a hotel to clear your head. Do you want me to bring the food I prepared?" she said.

"That is so kind of you, but I am going to order room service. Why are you so kind to me? Mothers-in-law and daughters-in-law aren't supposed to get along this fabulously."

There is a pause on the other end of the line, heavy with unspoken understanding. When Mama Witherspoon speaks again, her voice is tinged with a sadness that makes my heart ache.

"The apple didn't fall too far from the tree, I'm afraid," she says softly. "I know what my son is like. I was married to his father. It's hard being married to men like them."

I listen, transfixed, as my mother-in-law opens up about her own struggles—the countless affairs, the fear for her health that led her to withdraw from intimacy altogether, the realization that she stayed because she was the only one who truly accepted her husband for who he was.

"I see myself in you, Pamela," Mama Witherspoon says. "By helping you, I feel like I'm healing the younger version of me. It's the least I can do after what my son has put you through."

The tears I've been holding back finally spill over. "I don't think I can handle this anymore," I confess, my voice barely above a whisper. "It's becoming too much. The failed pregnancy, my mother, the other women...and the way he treats Marissa. I can't take it."

"Other women?"

"Yes, Kyle got Chloe pregnant."

"He did what?"

"I know. I couldn't believe it myself."

"Now don't make any rash decisions," the older woman cautions. "This is nothing a little therapy can't fix."

My head snaps up, eyes widening as I recognize the approaching figure. "I'll call you back, Mama Witherspoon," I say, hurriedly ending the call. I quickly dry my eyes and throw on some shades.

The man walking into the bar is one of Kyle's friends I saw a few days ago.

"Pamela? Is that you?" When I look up, it is Jake. His voice is deep and rich, with a hint of a Southern drawl.

"Hey Jake, don't mind the shades. My contacts are acting up and my eyes are super red."

"I understand. I think I'm going to get Lasik so I don't have to mess with them anymore," he says.

"That's on my never ending to do list," I reply.

"Hey, how are you? And how is Kyle? I never saw him get that angry before. We play around all the time at the gym, so it was weird to see him like that."

"Yeah, I apologize for that. He's kind of possessive of me."

"I see. What brings you to the Hilton? I'm here to get information about the amateur bodybuilding competition."

"You could definitely be a bodybuilder." Jake looks to the left and then the right.

"You better make sure Kyle isn't here before you start dishing out compliments." We both chuckle.

"Kyle was just projecting his guilt onto me. I found out he was sleeping with the nanny."

"Saint Kyle? I find that hard to believe, Pamela.

Women hit on him all the time at the gym, but he turns them down left and right. All he does is talk about how great a woman you are and how he can't wait to have children with you."

"Kyle said that?" I ask.

"Yeah, he sings your praises so much. He said you are the person that encouraged him to drop out of med school and to start coaching and personal training."

"Kyle Witherspoon sings my praises?"

"Yeah, he talks about how he gave up his career in medicine to really help people eat better and change their bodies. He said you were a big encouragement. To be honest, the way he talks about you made me jealous that I hadn't found someone like you."

"That's very sweet of you to say, Jake. I really needed to hear that."

Jake takes out a business card and hands it to me. "If you ever need a shoulder to lean on or cry on, I'm here."

I take the business card, and as our hands brush against each other, I feel a chill of excitement. Our eyes lock, and we stare for a while until I break the gaze.

"Well, I will hit you up if I need an ear."

"It was great seeing you again, Pamela."

"You too, Jake." I watch as he walks away, and for the first time in years, I allow myself to take in the beauty of another man, to imagine myself in his arms. Jake is tall, dark, and handsome. He isn't pretty—he is handsome and exudes masculinity. He is more muscular than Kyle, and I feel safe in his presence. For a moment, I forget about my chaotic life and imagine a simpler and less problematic life, but then I come back to reality. I grab the tapes, my drink, and head to the hotel room.

As I pass through the revolving doors, I cannot shake

the feeling that I am stepping into a new chapter of my life—one with danger, secrets, and the potential for both heartbreak and long-awaited truth.

The elevator ride to my floor is endless, the soft music a stark contrast to the chaos of my thoughts.

I look at my reflection in the mirrored elevator. The woman who stares back at me is changed. Whatever comes next, I will face it head-on. For Marissa. For myself. And for the truth that has been hidden for far too long.

I step into the hotel room and quickly set up the VCR. My hand trembles as I insert the VHS tape with the earliest date. The grainy footage flickers to life, revealing a younger Kyle seated in a dimly lit hospital room. His eyes, cold and focused, are fixed on something off-screen.

As the video progresses, I realize with growing horror that Kyle is watching a series of disturbing scenes. When the video first starts there is a lady on a hospital table with her legs open. Next it flashes to a young angry boy, sitting in a hospital room floor stabbing a doll with a plastic knife, who I now recognize as Kyle. When he stabs the doll a substance that looks like blood comes from it. As the fake blood oozes from it, his anger appears to subside.

Sitting next to him is Mama Witherspoon—a much younger version. She reaches out and grabs his hand. At first, I think, *why would a mother let her son watch a woman giving birth at such a young age?* I also think, *why a mother would let her child stab a doll?* Then I think maybe this is what wealthy people do. Expose their kids to their career choices at an early age. Maybe he has shown interest in being a gynecologist or surgeon.

I change my theory when I realize the woman on the

table has her feet in stirrups like you would for a pelvic exam, next I see the doctor insert an instrument inside the woman and apply what appears to be an anesthetic. I watch as the doctor then inserts multiple tools of which I am not familiar and remove what appear to be parts of a fetus's body. Kyle's expression changes from anger to excitement as he sees the multiple fetus parts. His eyes... they gleam with an unsettling intensity that makes my skin crawl. Kyle stands up and walks toward where the dead fetus parts are and looks at it in awe.

"Beautiful," he whispers. "So, fucking beautiful." Mama Witherspoon kneels in front of Kyle.

"Kyle how do you feel?"

"I feel good, happy."

"You don't feel like you want to hurt animals or people?"

"No, I feel fine." Mama Witherspoon lets out a long sigh of relief." I continue watching the tape and a doctor wearing a name tag that says Dr. Lawson appears on the screen.

"Beatrice we will have Kyle watch a live abortion once a month, but in-between the live sessions we will have him watch the tapes. This is his prescription. If the tapes work like I think they will. He may never have to attend the live sessions but let him decide that. Only time will tell." I cannot believe it. My husband gets off on watching abortions. *Is this what he was watching in the attic all these years? Is this what Chloe saw on his computer?* The are no words to describe the disgust I feel. I think about not putting in the next tape afraid of what I will find, but I need to know the truth. I need to know what I am dealing with.

I insert the next tape. It's the tape with the latest date

on it. It is the same hospital room, but on this tape, I see my best friend, Sheila. I shudder when I hear her voice. "I change my mind. I want to keep my baby. I don't want a late-term abortion." Tears fall from her eyes, and she continues to beg but no matter what she says the doctor doesn't stop. They continue against her will.

"It's too late, my dear. You have signed paperwork and been paid," Mama Witherspoon says.

"Please I'll do anything if you let me keep Marissa." Mama Witherspoon motions for the doctor to stop the procedure.

"Anything?" Mama Witherspoon asks. I paused the tape.

"What?" I said. "Are my ears playing tricks on me? I rewound the tape and played it repeatedly. I looked at the date on the tape and it said 6/25/2018. If my calculations are correct, it means that Kyle has been cheating with Sheila for over six years and it appears that Marissa, the daughter we adopted is Kyle and Sheila's biological daughter. I can't believe it. My whole life has been a lie. The little girl I have been raising for the last three years is my husband's and best friend's daughter. Tears flow from my eyes like mini waterfalls. An emotional pain I didn't know existed rises from the soles of my feet to the pit of my stomach. I fall to the floor too weak to stand and then I see someone step out of the bathroom and into the hotel room.

I scream at the top of my lungs when I realize who it is.

It's my psychotic husband Kyle dressed in a bell hop uniform.

CHAPTER 24
KYLE

I PRAYED that this day wouldn't come but deep down a part of me knew that Pamela would discover the truth no matter how hard I tried to cover it up. I imagined it would be decades from now, but she just kept insisting on wanting to have a baby and that triggered me into a life I had hoped to leave behind.

"Pamela I am going to give you five seconds to be quiet. If you don't, I'm going to have to drug you." Pamela immediately shut up. "I tried to be the good husband. I tried to be perfect for you, but you kept pushing my buttons."

"You lied to me. You said you weren't having an affair with Sheila. You said that Sheila wasn't pregnant with your child."

"She isn't. I haven't fucked Sheila in years. I had sex with Sheila over six years ago. The only reason I even allowed you all to be friends is because she threatened to spill the secret that she was Marissa's biological mother, and I didn't want to take that away from you."

"You're fucking sick! You get off on watching abortions."

"I'm not sicker than any of the doctors that perform abortions. I am only watching them perform a procedure. It beats the alternative. Killing innocent animals and people."

"Now that you know the secret. Hopefully, you can continue raising Marissa and we can go back to our happy lives."

"If you think I'm going to stay married to you; you're crazy."

"Hmm, mother told me that this wouldn't go how I planned. "Pamela put in the last tape there is something I want you to see."

"I'm not watching anymore of that sadistic shit."

"Pamela, I'm being very nice and levelheaded. You have gotten the good side of me for almost ten years please just do what I say because I'd hate for you to see the side of me that you saw in the hospital."

Pamela took a deep breath and put in the last tape. The tape I fear she had been avoiding. The one with the date that she was raped. She watched as a man she hadn't seen in over a decade appears on screen. On the tape was her stepfather, Stanley, the guy who raped her as a kid and came to her college campus and did it one final time. He's on his knees and I have a gun to his head. "Please Kyle don't do it; I promise I'm not a bad guy. I needed the money."

"You hurt my Pamela and since you hurt my Pamela, I have to hurt you," I say on the tape. I take the gun and shoot him in the head and Stanley falls to the ground.

I slam the power button and watch as Pamela immediately covered her mouth and screams. I watch as she stumbles to the bathroom, barely making it before she hurls over the toilet, throwing up everything she'd eaten. As she slumps against the cool tile, I stand behind her.

"If you go to the police or even think about trying to divorce me. This is what I will do to Marissa." I don't love her because I see the darkness that's in me, in her, and the only reason, she is alive and the only reason I killed your stepfather, Stanley, is because I love you.

Pamela releases a wail of denial, horror, and grief so loud that I have no other option but to silence her.

"Oh, Pamela," Kyle whispers in my ear, soft and almost sad. "Why couldn't you just leave well enough alone?" I place a needle in her neck and watch as she passes out in my arms.

CHAPTER 25
PAMELA

THE RAIN PELTS against the windshield as Kyle navigates the winding road leading to Mama Witherspoon's estate. I know this is where we're going because I've been to this house many times over the years. He grips the steering wheel with an intensity that matches the storm raging both outside and within me. The wipers struggle to keep up with the downpour, creating a hypnotic rhythm that only heightens my sense of unease.

I glance at my husband with new eyes. This man is a demon wrapped in a beautiful package—the personification of Satan reimagined.

"I told you not to scream."

"Kyle, did you drug me?"

"It was just an animal tranquilizer. You are fine."

I look down at my wrists. They're bound. My thoughts immediately go to my daughter.

"Where is Marissa? I promise if you've hurt her—"

"Calm down, Pamela. I haven't killed anyone in over a decade. Marissa is at home with Donna. She's fine. If you follow the rules, she will be okay."

"I can't believe you killed my stepfather. Everything makes sense now. How the cops never found him and how he just disappeared. No wonder the cops thought I killed him."

"He deserved it," Kyle continues, "so don't get all bent out of shape."

I can't believe the words coming out of my husband's mouth. So many times, I thought about killing that man, but didn't have the courage. He did the thing that my mother should have done. I'm conflicted. I'm angry at him, but I also feel a sense of relief knowing that my attacker, my abuser is no longer alive.

The wrought-iron gates of the Witherspoon estate slowly come into view—a fortress of wealth and secrets. As we approach, lightning decorates the sky, casting an eerie glow on the perfectly manicured grounds. The security guard's face is impassive as he recognizes us, buzzing us through without a word.

The mansion emerges from the darkened gloom, its windows like cautious eyes peering at everything within its grasp. I can't shake the feeling that I'm walking into the lion's den, about to receive answers from the source of my nightmares. But what choice do I have? The weight of the hidden tapes in my bag seems to grow heavier with each passing moment.

As we pull into the circular driveway, movement catches my eye. A sleek black car is just leaving, and I catch a glimpse of an older woman behind the wheel. Our eyes meet for a brief, electric moment before she turns away. The look she displays is one of empathy. My mind races. *Who is she? What* does *she know?* I take a deep breath, preparing myself for what lies ahead but making sure to commit the license plate to memory. The valet appears, seemingly unfazed by the downpour.

For the first time ever, the grand entrance doesn't welcome me. Its double doors taunt me and make me want to run in the other direction. It's at this time that Kyle removes the chains from my hands and legs. I think about making a run for it, but there's nowhere to go. I take my hand and slap him clean across the face.

"How dare you chain me up and drug me like I'm one of your damn victims."

Kyle doesn't hit me back; he just takes it.

"I had to tie you up because I didn't need you going to the police without having all the information."

I stomp toward the door and raise my hand to knock, but the door swings open before I can make contact. Henry, the ever-present butler, stands there with his usual stoic expression.

"Welcome, Mrs. Witherspoon. Lady Witherspoon awaits you in the sitting room."

I eye him up and down, my face adorned with disgust.

"Shut the fuck up, Henry, you sick bastard." I try to slap him, but he grabs my hand.

I snatch my hand from Henry and push past him into the corridors, my heels echoing on the marble floors. The opulence that once dazzled me now feels suffocating.

We reach the sitting room, and there she is—Beatrice Witherspoon, Kyle's mother, perched on an antique chesterfield like a queen on her throne. The first thing I notice is a painting of a bloody seahorse on the wall above the mantle. It matches the seahorse in rubies that hangs on her necklace. Her face breaks into a practiced smile as she rises to greet me.

"What a pleasant surprise," she coos, air-kissing my

cheeks. "Though I must say you look frightened. Is everything alright?"

I sink into the chair across from her. Without a word, I reach into my bag and pull out the tapes, letting them fall to the floor between us with a dull thud.

Beatrice's perfectly manicured hand remains composed as she reaches for her teacup. "I told you to leave him, dear. But you were blinded by the bling—is that what the kids say nowadays?"

"Cut the bullshit, Beatrice. What the fuck is going on, and why is Sheila on one of these tapes?"

"Kyle, leave us. And Henry, shut the door."

I watch as her son and butler obey her command like obedient, well-trained dogs. Once the door is closed and we're alone, Beatrice sets down her cup with a clatter, her eyes darting to the door as if checking for eavesdroppers. When she speaks again, her voice is filled with a strange mix of resignation and relief.

"Kyle is a recovering serial killer, but don't worry—we've found a way to control it."

The room spins around me as I struggle to process her words. My husband—a serial killer? It's too horrific to comprehend, and yet, deep down, a part of me has always sensed something wasn't right.

"Control it?" I whisper, my voice trembling. "What do you mean, control it?"

Beatrice's eyes take on a fervent gleam. "It's quite remarkable, really. We discovered his...tendencies early on. But with the right combination of medication and, shall we say, controlled outlets, we've managed to keep his darker impulses in check."

"Controlled outlets?" I repeat, vomit rising in my throat as I think of the tapes, the hidden room in our attic.

"Yes, dear. Those tapes you found—they're part of his therapy. A way for him to experience those urges without actually harming anyone." She says it so matter-of-factly, as if we're discussing a harmless hobby.

I stand up abruptly, knocking over my untouched teacup. "Therapy? You call that therapy? Do you have any idea what's on those tapes?"

Beatrice's face hardens. "Of course I do. I've overseen every aspect of Kyle's treatment. It's kept him safe all these years."

"Safe?" I laugh, a hysterical edge to my voice. "You call living with a monster safe?"

"Now, now," Beatrice says, her tone patronizing. "Kyle loves you. Marissa, not so much. He's worked so hard to overcome his nature. You should be proud of him."

I stare at her in disbelief. "Proud? You want me to be proud that my husband hasn't murdered a woman's child?"

"He's no more a murderer than the doctor or the lady who signed the paperwork. He's just an innocent bystander. He's just watching abortions. Besides, you don't understand," Beatrice hisses, dropping all pretense of civility. "Do you have any idea what would happen if he continued on the path of killing adult humans? The scandal, the ruined reputation—everything we've worked for would be gone!"

And there it is—the truth laid bare. It has never been about protecting Kyle, or me, or anyone else. It's all about preserving the Witherspoon legacy, their precious reputation.

"Who are the women on the tapes?" I demand,

thinking of the haunting image that has been seared into my brain.

Beatrice waves her hand dismissively. "Just women who agreed to our terms and conditions. No one important. Kyle never harmed them; I made sure of that. It was all...arranged and consensual. Just be glad that Kyle loves you."

"What do you mean, be glad that he actually loves me?"

"When Dr. Lawson and I came up with the idea to show Kyle an abortion as a cure to his killing addiction. We tried a plethora of other methods in which to cure him. We took him hunting and allowed him to kill animals, he watched executions at jails, we had him watch videos of people being killed in war to see if anything could replace the need to kill human or animal life.

All those methods were short lived. He would view it, but the urge would come back. But when he watched a live abortion for the first time. The results were astounding. Kyle's urge to kill only came once a quarter but when he watched the tapes, he had no desire to view live abortions. If he watched the tapes a few times a week, his desire remained dormant.

Then you started talking about wanting a baby and Kyle got nervous. Every time you got pregnant, he started to get excited about seeing a live abortion again, but he was normal for the first time in his life and your desire for pregnancy was triggering him back into a life he had no desire to return to. That's why he was mean to you Pamela. He started harming animals again, cheating with other women and hoping they get pregnant.

All his old behaviors started to surface. He didn't want to be a monster. He didn't want to get pleasure from you being pregnant. He didn't know how he would respond and if that dark part of him would take over and demand for you to have a live abortion. He also didn't want to risk passing on his proclivities to another human. You being pregnant was making it easy for him to go back to that old life."

"So, you're blaming me for your son's sickness."

"I'm not blaming you. I'm just trying to explain."

"If he was so adamant about not having children, why did you let Sheila have Marissa."

"On the tape, Sheila changed her mind at the last minute, so Kyle agreed to let her keep the child if she kept it away from him and took on full custody, but when we found out her husband was beating her. That girl really knows how to pick them doesn't she? I didn't want my granddaughter raised in such an awful environment, so we decided to kill two birds with one stone. We took Marissa away from Sheila and acted like it was an adoption hoping that this would satisfy you and keep Marissa from living in an abusive home. For a serial killer he really cares. He doesn't want to be a killer and he's trying hard, but you are making it hard for him Pamela."

"So, Kyle caused my miscarriages?"

"Honey, no that was all me. Well, the first one that involved the car accident was unfortunate, but the second one that appeared like a normal miscarriage was due to an oral medication that Chloe administered. The third one happened when Chloe put a few Legos on the step so that you and Kyle would blame Marissa. That one she did on her own. I do not condone extreme violence. We couldn't risk triggering him to want to kill, so we had to make sure you didn't get pregnant. Kyle fought us tooth and nail on that part—he didn't want us to harm you. That is why he tried so hard to get you to give up the idea of pregnancy. He hated seeing you miscarry.

You can thank Chloe as well for miscarriages. She made sure that your birth control pills were put in all your meals, so that you wouldn't conceive. That girl needs an Academy Award. She played her part better than I could imagine. She was hired to keep an eye on you and Kyle and to keep the plan moving along perfectly."

The room tilts dangerously as the full weight of her words hits me. She has been controlling everything—my body, my future, my entire life—all to protect her precious son and their family name. I grab the glass vase off the end table and throw it at her, but she moves out of the way, and I miss.

"You're insane," I yell. "All of you."

Beatrice's eyes flash with anger.

"We gave you everything—wealth, status, a beautiful home. All we asked in return was for you not to get pregnant, and you kept pushing. We even obliged and let you adopt Marissa, but you didn't listen. And because you didn't listen, you suffered. Was that so much to ask? You've heard the phrase, you can't get something for nothing, you know."

I back away from her, my hand fumbling for my purse. "I'm leaving. I'm taking Marissa, and we're getting as far away from this sick family as possible."

Beatrice's laugh is cold and brittle. "Oh, my dear. Did you really think it would be that easy? You signed a prenup, remember? Ten years of marriage before you can leave with anything. And even then, do you really think I'd let you take my granddaughter?"

The threat in her words is unmistakable. I turn and run, not caring about decorum or propriety. I have to get out, have to get to Marissa, have to find a way to escape this nightmare.

I burst out of the mansion; the rain has stopped, leaving behind an eerie stillness. I fumble for my keys, my hands shaking so badly I can barely grip them.

A movement in my peripheral vision makes me freeze. There, standing by my car, is Kyle. I back away, my heart pounding. "Stay away from me, you monster."

"Pamela, everything I've done was for you... for us," Kyle's voice breaks, raw with desperation.

"Don't you see? This is why I didn't want you pregnant. I was terrified it would awaken that...that monster inside me again. I've fought so hard not to be that man anymore."

His words hang heavy in the air, each syllable weighted with years of hidden struggle.

"You were the first person I truly loved, the only one who made me want to change. Those tapes... I watch them daily as a reminder, a warning to myself of what I used to be and a cure to my sickness. Your love helped me suppress those dark urges. It gave me the courage to keep watching. You gave me hope for a normal life." Kyle's eyes, brimming with tears, lock onto mine. The naked vulnerability in his gaze is almost unbearable. "Pamela, I can't do this without you. I can't be normal or live a regular life alone. I need you. I killed your stepfather, because he hurt the person, I loved the most, you."

The weight of his confession crashes over me like a tidal wave. My legs buckle, no longer able to support me. As I crumple to the floor, my vision blurs and darkens. The last thing I register is the sensation of falling—falling into an abyss of uncertainty and shattered trust. Then, mercifully, darkness overtakes me.

CHAPTER 26
PAMELA

15 YEARS ***earlier***

The fluorescent lights of the clinic waiting room buzz incessantly, casting sickly shadows across my face. I sit rigid in the uncomfortable plastic chair, my fingers twisting the hem of my oversized sweater. The air feels thick, heavy with unspoken fears and difficult decisions. My mind races, replaying that night in vivid, horrifying detail.

I squeeze my eyes shut, willing the memories away. But they cling to me like a second skin, a constant reminder of why I'm here. Taking a deep, shaky breath, I stand. My legs feel like soggy pretzels as I approach the reception desk. As I near, I look up and find myself captivated by a pair of startlingly green eyes.

The young man behind the desk can't be much older than me, maybe early twenties. His warm smile seems out of place in the sterile, somber environment of the clinic.

"Hi there," he says, his voice low and gentle. "How can I help you?"

I open my mouth to speak, but no words come out.

The lump in my throat threatens to choke me. The man's smile never falters as he slides a clipboard across the desk.

"It's okay," he says softly. "Take your time. Just fill this out when you're ready, and we'll take care of you."

Our fingers brush as I take the clipboard, sending an unexpected jolt through my body. For a moment, the weight on my shoulders feels a little lighter.

"Thank you," I manage to whisper before retreating to my seat.

As I fill out the form, I find my gaze drawn back to the receptionist. His presence seems to calm the chaotic swirl of my thoughts. I notice his name tag: Kyle.

When I return the clipboard, Kyle's eyes meet mine with a depth of understanding that takes my breath away.

"Pamela," he says, reading my name from the form. "That's a beautiful name."

A blush creeps up my cheeks, surprising me. How can I feel anything close to happiness in a place like this, at a time like this?

"Listen," Kyle says, leaning in slightly. "I know this is a difficult time. But you're not alone, okay? We're here to support you, whatever you decide."

I nod, unable to speak past the lump in my throat. As I turn to go back to my seat, Kyle calls out softly.

"Pamela? Would you like some tea while you wait? It might help calm your nerves."

The simple act of kindness breaks something inside me. Tears well up in my eyes as I nod. Kyle's smile is gentle as he steps out from behind the desk, gesturing for me to follow him to a small kitchenette area.

As Kyle prepares the tea, I find myself opening up. The words pour out of me—the break-in, the assault, the crushing fear and uncertainty I have because they can't find him. Kyle listens without judgment, his green eyes full of compassion.

"I'm so sorry that happened to you," he says when I finish, handing me a steaming mug. "You didn't deserve that. No one does."

I wrap my hands around the warm ceramic, letting its heat seep into my cold fingers.

"I don't know what to do," I confess, my voice barely above a whisper.

Kyle leans against the counter, his face serious. "That's okay. You don't have to know right now. This is a big decision, and it's yours to make. No one else's."

As we talk, I feel some of the tension leave my body. Kyle's presence is comforting, his words reassuring. For the first time since that horrible night, I feel like I might be okay.

The days that follow are a blur of appointments, counseling sessions, and difficult conversations. Through it all, Kyle is a constant presence, offering support and a listening ear. I find myself looking forward to our interactions, brief as they are.

One afternoon, as I leave a particularly emotional counseling session, I find Kyle waiting for me in the hallway.

"Hey," he says, his voice soft with concern. "Rough day?"

I nod, wiping at my eyes. "Yeah, you could say that."

Kyle hesitates for a moment, then asks, "Listen, my shift is almost over. Would you maybe want to grab a coffee? Talk somewhere that's not...here?"

My heart skips a beat. I know I should say no. Getting involved with someone right now is the last thing I need.

But something in Kyle's eyes, in the genuine care I see there, makes me nod.

"I'd like that," I say, surprising myself with how much I mean it.

We end up at a small café near campus, tucked away in a quiet corner. As we talk, I feel the walls I've built around me start to crumble. Kyle listens as I pour out my fears, my doubts, my dreams for the future. In turn, he shares his own story—how he started working at the clinic as preparation for medical school.

"I just wanted to help," he explains, his eyes earnest. "To make sure no one felt alone."

As the weeks pass, we grow closer. Our coffee dates become a regular occurrence, a bright spot in the darkness that has enveloped my life. I find myself smiling more, laughing even. The crushing weight of my decision still looms, but with Kyle by my side, it feels a little less overwhelming.

On campus, people start to notice the change in me. The girls who had once been my friends now watch me with narrowed eyes, whispering behind their hands. The guys, who had mostly ignored me before, suddenly find reasons to talk to me in class or at parties.

I try to ignore the stares and whispers, but they wear on me. One day, following a particularly nasty encounter with my former roommate, I break down in Kyle's arms.

"Why are they being like this?" I sob, my face buried in his chest. "I didn't do anything wrong."

Kyle holds me close, his hand stroking my hair. "They're jealous," he says softly.

"They're jealous of me? Why are they jealous of me?"

"I could think of a few reasons. You're beautiful, sexy,

smart, and you just so happen to be dating a guy whose father's last name is on the School of Economics."

"You're a Witherspoon?"

"Guilty as charged."

As the deadline for my decision approaches, I feel the weight of it pressing down on me. I spend hours talking it through with Kyle, weighing my options, considering my future.

In the end, the choice is mine alone.

When I finally make my decision, Kyle is there, holding my hand as I sign the papers. Whatever comes next, I know I won't face it alone. On the day that I decide to get the abortion, Kyle is there but refuses to go into the room with me. He says he doesn't want the first time we see each other naked to be like this. Once the procedure is over and we leave the clinic for the last time, Kyle turns to me, his green eyes serious.

"I know this isn't the most romantic timing," he says, a nervous smile playing at his lips. "But I care about you, Pamela. A lot. And I was hoping...maybe we could make this official? Be together, for real?"

My heart soars, even as a small voice in the back of my mind warns me to be cautious. But looking into Kyle's eyes, seeing the sincerity there, I push my doubts aside.

"Yes," I say, my smile bright despite the tears in my eyes. "I'd like that."

As Kyle pulls me into a kiss, I feel a sense of hope I haven't experienced in months. The road ahead won't be easy, but with Kyle by my side, I feel ready to face whatever comes next.

CHAPTER 27
PAMELA

THE CLOCK in the corner of Beatrice Witherspoon's opulent sitting room chimes three times, each resonant toll feeling like a death knell. I wake up, my mind reeling as I try to process the horrifying revelations thrust upon me. The room is spinning.

Beatrice's piercing gaze never wavers as she watches my face cycle through shock, disgust, anger, and finally a bone-deep fear that settles into every line of my body. Her lips curve into a small, satisfied smile. I sense this is the moment she has been preparing for.

"Well, hello there sleeping beauty. You had us worried for a moment. I know all of this is difficult to hear, my dear," Beatrice begins, "but you must understand this is the only way to help my son. To help our family."

The door creaks open, and Kyle steps into the room. His presence, once a source of comfort, now fills me with revulsion. I jerk back, nearly toppling my chair in my haste to put distance between us.

"Don't you take another step toward me," I spit, my voice trembling with a mix of fear and rage.

"Kyle," Beatrice intervenes smoothly, "perhaps you should give us some more time. Pamela needs a moment to...process all of this."

Mother and son lock eyes in a silent battle of wills. For a moment, I think Kyle might refuse, might lunge forward and reveal the monster that has been hiding beneath the surface all along. But then he nods curtly and leaves the room, the door closing behind him with a sound of finality. Beatrice turns back to me, gesturing for me to sit. "Now, my dear, I know you probably think I'm a horrible person. But let me ask you this—what would you do if you found out Marissa was a killer?"

The mention of my daughter's name sends a jolt of panic through me. "I'll tell you what you'd do," Beatrice continues, her voice hardening. "You'd do everything in your power to help her. And that's exactly what I'm doing for my son. That's what we mothers do."

My hand instinctively goes to my phone, desperate to call someone, anyone, who could help me escape this nightmare. But before I can even unlock the screen, Beatrice nods almost imperceptibly. One of her security guards snatches the device from my grasp.

"Give me back my phone!" I cry, my voice rising with panic.

Beatrice's smile never wavers. "Everything will return to normal once you calm down and we discuss Kyle's treatment."

"I'm not discussing anything with you," I snarl, rising to my feet. "You're all sick. I'm leaving."

"Sweetie," Beatrice's voice takes on a dangerous edge, "where exactly do you think you're going to go? To your mother's? This is your family now, and you need to protect it."

I feel the walls closing in, the reality of my situation becoming painfully clear. I'm trapped.

"Let me paint you a picture," Beatrice continues, her voice dropping to a near whisper. "If it comes out that my son is a killer—which it won't, but let's entertain the possibility—there will be lawyer fees, lawsuits, an intense scrutiny of your life. Who's going to pay for all of that? Who's going to take care of your precious Marissa? And your dependent mother?"

My breath catches in my throat as Beatrice's implications become clear.

"And what if they say you were complicit? That you knew about it all along and were just waiting until you reached your tenth year of marriage to cash out? That means jail time for you, my dear. And then what becomes of Marissa? Your pitiful excuse for a mother raising her, passing down all those lovely generational curses?"

Beatrice leans forward, her eyes glittering with malice. "How do you think your daughter will fare with two parents branded as serial killers and a grandmother who will let her next boyfriend touch her inappropriately? Her life will be ruined before it even begins."

The weight of Beatrice's words crashes down on me like a physical force. I sink back into my chair, the fight draining out of me as the hopelessness of my situation becomes clear.

"So," Beatrice concludes, her voice returning to its usual saccharine sweetness, "I suggest you sit down, shut up, and listen to what comes next."

I feel hollowed out, a shell of the woman I had been just hours ago. "Why?" I whisper. "Why would you keep something like this from me?"

Beatrice's laugh is cold and brittle. "Oh, my dear. We

always planned to tell you one day. We just had to get the right puzzle pieces in order. We've known this day would come. Why do you think we moved you away from your family? Do you really believe it was mere coincidence that my son met you in that abortion clinic?"

My head snaps up, my eyes wide with shock.

"Oh yes," Beatrice continues, relishing my distress. "I arranged that. I chose a broken girl for my broken son." Beatrice leans forward and whispers. "I broke you so that you would be broken for my broken son. It was all so perfectly orchestrated. You need to understand, my dear —this has all been meticulously planned. Well, almost all of it. I didn't plan on Chloe falling for Kyle, finding out his secret, getting pregnant by him, and running away, but even all that is under control."

"What do you mean you broke me?"

"Well, you were already fragile, but I had to break you, so I hired your stepfather Stanley to rape you while you were in college so that you and Kyle would bond." Something took over me and I balled up my fist and socked Beatrice in the face. I hit her so hard that she fell from her chair.

"You evil bitch!" Once Beatrice recovered from the punch that caused her to draw blood and fall to the floor. She wiped her lip sucking the blood until it stopped bleeding. She put up her hand halting her security to keep from grabbing me.

"You only get one of those. I deserve that. I felt bad about that and its's why I allowed Kyle to kill him."

My mind races, pieces falling into place with sickening clarity. "All these years I blamed myself for having too much to drink, for not being responsible and it was you all along."

I lunge at Beatrice but fall to the ground when I feel electricity surging through my body. I've been tased by security.

"I told you only one of those."

Beatrice takes a deep breath and leans down toward me as I recover on her living room floor, her next words shattering my world into a million pieces. "You see, we need to proceed to the second part of curing my son, and it simply wouldn't happen without your help. Kyle needs unconditional love. We believe that once he has that, his... urges...might dissipate, completely."

Panic claws at my throat. "Where is Marissa?" I demand, my maternal instincts overriding my fear. "If you harm my daughter, I swear I'll kill you."

Beatrice laughs, genuinely amused. "See? That's exactly what I mean. Look at what mothers will do for their children."

"She's with Donna. But don't worry, Donna is ignorant of Kyle's proclivities. I needed at least one normal child."

I feel as if I'm drowning, each revelation pulling me further into the depths of this nightmare. "Kyle...he's really been trying not to kill anyone?"

"Oh yes," Beatrice assures me. "That's why he didn't want children. He was terrified of passing on his...proclivities. But you couldn't just be happy with him, could you? You had to push for a child. Even after he relented and agreed to adopt, it wasn't enough for you."

Tears well up in my eyes as the full weight of my situation crashes down upon me. I'm trapped with no clear way out.

"He's been doing all of this because he loves you," Beatrice presses on. "He has my love, of course, but he needs yours, Pamela. You hold the key to my son's humanity." She pauses, letting her words sink in. "So will you help me cure him?"

I sit in stunned silence, my mind racing through possible scenarios, searching desperately for a way out. But with each passing second, the reality of my situation becomes clearer. I'm outnumbered, outmaneuvered, and utterly alone.

"I know it's a lot to process," Beatrice adds, her voice softening. "But this is why I'm telling you now. I feel so terrible about having to lie to you all this time. I feel horrible about what I have done to you."

I look up, meeting Beatrice's gaze. At that moment, I make my decision. It isn't surrender, not really. It's survival. I will play along, bide my time, and find a way to protect myself and Marissa. No matter what it takes.

"Yes, Beatrice," I say, my voice barely above a whisper. "I'll help."

"Good because there is something else, I need to tell you about Kyle."

As Beatrice begins outlining the next steps in Kyle's "treatment," and divulges intimate family secrets, I can hardly believe what I'm hearing. The secrets this family harbors are too much for one person to handle. A resolve hardens within me. I will play their game for now. But deep down, a fire has been lit—a determination to not only survive this nightmare but to find a way to escape it. For myself, for Marissa, and for all the nameless victims who have suffered at her hands.

The clock chimes again, marking the passage of another hour. But for me, it feels like the tolling of a bell signaling the death of my old life and the birth of something far more dangerous and unpredictable. The game has changed, and I am now a player, whether I like it or not.

CHAPTER 28
KYLE

2.5 MONTHS ***later***

I sit on a plush leather couch, my hand intertwined with Pamela's—a picture of marital harmony. To an outsider, we might seem the perfect couple—successful, attractive, and deeply in love. But beneath the surface, secrets threaten to tear apart our carefully constructed guise at any moment.

Relief washes over me as I gaze at my wife. For over a decade, I have carried the weight of my dark proclivities, lying to the woman I claim to love with all my heart. Now, here we are in counseling, Pamela by my side, holding my hand, offering a reassuring smile. It seems almost too good to be true.

Dr. Cassandra Barker, our family psychologist, is retired but offers her services to us as a favor to my mother—for a small fortune, of course. Discretion is paramount. She's a tall, austere woman with steel-gray hair and piercing blue eyes. She leans forward in her chair, her gaze moving between us. "Pamela," she begins, her voice measured and calm, "how would you describe your relationship with Kyle at this point?"

Pamela's smile doesn't waver. "It's better—so much better. Once you helped me understand his...condition, and I accepted him for who he is, things improved dramatically." She squeezes my hand and turns toward me, her smile comforting. "I now understand why he was so hesitant about having children. It wasn't that he hated kids—he just didn't want to risk bringing anyone like him into the world and he didn't want to awaken that dark part of him again."

I feel a twinge of comfort at her words. *Is Pamela truly loving me despite my darkness?*

"When I first learned the truth," Pamela continues, her voice almost dreamy, "I couldn't accept it. But now I admire him for taking charge, for being so responsible." She turns to me, her eyes shining with unshed tears. "I've learned to forgive him. It took some time, but we're finally healing."

I lean over, bringing Pamela's hand to my lips and pressing a gentle kiss against her skin.

Dr. Barker nods, her expression unreadable. "And Kyle," she says, turning her penetrating gaze on me, "how often have you been watching the tapes? Has there been any change since Pamela discovered the truth?"

I swallow hard, fighting the urge to loosen my collar. "It's decreased significantly," I reply, my voice steady despite the sudden dryness in my mouth. "I'm down to once a week now. That, coupled with the medication Dr. Lawson prescribed, has helped me train my thoughts. I rarely experience those...desires anymore."

Dr. Barker makes a note on her pad, her pen

scratching against the paper, the only sound in the room for a long moment. "I've noticed you've gained some weight," she observes, her tone neutral. "It looks good on you—healthy."

I feel my cheeks flush, self-consciousness washing over me. I've always prided myself on my physical fitness, seeing it as another form of control over my dark urges. The idea that I've let myself go, even slightly, is deeply unsettling.

"Yeah," I mumble, shifting in my seat. "I haven't been to the gym much lately. There's been a lot of stress eating as Pamela and I worked through my issues. It doesn't help that my wife is a great cook and is cooking me fantastic meals for breakfast, lunch and dinner. I didn't know this healing work would affect other areas of my life. But I'm starting back first thing Monday morning."

Dr. Barker nods, making another note. "Well," she says, closing her notebook with a decisive snap, "that concludes our three sessions for this week. I'll see you both next Wednesday."

As Pamela and I exit the office, stepping into the hushed hallway of the medical building, I lean close to her. "Is my weight gain really that noticeable?" I whisper, unable to keep the anxiety from my voice.

Pamela turns to me, her expression softening. "Kyle, I wouldn't worry about it," she says, reaching up to cup my face in her hands. "When you've been as fit as you have your whole life, it's hard for people to see you any other way. Don't make a mountain out of a molehill." She leans in, pressing a soft kiss to my cheek. "I love you whether you're slim or chubby," she murmurs, her breath warm against my skin. Then, to my surprise, she places her hand on my stomach, pinching the small roll of fat that has begun to form there.

For the first time in my adult life, I feel truly self-conscious about my appearance. The gym suddenly seems like a lifeline—a way to regain control, not just over my body but over my entire life. *Did my wife just call me chubby?*

As we make our way to the parking garage, my mind races. On the surface, everything seems to be improving. Pamela knows the truth and has chosen to stay. My urges are under control, managed through a combination of therapy, medication, and those damned tapes. I should feel relieved, grateful even. So why do I feel so... hollow?

The drive home is silent, each of us lost in our thoughts. I can't shake the feeling that something is off, that this new equilibrium we have achieved is as fragile as glass. One wrong move, one misstep, and it will all come crashing down.

As we pull into the driveway of our home, I notice a familiar car parked across the street. My mother's sleek black Mercedes sits there, its tinted windows revealing nothing.

"Your mother's here," Pamela observes, her voice carefully neutral.

I nod, my jaw tightening. "I see that."

We exit the car, and as if on cue, my mother emerges from her vehicle. She glides toward us, every inch the elegant matriarch, her Chanel suit impeccable despite the summer heat.

"Darlings," she calls out, air-kissing each of us in turn. "I thought I'd drop by for a visit. I hope I'm not interrupting?"

I force a smile. "Of course not, Mother. Come in."

As we enter the house, I feel like a puppet on strings with my mother as the master puppeteer. I watch as Pamela moves to the kitchen to prepare tea, her movements graceful but tense.

Beatrice settles in the living room, her sharp gaze taking in every detail. "It looks like you have decorated in here. I'm loving the new full-length mirrors."

"Yeah, Pamela says it opens the place up. I don't like them though. It's a constant reminder of all the weight I've gained."

"I didn't want to say anything, but you have gotten a bit chubby, and your hair could use a trim. You are starting to look like you did as a kid, like a cute little chubby mixed girl," Beatrice replied.

I give my mom the stare of death. I immediately become self-conscious remembering the way kids use to taunt me for being overweight. We agreed that we would never bring up those days because of how painful they were towards me. It's the reason I got into fitness. I was determined to never be that little fat boy again. I've been avoiding the scale like the plague afraid of what it might say. Pamela bought a new fancy scale that measures body fat percentage. She's lost a fair amount of weight and is always excited to see her decreasing numbers.

"Mom, please don't bring that up," I whisper.

"I forgot you're very sensitive about that time in your life. I'll do my best to never bring it up again."

"Thank you," I say.

"How are the therapy sessions going?" she inquires, her tone casual, but her eyes keen.

"They're going well," I reply, sinking into an armchair across from her. "Dr. Barker thinks we're making progress. It was smart of you to switch therapists and doctors."

Beatrice nods, a small smile playing at the corners of her mouth. "And Pamela? How is she adjusting to... everything?"

Before I can respond, Pamela enters with a tray of tea and cookies. "I'm adjusting just fine, Beatrice," she says, her voice steady as she sets the tray down. "It's been a lot to process, but I think we're on the right track."

Beatrice's smile widens, but it doesn't reach her eyes. "I'm glad to hear that, dear. I knew you were the right choice for my Kyle."

As Pamela pours the tea, I notice the slight tremor in her hands. Is it fear? Anger? Or something else entirely?

The conversation flows, touching on harmless topics —the weather, local gossip, plans for the holidays. But beneath the surface, tension swirls like an undertow, pulling at us.

As the visit ends, Beatrice rises to leave. "Oh, before I forget," she says, reaching into her purse. "I brought something for you, Kyle."

She withdraws a small, unmarked DVD case and holds it out to me. I feel my blood run cold, knowing exactly what it contains.

"I had your VHS tapes turned into DVDs. I think it would be better to monitor how often you watch. I'll give you one a week. Keep a log of how often you partake," Beatrice says, her voice low.

I take the case, my fingers feeling numb. "Thank you, Mother," I manage, my voice sounding distant.

As Beatrice makes her goodbyes, I catch Pamela's eye. For a moment, I see something flicker there—fear, revulsion, and...determination?

The moment passes, and Pamela is all smiles again, waving as Beatrice's car pulls away.

As the door closes, I feel the weight of the DVD case in my hand. It seems to pulse with dark energy—a Pandora's box of horrors that I both crave and despise.

"I'm going to take a shower," Pamela announces, her voice unnaturally bright. "Why don't you go ahead and... watch your weekly video?"

I nod mutely, waiting until I hear the bathroom door close and the shower start before heading to the attic, DVD in hand.

As I settle into the worn leather recliner facing the large-screen TV, which has become both my salvation and my prison, I feel a familiar mix of anticipation and self-loathing. I insert the disc with trembling fingers, my breath catching as the first images flicker to life.

CHAPTER 29
PAMELA

THE WATER CASCADES over my body, scalding hot and relentless. I stand still beneath it, letting the droplets pound my skin until it turns an angry red. A wail escapes my throat as tears stream down my face. Steam fills the bathroom, fogging the mirrors and creating a cocoon of temporary safety. Here, in this small sanctuary, I can finally drop the mask.

Almost three months. It's been almost three long, excruciating months since my world shattered into a million jagged pieces. The words echo in my mind like a never-ending nightmare: My husband is a fucking serial killer. *How many people has he killed? How many abortions has he watched? How many crimes has he committed? Am I safe? Is Marissa safe?*

I press my forehead against the cool tile, struggling to keep my breathing steady. I can't afford to break down—not even here. The house is bugged; every room listens to my every word. My phone has been replaced with one I can't control. I'm always under surveillance. Even Chloe, the young woman I thought was helping me, turned out to be just another pawn in this sick game, reporting my every move back to Beatrice Witherspoon and almost killing me by making sure I fell down the steps. I wonder how many people have been in on this.

The shower is the only place I can let my guard down, even slightly. But even this small reprieve is tainted by the knowledge of what awaits me outside these steamy walls.

With a shuddering breath, I reach for the soap, mechanically going through the motions. My skin crawls at the memory of Kyle's touch, of having to pretend I still love him, still desire him. But now, it takes all my will not to recoil every time he comes near me.

Kyle has changed too. His 35th birthday has come and gone, shifting his priorities. No longer needing to work to maintain our lifestyle, coupled with all the new developments in his therapy, he's let himself go. The once-sculpted physique that drew admiring glances is softening, a layer of fat creeping over his muscles.

I feel a wave of revulsion. If he had only gained weight, I could handle it. Love isn't about physical perfection. But coupled with the knowledge of what he truly is? It's almost more than I can bear. I think of fictional killers on TV—Dexters and Joe Goldbergs. At least they had the decency to be attractive. Now I'm trapped with an overweight murderer, expected to play the role of the loving, supportive wife.

The water cools, signaling the end of my brief escape. I turn off the shower, each movement like donning armor for battle. I dry myself methodically, avoiding my reflection in the mirror. I can't bear to see the stranger looking back at me. The only thing saving me is the gym. I've been working out to deal with the stress, and as a result, I've lost over thirty-five pounds in the last three months.

At least my body looks better than ever—the only positive thing to come from this.

Wrapped in a plush robe, I pad silently to the bedroom. Kyle is already in bed. He looks up as I enter, his expression a mix of hope and trepidation.

"Pamela," he begins, his voice hesitant. "Do you think we'll ever have sex again? I know what my mom and I have done is horrible. I don't deserve you, but... do you think you could ever love me again?"

The question hangs between us, heavy with implication. My heart races, knowing my response could mean the difference between life and death—for me and for Marissa.

Taking a deep breath, I turn to Kyle, forcing a smile. I lean in, pressing a kiss to his lips, desperately trying to recall our first kiss. It had seemed so magical then, full of promise and passion. Now it tastes like filth.

For the rest of the night, I push every thought from my mind, focusing only on the physical act. I make love to my husband with a fervor born of desperation, knowing that if I can't convince him of my love, Beatrice will hear about it. And I've made a deal—I will help "heal" Kyle.

As we move together in the darkness, I feel a grim satisfaction. After discovering the truth about the tapes, I took matters into my own hands. A discreet visit to my gynecologist ensured I would never bear Kyle's children. It's a small act of rebellion, but it gives me a sense of control in a situation where I have little.

In the aftermath, as Kyle's breathing evens out into sleep beside me, I stare at the ceiling, my mind racing. How could I have not known? Has this been the only reason he chose me—because I was the perfect cover for his secret? I feel sick, realizing how thoroughly I've been manipulated, nothing more than a pawn in the Witherspoon family's twisted game.

But even as despair threatens to overwhelm me, a spark of determination flickers to life. I have a plan, one that has been forming in my mind for weeks. Kyle has never taken my baby food business seriously, dismissing it as a hobby. But over the years, as I've sold to the other wives at the school, I've built up a sizable nest egg.

It isn't much, but it will be enough. Enough to leave this family, to take Marissa, and start a new life far away from the Witherspoons. The pieces are falling into place, a jigsaw puzzle of escape slowly taking shape.

As I lie here, still entangled with Kyle, I replay every moment of our relationship in my mind. The exaggerated masculinity, the deep voice, the barely contained anger—it all makes sense now. He's been overcompensating, hiding his true nature behind a disguise.

I know I have a choice to make. If the Witherspoons have silenced all those women, there's no telling what they might do to me if I don't play along. I need a foolproof plan, one that guarantees Marissa's and my safety.

I turn my head slightly, studying Kyle's sleeping face. He looks almost innocent, like the man I thought I had married. But I know better now. I know the monster beneath the surface.

CHAPTER 30
PAMELA

THE NEXT MORNING dawns bright and clear, mocking the darkness that permeates the Witherspoon household. I go through my routine on autopilot, fixing breakfast for Kyle and Marissa, packing lunches, all while my mind races through the details of my escape. At the kitchen sink, washing dishes, I feel Kyle's presence behind me. His arms encircle my waist, and I fight the urge to flinch.

"Last night was amazing," he murmurs, his breath hot against my neck. "I've missed you so much, Pam."

I force myself to lean into his embrace, tilting my head to give him better access. "I've missed you too," I lie, the words tasting bitter on my tongue. Kyle's hands start to wander, and I brace myself. But before things progress further, the doorbell rings, slicing through the moment.

Kyle pulls away with a frustrated sigh. "I'll get it," he says, kissing my cheek before heading to the front door.

I let out a breath, and grip the edge of the sink. I hear muffled voices from the foyer, then the sound of heels on the hardwood.

"Pamela," Beatrice Witherspoon's voice rings out, saccharine sweet. "I hope I'm not interrupting anything."

I turn, plastering on a smile that feels more like a grimace. "Of course not, Beatrice. We were just finishing breakfast. Can I get you some coffee?"

Beatrice waves away the offer, her sharp eyes scanning every detail of the kitchen. "No need, dear. I just stopped by to see how things are going. Kyle tells me you two had quite the evening last night."

My cheeks flush, a mix of embarrassment and anger. Of course, Kyle told his mother. There are no boundaries in this family, no secrets—except the ones we keep from each other.

"Yes," I manage, my voice steady despite the turmoil inside. "Things are... improving."

Beatrice's smile widens, showing too many teeth. "I'm so glad to hear that, dear. I knew you'd come around eventually. You're such a good influence on our Kyle."

The conversation continues, a dance of polite small talk and veiled threats. I feel like I'm suffocating. But beneath the surface, my resolve strengthens. I will play their game for now, but soon, very soon, I will make my move.

As Beatrice prepares to leave, she pulls Kyle aside. I busy myself with the dishes, straining to hear.

"...new medicine," Beatrice says in a low voice. "Dr. Lawson thinks it might help with the urges."

When Beatrice finally leaves, she leaves behind a cloud of expensive perfume and unspoken threats. I retreat to the bathroom again, staring at my reflection, searching for any sign of the woman I used to be.

"You can do this," I whisper to myself. "For Marissa. For yourself."

CHAPTER 31
KYLE

THE DARKNESS in the bedroom is oppressive, a thick blanket of shadows pulsing with each labored breath I take. My stomach churns, threatening to revolt at any moment. Sweat beads on my forehead as I stumble through the blackness, one hand outstretched, searching for something to steady me in a world that feels suddenly alien and hostile.

The sharp corner of the dresser finds my toe with unerring accuracy, sending a bolt of pain shooting up my leg. I bite down hard on my lower lip, tasting copper as I suppress a scream. The last thing I want is to wake Pamela or Marissa. They don't need to see me like this—weak, vulnerable, a far cry from the strong, dominant figure I've always portrayed.

My fingers finally find the cool metal of the doorknob. I nearly fall into the bathroom, collapsing toward the toilet as my stomach empties itself again. For the third time tonight, my body convulses, expelling what little remains.

The harsh fluorescent light flickers to life, momentarily blinding me. Squinting against the glare, I see Pamela's silhouette in the doorway, one hand on the light switch, the other rubbing sleep from her eyes.

"What's going on, Kyle?" Her voice is thick with sleep, but there's an undercurrent of something else—concern? Irritation? I can't quite place it. I spit into the toilet, trying to rid my mouth of the acrid taste of bile. "Pam, I think I need to go to the doctor or call Dr. Lawson. I don't feel well at all."

Pamela's brow furrows, a hint of exasperation creeping into her tone. "It's probably just a stomach bug, Kyle. I don't want to call her this early in the morning."

"I think something is really wrong with me," I insist, desperation creeping into my voice. "I've never been this sick."

Pamela shakes her head, a flash of disgust crossing her features before she schools her expression back to neutral. "Men are such babies. As soon as you're sick, you act like the world is ending."

"Just call her, please," I plead, too miserable to be offended by her dismissive attitude.

With a sigh, Pamela relents. "I'll call her and put her on speaker. Where's your phone?"

"It's in my jacket pocket—the navy blue one in the closet," I reply, grateful for the small concession. As Pamela retrieves the phone, I lean back against the cool tile wall, closing my eyes against another wave of nausea. I listen as Pamela dials Dr. Lawson, praying this isn't serious. The irony isn't lost on me—a man who has taken lives, now terrified of losing his own.

"I hate to bother you, Dr. Lawson, but Kyle insisted I call. He's adamant about seeing you. He doesn't feel well," Pamela says.

Dr. Lawson's voice crackles through the speaker, distant and thin. "Kyle, what other symptoms are you experiencing?"

"Just the vomiting," I reply, trying to catalog my body's complaints.

Dr. Lawson pauses. "Vomiting, coupled with the weight gain I've noticed over the last few months, could mean a few things. Have you been having mood swings?"

"Yes," Pamela answers for me.

"Are your nipples sore?"

The question catches me off guard, and I touch my chest tentatively. "Yeah, they're a little tender," I admit, confusion creeping into my voice.

There's a moment of silence before Dr. Lawson speaks again, her tone carefully neutral. "It sounds like you might have Couvade syndrome."

"What the fuck is that?" I ask, fear blooming in my chest.

Dr. Lawson's explanation does little to soothe my concerns. She says I have Couvade Syndrome – a psychosomatic condition where you experience pregnancy symptoms? It seems too bizarre to be real, yet as she describes the symptoms, I feel a chill of recognition.

"It should resolve itself," Dr. Lawson assures me. "It's probably a combination of losing the baby and confronting your truth. If it doesn't resolve in a few weeks, we'll do more tests. But I've seen this before. Men don't talk about it because they're embarrassed, but it's common. Try to relax, and you'll feel better soon."

My mind reels. "Living in my truth"? Does she mean my confession to Pamela? The tapes, the years of deception laid bare? And the baby—the one we lost, the one I was secretly relieved about. Is my body rebelling, forcing me to confront buried emotions?

"Could this explain the weight gain?" I ask, self-conscious of the softness creeping over my once-chiseled body.

"Yes, Kyle. Some men do experience weight gain," Dr. Lawson confirms, her voice maddeningly calm.

As the call ends, I pull myself up from the toilet, my legs shaky. I stumble back to the bedroom, collapsing onto the bed with a groan. Pamela quickly grabs the trash can and places it beside me.

"Honey, please don't throw up on the sheets," she says, her voice tight. "Actually, could you sleep on the couch tonight or in another room? I don't want to wake up with vomit in my hair. If I do, I'll be one mad black woman."

The request stings more than I care to admit. I gather my things, shooting Pamela a wounded look as I head for the couch. To my surprise, a small smile plays at the corners of her mouth.

"What's so funny?" I snap, anger momentarily over-riding my nausea. "Why are you smiling?"

Pamela's smile widens, a chuckle escaping her lips. "It's ironic you have pregnancy symptoms after what you did to those women."

"I didn't do anything to those women. They made their choices."

"But didn't you prey on poor women who needed money? Their children might be alive if not for you."

"I didn't choose the women. They would have had the abortion whether I was there or not."

"If you say so," Pamela replies.

The urge to lash out surges through me. Without another word, I storm out, slamming the door behind me.

As I settle onto the couch, my mind races. *Is my guilt manifesting physically? Am I so attached to that unborn child that I'm feeling its loss? Or is this some cosmic joke, a punishment for the lives I've taken?*

The nausea returns, and I barely make it to the bathroom before my stomach empties again. Kneeling on the cold tile, my forehead against the porcelain, I feel more alone than ever.

In the pre-dawn hours, as light begins to creep through the windows, I finally drift into a fitful sleep. My dreams are chaotic—faceless victims, Pamela's laughter, and a shadowy figure that might have been the child we lost.

When I wake, the house is quiet. Pamela and Marissa are likely still asleep upstairs, unaware of my night of misery. I pull myself up and head to the kitchen, fumbling with the coffee maker. As the rich aroma of brewing coffee fills the air, my gaze falls on the laptop sitting on the counter. I open it with shaking hands and type, "Couvade syndrome."

I scroll through the results—scientific articles, personal anecdotes—and feel a growing sense of calm. The symptoms match mine—nausea, weight gain, mood swings, even the sore nipples. But it's the psychological aspects that chill me. Many sources link Couvade syndrome to anxiety about impending fatherhood, unresolved grief over pregnancy loss, or deep-seated guilt.

Guilt. The word pulses on the screen. I slam the laptop shut, unable to face it. The sound of footsteps on the stairs jolts me. Pamela appears, her expression unreadable as she takes in my disheveled state.

"Feeling any better?" she asks, her voice neutral.

I nod, not trusting myself to speak. Pamela moves around the kitchen, preparing breakfast. There's a distance between us now, a chasm growing wider each day.

As she hands me a cup of coffee, sweetened just the way I like, she says, "I'm sorry about what I said last night. It was insensitive."

"It's okay," I reply. "It pales compared to what I did to you."

Just as Pamela is about to respond, another wave of nausea hits me again. As I retch, I feel Pamela's hand on my back—a gesture of comfort that feels more like a brand. In that moment, as my body rebels and my mind grapples with my sins, I realize my world is crumbling. And maybe this is what I deserve.

CHAPTER 32
PAMELA

THE MOMENT I agree to help "cure" Kyle, my surveillance begins in earnest. I've always been watched, but now I know it. I lose access to my phone, so before Donna and her husband leave for the Peace Corps, I ask her to get me a burner phone. I tell her to keep it quiet—I don't want Kyle or Beatrice to know. My excuse? Kyle is cheating, and I need the phone to set him up. Donna agrees, still reeling from her own recent infidelity scandal.

I know I shouldn't trust my sister-in-law, but since she and Kyle are only half-siblings, I figure she might have some loyalty to me. I truly believe Beatrice wants to keep Donna in the dark about Kyle because Donna provides the family with a veneer of normalcy—something Beatrice craves. It might be naive, but I don't have many choices. I have no one else I can trust not to run back to Beatrice.

I need the phone to find out about the older woman I saw leaving the house the night Kyle drugged and kidnapped me. I call Detective Kendall—the detective who provided pictures of the redhead flirting with Kyle. I give him the license plate and wait for his call. I have a plan.

To not get caught, I hide the phone under the bathroom sink, taping it to the top of the cabinet. I only make calls when I'm in the shower.

As I sit on the bathroom toilet with the phone in my pocket, it suddenly vibrates against my thigh, making my heart leap into my throat. I fish it out with trembling fingers and glance around the bathroom to make sure I'm alone. The screen lights up with a message from Detective Kendall. An address glows on the display, followed by two words: "Be careful."

My breath catches in my chest. This is the lead I've been waiting for. The mysterious woman I saw leaving the Witherspoon residence—the one who might hold the key to unraveling their secrets—lives just a few blocks away.

But caution nags at the edges of my excitement. The Witherspoons are watching my every move, their invisible surveillance reaching far beyond the confines of their mansion. One misstep, one hint that I'm digging into their past, and everything could come crashing down.

Desperation fuels my plan. I call my hairdresser and book a hair appointment at my usual salon, a place where I've spent countless hours maintaining the perfect image of a Witherspoon wife. But this time, my intentions are far from cosmetic.

The salon buzzes with activity as I step inside, the air thick with the scent of chemicals and lavender shampoo. I plaster on my best society smile, exchanging pleasantries with the receptionist as I settle into a waiting chair. My fingers drum an anxious rhythm on my knee, hyper-aware of every tick of the clock on the wall.

Finally, my stylist approaches—a petite woman with jet-black hair that hangs to her waist. Her smile is jovial as she hands me a glass of champagne and leads me to the back room. As we pass the wash stations, she leans in close, her voice barely audible over the hum of blow dryers.

"Everything's set," she murmurs. She quickly styles me in a long wavy blonde wig while I change into a different pair of clothes. I put on a pair of sunglasses and give myself a quick once over in the mirror. I look nothing like a Witherspoon. "There's an Uber waiting out back. You've got about an hour. That will give me an hour to give you a quick hairstyle so that nothing seems suspicious. You are normally here for two hours so that should suffice."

Relief washes over me. "Thank you, Dena," I whisper. "I owe you one."

"You don't owe me anything. I'm just upset that I can't do more. Are you sure you don't want to call the police?"

"No police. I have a plan, and I just need you to trust me."

"Uh-huh, but if I ever see you come in here with bruises, I'm calling the police." She gives me a fierce hug.

"Thanks for caring, and if I need you, I will definitely let you know," I reply. I've known Dena for over ten years. She used to do my hair in college. When I married Kyle, I invested in her business and ever since then she's been trying to find a way to pay it forward. Today was that day.

Slipping out the back door feels like stepping into

another world. The grimy alley is a far cry from the polished streets I usually traverse, but today it represents freedom. I climb into the waiting car, my heart pounding against my ribs. The city blurs past the windows, familiar landmarks giving way to unfamiliar neighborhoods. In fifteen minutes, we pull up in front of a towering luxury condominium, its glass and steel exterior gleaming in the afternoon sun.

I step out, smoothing my designer costume with trembling hands. I take a deep breath, preparing for what's to come. The doorman eyes me suspiciously as I approach, but a flash of my most charming smile and a $1,000 bribe grants me entry.

The elevator ride to the 17th floor feels eternal. My reflection stares back from the polished doors—a woman on edge, her makeup unable to hide the fear and determination in her eyes.

When the doors slide open, I stride down the hallway, searching for apartment 1726. My red-bottom heels click against the marble floor, each step bringing me closer to answers... or more questions.

I raise my hand to knock, hesitating for just a moment. This is it. No turning back now. The sound of my knuckles against the wood echoes in the quiet hallway. One second passes. Two. Three. Just as I'm about to knock again, I hear movement from within. The door opens a crack, revealing a sliver of a face. A woman's eye, lined with expertly applied eyeliner, peers out at me. Recognition flashes in her gaze, followed quickly by fear.

"You shouldn't be here," the woman hisses, her voice low and urgent. "Go away."

My carefully prepared speech dies on my lips. I hadn't expected such immediate hostility.

"Please," I say, my voice cracking. "I just need to talk to you. About the Witherspoons."

The eye widens, then narrows. "I don't talk about the Witherspoons," she snaps. "Not to anyone. Especially not to you."

Before I can protest, the door slams shut. The sound reverberates through the hallway, a finality that sends a chill down my spine.

I stand frozen in disbelief. I've come so far, risked so much, only to be shut out at the final hurdle. Desperation claws at my throat as I raise my fist to knock again.

"Wait!" I call out, not caring who might hear. "Please, I'm begging you. I need to know the truth. About Kyle, about all of it. My daughters and my life could be at stake."

Silence stretches out, broken only by my pounding heart. Then, miraculously, I hear a lock turning. The door opens wider, revealing the woman in full. She's older than I expected, maybe in her late fifties, with ageless beauty that speaks of expensive skincare and exclusive spas. Her silver hair is swept up in an elegant bun, and her silk robe whispers against her skin.

But it's her eyes that capture my attention. They're a striking shade of green—the exact same color as Kyle's.

"How did you find my address? It's unlisted."

"I'm a Witherspoon."

"You're making a mistake," the woman says, her voice softer now, tinged with pity. "There are some truths better left buried."

I swallow hard, fighting back tears. "I can't live with not knowing anymore," I whisper. "Please. I'll do anything."

The woman studies me for a long moment, her gaze

piercing my soul. Finally, she steps back, opening the door wider.

"Come in," she says with a sigh. "But remember, I warned you. Once you know, there's no going back."

I step over the threshold, my heart racing. The apartment is a study in understated luxury—cream-colored surfaces, gleaming chrome, and splashes of color from abstract paintings.

The woman leads me to a pristine white couch, gesturing for me to sit. As I do, my eyes are drawn to a photo on a side table. It shows a younger version of the woman, her arm around a teenage boy with familiar green eyes and long curly hair. He's chubbier and if I didn't know he was my husband I'd think he was a girl.

"That's Kyle," I breathe, reaching for the frame.

The woman's hand shoots out, stopping me. "Don't touch that," she says sharply. Then, more gently, "Yes, that's Kyle. My nephew."

"But that would make you...?"

"Eleanor Witherspoon, his aunt," the woman finishes. Questions flood my mind, each more urgent than the last. She gets up and pours me a glass of sweet tea and then pours herself a glass.

"Now what do you want to know?"

"I guess I want to know more about Kyle and how all this got started. I need to know what I'm up against."

"Kyle was brilliant, charismatic, and gifted. Everything they hoped for. But he also had...darker tendencies. A lack of empathy, a desire for control that bordered on obsession." She leans forward, her voice dropping lower. "There was an incident when Kyle was about nine years old. A girl...she didn't survive. That's when I wanted to alert authorities and get him help."

"What happened?" I ask, my heart racing.

"Kyle killed her. He drowned her in a pool because she called him fat and said he looked like a girl." I clasp my hand over my mouth in disbelief of what is being said. "They silenced me when he confessed to me. He always confessed to me. He trusted me and she hated the bond we had; Eleanor says bitterly. I tried to get them to get him real help, but Beatrice insisted on 'other methods.'

"What happened. Why didn't he get caught?"

"The police ruled it an accident because there was no witnesses. She said if I ever spoke a word, they'd make me disappear. So, I've been in this glass prison, watching as Beatrice tries to cure Kyle. I believe she had something to do with my brother's death." My mind reels. Eleanor nods grimly.

"You think Beatrice killed your brother?" I ask.

"I do, but I can't prove it."

"Why are you at Beatrice's mercy? You're a Witherspoon—you should be financially stable."

"My father, Thomas Witherspoon, left everything to my brother Kenneth and Kenneth left everything to his wife Beatrice. My father hated me. Said I looked like his cheating mother, so yes, I'm financially at Beatrice's mercy."

"I'm sorry that happened to you."

"It's fine. But tell me, how have you avoided getting pregnant?"

"They've been sabotaging my pregnancies."

"I tried to warn you, but I could only send one text. It was from a random stranger's phone."

"What do you mean?"

"The text you got that told you to get out while you still could. That was me. They monitor my calls but apparently, they are not monitoring my home. I had this whole building checked for wires and surveillance. That's the only reason I feel, comfortable letting you in.

"Why are you helping me?" I ask.

Eleanor grasps my hand. "Because I see in you the strength to do what I couldn't—stand up to them, expose the truth. But be careful. The Witherspoons will stop at nothing to keep their secrets."

My phone buzzes with another text from Kyle: "Coming home soon? We really need to talk."

"Who is it?" Eleanor asks.

"It's Kyle," I reply. Eleanor's eyes widen.

"He suspects something. You need to go now. And Pamela...trust no one. Not even those closest to you."

"Will you do me a favor?"

"It depends on what the favor is."

"Promise me you will take care of Marissa if anything happens to me." Eleanor pauses before responding."

"I can't even believe I'm agreeing to this, but yes I promise."

CHAPTER 33
KYLE

PAMELA WALKS THROUGH THE DOOR, looking amazing. I love when she comes back from the beauty salon; she looks angelic. I'm gaining the weight she's losing. She's almost down to her college weight, and all I want to do is love her. Just as I'm about to greet her, I feel the urge to hurl and rush to the toilet, vomiting everything I've eaten that day. Nothing stays down. I collapse to my knees, curling into a fetal position from the intense stomach cramps. It's like nothing I've ever felt.

"Please, take me to the hospital. Something isn't right."

As my heaving subsides, I become acutely aware of Pamela's hand on my back. Her touch, once comforting, now feels like an accusation. I straighten up slowly, avoiding her gaze as I rinse my mouth at the sink.

"You're right. We should call Dr. Lawson again," Pamela says, her voice tinged with concern and something else—suspicion? "This seems more severe than just a typical case of Couvade Syndrome."

I nod weakly, unable to muster the energy to have a

full conversation. As Pamela dials the number, I sink into a kitchen chair, my head in my hands. The room spins around me, a dizzying carousel of guilt and fear.

Dr. Lawson's voice crackles through the speakerphone, sounding more alert than during our pre-dawn call. "Kyle, Pamela, what's going on?"

Pamela takes charge, detailing my symptoms with clinical precision, making me feel more like a specimen than a husband. As she speaks, my gaze drifts to the knife block on the counter. The pain is so severe that my mind often contemplates just ending it all.

"I see," Dr. Lawson says, when Pamela finishes. "Kyle, I think it's time you came in for some tests. This level of symptoms is unusual, even for Couvade Syndrome. I want to rule out any other underlying conditions."

The word "underlying" hangs in the air. A cold sweat breaks out across my forehead. What if they find something? What if my body is betraying my secrets, manifesting my guilt in ways that even the most skilled liar can't hide?

"We'll be there," Pamela answers for both of us.

"When's the earliest you can see us?"

As Pamela finalizes the appointment details, my mind wanders. I think of the tapes hidden in the attic, the secrets buried beneath floorboards and behind false walls. What if this is just the beginning? All the dead fetuses, the people and animals I killed as a kid—*What if my body continues to rebel, broadcasting my sins to the world?*

The rest of the morning passes in a haze of nausea and paranoia. I jump at every sound, flinching away from Pamela's touch. Even Marissa's innocent questions about why Daddy is sleeping on the couch feel like interrogations.

As we prepare to leave for Dr. Lawson's office, I catch a glimpse of myself in the hallway mirror. The man staring back at me is a stranger—pale, sweating, and overweight with dark circles under his eyes. For a moment, I think I see something move in the reflection behind me—a shadowy figure that might be a child. I whirl around, heart pounding, but the hallway is empty.

The drive to Dr. Lawson's office is tense, the silence between Pamela and me thick with unspoken words. As we pull into the parking lot, Pamela turns to me, her expression unreadable.

"Whatever's going on, Kyle, we'll get through it," she says, her voice steady. I nod, not trusting myself to speak. As we walk into the medical building, I can't shake the feeling that I'm walking to my own execution.

Dr. Lawson's office is filled with anatomical charts that suddenly seem sinister to my fevered mind. For the first time, I notice a painting of a seahorse on the wall. My gaze breaks when the doctor enters, clipboard in hand, and I feel my heart rate spike.

"Alright, Kyle," Dr. Lawson begins, her tone professional. "I'm going to run a series of tests—blood work, hormone levels, the works. We need to get to the bottom of what's causing these extreme symptoms."

As she draws blood, I watch the vial fill with detached fascination. *Is my guilt visible in those crimson drops?* The examination seems to last for hours, each new test bringing fresh waves of anxiety. When Dr. Lawson finally finishes, she sits across from us, her expression grave.

"I'll need to wait for the lab results to come back before I can give you a definitive answer," she begins.

"But I have to be honest—I'm concerned. These symptoms, coupled with the recent stress you've been under, could indicate a more serious condition."

The room tilts around me. "What kind of condition?" I manage to ask, my voice barely above a whisper.

Dr. Lawson hesitates, her eyes flicking between me and Pamela. "It could be nothing," she says carefully. "But there's a possibility we're looking at early signs of a neurological issue. The extreme stress you've been under, combined with... other factors... could have triggered something."

"I'd like to schedule an MRI," Dr. Lawson continues. "And in the meantime, I want you to take it easy. No work, no stress. And Kyle," she pauses, her gaze boring into me, "I need you to be completely honest with me about everything. Your physical health, your mental state—it's all connected."

"We need to call your mother," Pamela says, her tone leaving no room for argument. A chill runs down my spine. My mother, Beatrice Witherspoon, has always been the puppet master, pulling the strings of my life from the shadows. The thought of involving her in this... this weakness... makes my stomach churn anew.

"Why?" I manage to croak, my throat raw.

Pamela's eyes narrow. "Because, Kyle, this is bigger than us. Dr. Lawson's tests, your symptoms...something isn't adding up. And if anyone knows what's really going on, it's your mother. She may know things about your childhood or family history that could be important here."

I want to protest, to insist that my mother be kept out of this. But the energy drains from my body, leaving me slumped in the seat, defeated. I nod weakly. Pamela wastes no time. She dials Beatrice's number, putting the phone on speaker as it rings.

"Pamela, dear," Beatrice's voice fills the room, syrupy sweet and laced with tension. "To what do I owe the pleasure?"

"Beatrice," Pamela begins, her voice steady, "something's wrong with Kyle. We've arrived at Dr. Lawson's office and—"

"What kind of tests did she run?" Beatrice interrupts, her tone suddenly sharp. My head snaps up, my eyes meeting Pamela's across the room. There's something in my mother's voice, a note of...fear?

"Blood work, hormone panels," Pamela replies, her brow furrowed. "She wants to do an MRI. Beatrice, what's going on?" There's a long pause on the other end of the line. When Beatrice speaks again, her voice is low, almost resigned.

"I'll be there as soon as I can. Have her start running the test immediately." The line goes dead before either of us can respond.

CHAPTER 34
KYLE

THE HOSPITAL ROOM closes in around me, its white walls seeming to pulse with the frantic beating of my heart. I pace back and forth, my footsteps echoing off the linoleum floor, each step a metronome marking the agonizing passage of time. Twenty minutes stretch into an eternity, each second laden with uncertainty and fear.

My mind betrays me. It races wildly, conjuring up a parade of horrors, each more grotesque than the last. Cancer, its insidious tendrils spreading through my body, devouring me from the inside out. A brain tumor pressing against my skull, ready to rob me of my faculties, my memories, my very self. Or perhaps something even worse —a nameless, faceless disease lurking in the shadows of medical science, waiting to claim me as its newest victim.

The nausea comes in waves, threatening to overwhelm me. I lean against the wall, pressing my forehead against its cool surface, willing the room to stop spinning. But even as the physical discomfort subsides, the panic rises anew. I've always prided myself on being in control, on knowing every angle, every possible outcome. But now, faced with the vast unknown of my own mortality, I feel utterly adrift.

A knock at the door shatters the silence, startling me so severely that I nearly jump out of my skin. The sound is like a gunshot, violently punctuating the tense atmosphere. I whirl around, my heart in my throat as the door swings open.

My mother, Beatrice, sweeps into the room, a vision of carefully cultivated poise and elegance. Her perfume precedes her, a familiar scent that has always meant home, security, and now—inexplicably—dread. Her face is a masterpiece of control, concern etched into every line, but something lurks beneath the surface. Something I can't quite name.

"Kyle," she says, her voice a soothing melody that does nothing to calm the storm raging inside me. Her hands, cool and soft, cup my face. "Let me look at you."

I stand there, frozen, as my mother's eyes roam over my features. There's an intensity to her gaze that I've never seen before, as if she's searching for something. And then, for just a moment, I see it—a flicker in her eyes. Whatever it is, it sends a chill down my spine.

Before I can question her, Dr. Lawson enters the room. The atmosphere shifts immediately, becoming heavy with anticipation. The doctor's face is a blank canvas, giving nothing away.

"The rush-ordered lab results arrived," she begins, her voice steady and professional. But then she hesitates, and in that split second, my world begins to crumble. "Kyle," Dr. Lawson continues, her voice gentling, a stark contrast to the chaos in my mind. She leans forward, her eyes searching mine. "Do you remember when you used to come here as a child? How you liked to play with both Barbies and trucks?"

The memory flashes, unbidden. Plastic dolls with impossible proportions. The satisfying weight of a toy truck in my small hands. The conflicting emotions, even then. "Yeah," I manage, my throat dry. "You told me it was normal."

"It was and still is." She replies. Dr. Lawson continues, her gaze never leaving mine. "Okay. Do you remember when you told me about your crush on that boy at school? How he used to rub your calf muscle during recess, and you'd do the same?"

Heat floods my face. I resist the urge to look at Pamela, shame and confusion warring within me. "Yes, but I was just a kid," I protest weakly. "What does that have to do with my diagnosis?"

"Just follow along with me, Kyle." Her voice is soothing, but there's an undercurrent of urgency that sets my nerves on edge. I take a deep breath.

"Okay," I whisper, my voice barely audible.

"Do you remember when you kept telling me that you wanted to commit suicide because you felt different?"

The old pain resurfaces, a dull ache in my chest. "Yes, but I wish you wouldn't have this conversation with Pamela here." I gesture helplessly towards my wife. "This is embarrassing, Dr. Lawson."

"Kyle," Dr. Lawson's voice takes on a hint of steel. "She needs to know this. There's a reason I'm telling you this in front of her."

I swallow hard, nodding for her to continue. The ticking of the clock on the wall seems impossibly loud.

"Your mother and I withheld some information from

you as a child," Dr. Lawson says, her words measured. "We didn't think you would be able to handle it back then, especially after your father died and you were dealing with... your other illegal proclivities." She pauses, and I feel the weight of unspoken words. "You were mentally fragile, and we never thought what has happened today would occur. It only happens to 1% of men."

A chill runs down my spine. "You're scaring me, Dr. Lawson."

She takes my hand, her touch surprisingly warm. I notice for the first time how old she looks, lines etched deeply around her eyes and mouth. How long has she carried this secret?

"Kyle, there's no easy way to say this," she begins, her voice barely above a whisper. I lean in, drawn by the gravity of her words. "You were born intersex, and it appears that you have... impregnated yourself."

The words hang in the air, absurd and impossible. I blink rapidly, certain I must have misheard. The silence in the room is deafening, broken only by the pounding of my heart and Pamela's sharp intake of breath.

"That's... that's not possible," I finally stammer, my voice sounding strange and distant to my own ears. "I'm a man; I can't..."

But even as I deny it, long-buried memories begin to surface. The hushed conversations between my mother and Dr. Lawson that would abruptly cease when I entered the room.

I recall overhearing my mother say, "Maybe we chose wrong..." to my father that ended with them fighting.

I look down at my body, suddenly foreign and unfamiliar. Who am I? What am I?

I force myself to look at Pamela. Her face is a storm of

emotions – shock, disbelief, and something that looks terrifyingly like betrayal.

I shake my head vehemently, words failing me. Dr. Lawson clears her throat, drawing our attention back to her. "We have a lot to discuss," she says softly. "About your past, your future together, and the choices that lie ahead."

I nod numbly. My entire identity, my understanding of self, has just been shattered. And yet, life continues. A child – my child – grows within me, defying everything I thought I knew about biology and myself.

"But... how?" My voice cuts through the fog in my mind, sounding small and lost.

"Dr. Lawson and Pamela could you give us some time?" Beatrice interrupts, her tone leaving no room for argument. The doctor and Pamela quietly exit, leaving me alone with my mother, and the weight of this revelation.

Beatrice takes a deep breath, before proceeding further. "Do you remember when you were at the pool the day those kids' made fun of you for being overweight and having girl boobs?"

"Yes, I remember."

"Well, I planned to tell you then, but then a week earlier that girl drowned in the pool at the pool party, and I knew it wasn't accidental. You told your Aunt Eleanor; you killed her and there was no way I was going to tell my child, a killer, that he was also intersex. It was too much for a nine-year old to handle. I thought you might kill yourself and I couldn't lose you, Kyle. So, I told you the pills you were taking were for depression and anxiety but they were really suppressing your estrogen levels so you would continue to look like a man. People couldn't tell if you were a boy or girl when you were born, but you had boy parts, so I decided to raise you as a boy. I thought it would be easier."

Her words wash over me, each one a blow to everything I thought I knew about myself. I stumble backward, sinking onto the edge of the hospital bed as the room swims around me.

"So, the pills I'm taking now..."

"They suppress your estrogen levels. It's why you are what they call a pretty boy."

"I couldn't let you be a killer and intersex," Beatrice continues, her voice breaking slightly. "It was too much for a child to handle, so I decided to hide it for as long as I could until I felt you could manage it. You got dealt a bad hand, son, and I played it the best way I knew how."

I feel something shift inside me. It isn't just nausea this time. As my world crumbles around me, I realize that my greatest victim might have been myself all along.

The silence that follows is deafening, broken only by the steady beep of hospital machinery and the pounding of my own heart. I stare at my mother—this woman I've known my entire life—and suddenly feel as though I'm looking at a stranger. The carefully applied makeup, the perfectly coiffed hair, the designer outfit—it all seems like a mask now, hiding the truth that's been lurking beneath the surface for years.

"How could you?" I whisper, my voice barely audible. The words hang in the air between us, heavy with accusation and betrayal. "How could you keep this from me for so long?"

Beatrice's face crumples, the perfect mother persona breaking under the weight of her secrets. "I thought I was protecting you," she says, her voice trembling.

"When you were born, the doctors...they didn't know what to do. They said we had to choose, and I... I couldn't bear the thought of you struggling, of being different."

I laugh—a harsh, bitter sound that seems to echo off the sterile walls of the hospital room. "Struggling? Being different? Do you have any idea what I've been through? The confusion, the self-hatred, the feeling that something was fundamentally wrong with me. The attraction to both sexes that I kept to myself. The crazy thoughts of suicide that still plague me."

Memories flood my mind—years of therapy, of medication, of trying to understand why I felt so disconnected from other people. The countless nights I lay awake, staring at the ceiling, wondering why I didn't fit in with the other children.

"And the pills," I continue, my voice rising with each word. "You've been drugging me? For how long? My entire life?"

Beatrice flinches at the accusation but doesn't deny it. "It was the only way to maintain the illusion," she says softly. "To keep you... normal."

The word "normal" hits me like a physical blow. All those years of striving for normalcy, of trying to fit into the mold my mother had created for me—it had all been based on a lie.

"Normal?" I spit the word back at her. "There's nothing normal about this, Mother. You've been lying to me my entire life. You've been manipulating my body, my hormones, my very identity!"

The realization hits me anew, stealing the breath from my lungs.

"This is insane," I mutter, running my hands through

my hair. "I can't... I can't be pregnant. I'm a man; I have a life, a career, for God's sake!"

The irony of the situation isn't lost on me. I, who have ended so many lives, am now faced with the prospect of creating one. The thought sends a shiver down my spine.

"Kyle," Beatrice says, taking a tentative step toward me. "I know this is a shock, but we can figure this out. We can—"

"We?" I interrupt, my voice cold. "There is no 'we' anymore, Mother. You lost the right to be part of any decisions about my life the moment you decided to lie to me about who I am."

Beatrice recoils as if slapped, her carefully manicured hand flying to her throat. "Kyle, please," she pleads. "I'm your mother. I only ever wanted what was best for you."

I stand up, my legs shaky but my resolve firm. "What's best for me? You don't have the faintest idea what's best for me. You never did."

"I did what I had to do to keep you safe," Beatrice says, her voice strong despite the tears in her eyes. "I've spent your entire life trying to protect you, Kyle. From your father, and from society."

I lean against the wall, suddenly feeling exhausted beyond measure. The weight of these revelations, of the life growing inside me, of the years of lies and manipulation—it's almost too much to bear.

"I need time," I say finally, my voice hoarse. "Time to process all of this, to figure out what it means for my life, for my future."

Beatrice nods, relief visible on her face. "Of course, dear. Whatever you need. I'll be here whenever you're ready to talk more." Beatrice walks out of the room and into the hallway. I needed to be alone.

CHAPTER 35
KYLE

I LEAN HEAVILY against the wall of the hospital room. My mind reels, struggling to process the diagnosis I've just received. The doctor's words echo relentlessly, each repetition feeling like a physical blow. Waves of emotion crash over me - fear, anger, disbelief, and a profound sense of loneliness. Dr. Lawson just stands there and allows me to have my moment.

My chest tightens, breaths coming in short, sharp gasps. The edges of my vision blur as hot tears well up, threatening to spill over. My legs wobble, no longer able to support my weight. I slide down the wall until I'm sitting on the cold tile floor.

A sob escapes my lips, quickly followed by another, then another. The floodgates open, and I find myself weeping uncontrollably. My body shakes with the force of my cries, hands clenched into fists as I pound them against the floor in frustration and despair.

In between sobs, flashes of anger surge through me. "Why me? It's not fair!" The words dissolve into unintelligible wails as another wave of grief washes over me.

As the initial surge of emotion begins to ebb, a numbing sense of shock settles in. I stare blankly at the opposite wall, my mind struggling to reconcile the life I'd known this morning with the uncertain future that now lies before me. I feel adrift, untethered from everything familiar and safe.

In this moment, sitting alone on the floor, I have never felt more scared or more alone in my entire life.

A memory flashes: Pamela's smile, her laughter when I first started feeling sick. I look up and see her walking back into the room. I turn to her, fury in my eyes.

"Did you know?" I demand. "Is that why you were smiling? When I was sick and miserable, did you find it funny?"

Pamela meets my gaze, guilt and defiance warring in her expression. "Yes," she admits quietly. "I knew."

The betrayal cuts deep, sharper than I ever imagined. I stumble back, the ground seeming to shift beneath me.

"How long?" I whisper, my voice rough. "How long have you known?"

Pamela hesitates before answering. "The night I found the tapes. Your mother told me everything then. She said it was necessary—to help me understand... to help me stay."

A bitter laugh escapes me, tinged with hysteria. "To help you stay. So, this was all just another manipulation? Another way to keep me in line?"

Beatrice, overhearing the commotion, steps back into the hospital room. "Kyle, you have to understand. I did what I thought was best. I was trying to give you a normal life."

"Normal?" I spit the word as if it's poison. "You call this normal? Lying to me about who I am, what I am?

Letting me believe I was a monster when all along... you're the monster. I'm glad dad's dead. At least he doesn't have to see what you've become."

"Your father didn't die," Beatrice snaps, her voice breaking. "He killed himself because he couldn't stand being a father to a boy/girl like you!" He left me alone to deal with this all by myself. I did the best I fucking could." Her face crumples as she realizes what she's said. She grabs her things and storms out, unable to face the truth she's just unleashed. *My dad killed himself because of me? This is too much.*

Dr. Lawson clears her throat, pulling me back to the present.

"Regardless of how we got here," she says, her voice steady, "we need to discuss your options, Kyle. This pregnancy is high-risk. There are decisions that need to be made. The chances of this child surviving are very slim, so we need to consider all options."

The word "pregnancy" sends a fresh wave of nausea through me. I place a hand on my stomach, feeling the slight swell I'd thought was just weight gain. Inside me, a life is growing—a life twisted from my own body, a grotesque reflection of the lives I've destroyed.

"I need...air," I mutter, stumbling toward the door. No one stops me as I flee the hospital room, my footsteps echoing down the empty hallway.

I burst outside, gulping the cool air like a drowning man.

Standing in the parking lot, I confront the shattering of everything I believed about myself. I'm not just a killer hiding in plain sight. I'm something else entirely—a grotesque blend of contradictions. I realize my journey into horror and self-discovery has only just begun.

Pamela walks outside. She hears my frantic voice, punctuated by the rapid tapping on my iPhone.

"This can't be right," I mutter, desperation lacing my tone. "There has to be a mistake."

Pamela takes a deep breath, preparing for the difficult conversation ahead.

"Kyle," she says gently, "we need to talk."

My eyes are wild, my hair disheveled from my constant pacing. "Pam, you won't believe what I've found," I say, my words rushing out. I show her my phone. "There are cases of pseudocyesis—false pregnancy. The body can mimic all the symptoms. That's what this is. We need a second opinion. Maybe a third. We can't trust just one doctor."

Pamela places a hand on my arm, feeling the tremors running through me.

"Honey," she begins, her voice firm yet soft, "I know this is hard to accept, but Dr. Lawson is thorough. Your mother even asked her to keep searching for other explanations, just to be safe. But if she says you're pregnant, then—"

"No!" I interrupt, my voice rising. "No, it's impossible. Men don't get pregnant, Pam. It's biologically impossible. There has to be another explanation."

Pamela sees the fear in my eyes, my desperate need to deny reality. She takes a deep breath, bracing herself.

"Kyle, listen to me," she says, her tone serious. "We need to be very careful about how we handle this."

My brow furrows. "What do you mean?"

Pamela glances around, making sure we're alone before continuing. "Think about it, Kyle. If word gets out about your condition, it'll be national news. Maybe even international. Reporters will camp outside our house, government agencies will want to study you, scientists will try to figure out how this happened. This might even cause them to start looking into your other proclivities."

My face drains of color as her words sink in. "But...we need answers," I protest weakly.

Pamela shakes her head. "And what about the other women Kyle? The ones you...were with. If they find out, they'll start asking questions, demanding more money to keep quiet. They might think something's wrong with them or they might tell the world about the horrible things you have done. You need to have this baby without anyone finding out. We need to figure out our next steps without involving anyone else."

"So I'm just supposed to accept this? Pretend everything's normal while I'm...while I'm..."

"Pregnant," Pamela finishes. "Yes. That's exactly what you need to do, at least for now. Until we figure out how to handle this without turning our lives upside down."

"What do we tell everyone?"

"We tell them you're dealing with private health issues. No visitors, no social media—nothing that could tip anyone off to what's really going on."

My hand drifts to my abdomen, an unconscious gesture I've developed over the past few months. "And after?" I ask. "What happens when the baby comes?"

Pamela meets my gaze, the weight of our shared secret heavy between us. "We tell them we adopted another child," she says finally. "For now, we focus on keeping this quiet and keeping you healthy."

I feel the fight drain out of me. Reality sets in, replacing my denial with a numb acceptance.

"I'm scared, Pam," I whisper.

Despite everything, I see compassion in Pamela's eyes.

She takes my hand. "I know," she says softly. "I am too. But we'll get through this. Together."

As the afternoon sun slants through the hospital room window, we sit in silence, lost in our thoughts. The world outside continues, oblivious to the nightmare unfolding within these walls. For now, our secret is safe. But I can't shake the feeling that this is just the beginning of a journey that will test us in ways we can't yet imagine.

The next few days blur together—medical tests, hushed conversations, and mounting tension. My mood swings wildly between acceptance and denial, sometimes within the span of an hour. Pamela walks on eggshells, unsure which version of me she'll find when she enters the room.

One afternoon, she finds me surrounded by medical journals and printouts.

"Kyle," Pamela says cautiously, "what's all this?"

I look up, my eyes bright with manic energy that makes her heart sink. "I've been researching," I say, my words tumbling out. "There are case studies of tumors that mimic pregnancy symptoms. That has to be what this is, Pam. It has to be."

Pamela sighs, setting her purse down and sitting beside me. "Kyle, we've been over this. Dr. Lawson has run every test imaginable. This isn't a tumor, and it isn't Couvade syndrome. You're pregnant."

I shake my head. "No, you don't understand. Look at this article. It talks about—"

"Enough!" Pamela snaps, her patience worn thin. "Kyle, I know this is hard, but you need to stop. Now."

She closes the laptop and pushes it aside. I stare at her, hurt and defiant. "You don't believe me," I accuse. "You think I'm crazy."

Pamela takes a deep breath, calming herself. "I don't think you're crazy. I think you're scared. But Kyle, this denial... it's not helping anyone, especially me. Do you know how hard it is seeing my husband with life growing inside him and constantly denying it. It's triggering me, Kyle. It's making me think you don't want this baby. Like you didn't want ours."

"Pamela, I'm so sorry. I never thought about how this could be affecting you."

She takes my hand. "I know this isn't what we expected. It's not fair, and it's not normal. But it's happening, and we need to deal with it."

My shoulders sag. "I don't know how," I admit.

Pamela squeezes my hand. "We'll figure it out together," she says. "But first, you need to accept this is real. Can you do that?"

I'm quiet for a long moment, my hand resting on my abdomen. Finally, I nod, a tear slipping down my cheek. "Okay," I whisper. "Okay."

Pamela wraps her arms around me as silent sobs shake my body. I wonder what the future holds for us. The road ahead is uncertain, filled with challenges we can't yet imagine. But for now, we have each other. And for now, that will have to be enough.

CHAPTER 36
KYLE

3.5 MONTHS Later

I shift on the couch, the rough fabric irritating my sweat-dampened skin. The weight in my abdomen feels heavier than ever, a constant reminder of this overwhelming journey.

Jewelry clinks, and the sharp click of high heels echoes through the house, disrupting the stillness. Pamela must be getting ready to go out. Again. I struggle to sit up, my swollen belly making every movement a chore. I pause, breathless, one hand on my lower back, the other on my stretched stomach. I'm six months pregnant and I'm as big as a house.

"Where are you going?" I call out, unable to mask the suspicion in my voice. The words come out strained, a mix of physical discomfort and emotional turmoil.

Pamela enters the living room, stunning in a vibrant yellow dress that highlights her dark skin. Her hair is straight, cascading down her back. The sight of her takes me back to our dating days, but now, instead of excitement, it only deepens the gulf between us.

"I told you, babe. I'm going out with the girls," Pamela says lightly, though there's a familiar edge to her tone.

Frustration flares, mingling with a sense of abandonment. "Which girls? And where exactly are you going?"

"Jasmine and Keisha. I met them when I started that new yoga class. We're checking out that new club downtown," she replies casually, grabbing her purse. The sequins catch the fading light, scattering tiny rainbows across the room.

"A club? Seriously?" My voice rises, fueled by resentment. "And who's watching Marissa?"

Pamela frowns, confused. "You are, of course. It's your night with her, remember?"

I struggle to my feet, supporting my aching back. A flutter in my belly makes me pause, steadying myself with a deep breath. "So you're just going to leave me here, six months pregnant, to take care of our daughter while you go party?"

"Kyle, it's one night," Pamela says, but her words only stoke my anger.

"One night? It's been one night a week for the past month! I haven't been out since I got pregnant, and you keep abandoning me!"

Pamela's expression hardens, her earlier lightness gone. "Abandoning you? I've been nothing but supportive! I work full-time, take care of Marissa, and go to every doctor's appointment with you. Am I not allowed any time for myself?"

Her words sting, and I lash out, my frustration boiling over. "Oh, poor you. It must be so hard supporting your freak of a husband. Sorry my pregnancy is cramping your social life!"

Regret hits immediately, but it's too late. I see the hurt flash across Pamela's face before anger takes over.

"That's not fair, and you know it," she snaps. "I've been here for you every step of the way. But I'm not putting my entire life on hold just because you're going through this!"

"This?" I gesture wildly at my stomach, feeling another flutter. "This is our child, Pamela! Our miracle! And you act like it's a burden!"

Pamela's eyes narrow. "Actually, that's your child, not mine. It has none of my DNA. You got yourself pregnant, Kyle and I don't think you should be calling it a miracle because you never wanted children. And let's not forget you and Beatrice robbed me of motherhood."

Her words hit me like a slap. I instinctively protect my swollen belly, the room spinning around me. "How... how can you say that?" My voice cracks, betraying my vulnerability. "We're supposed to be partners!"

"Partners? Were we partners when you fucked the nanny and got her pregnant? When you hid your inner demon from me? When you called me fat and told me to get rid of our baby? No, we weren't partners. You were selfish, and if anyone needs a little time alone, it's me."

"I apologized for that, and I thought you forgave me."

"I forgave you so I wouldn't be bitter, but I haven't forgotten."

"And what about the support I need?" My voice rises again. "The doctor's appointments, cravings, mood swings? I haven't had a normal day in months, Pamela. I haven't seen friends, had a drink—I can barely move without pain. And you think you're the one who needs a break?"

"Kyle, millions of women do this all the time. It's

temporary. In a couple of months, you'll be free. So chill. You sound like a little bitch."

Just as I'm about to respond, the door creaks open, and Marissa peeks out, her eyes wide with concern. "Mommy? Daddy? Why are you yelling?"

Her small, worried face stops us cold. We exchange guilty looks. Pamela takes a deep breath, forcing herself to calm down.

"It's nothing, sweetie," she says gently. "Go back to your room. Mommy and Daddy are just talking."

As Marissa retreats, closing the door softly behind her, I collapse back onto the couch, drained. The anger has left me hollow and sad. The room falls into a heavy silence, broken only by the ticking clock and my labored breathing.

"Just go," I murmur, not meeting Pamela's eyes. The fight has drained from me, leaving only exhaustion. "Have fun with your friends."

Pamela hesitates, torn between her plans and staying. The tension is suffocating. Part of me wants her to stay, to comfort me, to say everything will be okay. But another part, hurt and angry, just wants her gone.

I sit there, feeling the weight of our unborn child and the burden of this strange, isolating experience. I wonder how we got here. How did our partnership become a battlefield of resentment and misunderstanding? I think back to when we first learned of my pregnancy, the shock, the excitement. We were united then, ready to face this unprecedented challenge together.

But as the weeks turned into months and my body changed, the strain grew. Somewhere along the way, we stopped being a team and started keeping score.

I glance at Pamela, still standing in her beautiful

dress, and I'm struck by how far apart we've drifted. There's an ocean of unspoken words between us, fears and frustrations we've kept buried.

"Pam," I begin, my voice barely a whisper. "I—"

But before I can finish, she turns away, grabbing her purse. "I'll be back when I get back," she says, avoiding my gaze.

Then she's gone, the front door closing with a soft thud, the sound echoing through the empty house. I'm left alone with my thoughts.

As the last light fades, I place my hands on my stomach. Despite everything—the fear, the pain, the uncertainty—I can't help but feel a surge of love for this child, our child, regardless of DNA.

"It's just you and me tonight, Kayla" I murmur, a tear slipping down my cheek. "But we'll be okay. We have to be."

In the deepening darkness, I make a silent promise—to myself, to Pamela, to our unborn child—that we'll find a way through this. Somehow, we'll bridge the gap that's grown between us. Because in the end, we're all we've got. And that has to be enough.

CHAPTER 37
KYLE

I WAKE up as the first rays of dawn creep through the linen curtains. Pamela's hand rests on my protruding stomach, her fingers layed across my caramel skin. I glance down at her hand, so delicate against my swollen abdomen, and feel a surge of conflicting emotions. I'm 28 weeks pregnant, a fact that still seems surreal. I want to push her hand off because I'm still angry about how she's been treating me.

My mind races with questions that have plagued me for months: Why me? Out of all the men in the world, why was I chosen for this bizarre twist of fate? I catch sight of my reflection in the mirror across the room. The man staring back at me is a far cry from the chiseled figure I once was. My stomach pushes against my tank top, creating a rounded silhouette that feels alien. I try to suck it in, but the bump remains, stubbornly visible.

With a soft groan, I place my hand over Pamela's, feeling a strange flutter beneath my skin. The sensation of something—someone—moving inside me is both awe-inspiring and deeply unsettling. I'm a man, for crying out loud. Men aren't built for this.

Pamela stirs beside me, her eyes meeting my troubled gaze. A warm smile spreads across her face as she props herself up on one elbow.

"Good morning, handsome," she murmurs, her voice husky with sleep.

I force a smile, trying to mask the turmoil churning inside me. "Morning," I reply, my voice strained. Pamela's hand caresses my belly, her touch tender, making my throat tighten with emotion.

"How are you feeling today?" she asks, concern evident in her eyes.

"I'm... managing," I reply, struggling to keep my voice steady. I sit up slowly, wincing at the unfamiliar aches in my lower back. Pamela watches me with a mixture of sympathy and something else—amusement?—in her eyes.

"You know," she says gently, "it's okay not to be okay all the time. This is a lot to handle."

I nod, not trusting myself to speak. Tears prick at the corners of my eyes, and I silently curse the hormones that seem intent on stripping away every shred of my masculinity.

Pamela gets out of bed and opens the curtains fully, letting the morning light flood the room. My gaze is drawn again to my reflection. I stand up slowly, supporting my lower back with one hand. I turn to the side, lifting my tank top to examine my profile.

The bump is undeniable now. I attempt to suck in my stomach again, but it's futile. My once-defined abs have given way to a smooth, rounded curve. I let out a frustrated sigh, letting the tank top fall back into place.

"Kyle," Pamela's voice cuts through my self-critical

thoughts, "remember, Marissa and I are going to Disney World with her class for the week."

I groan, rubbing my temples. "You're leaving me alone again?" The thought of being alone makes my stomach churn—and not from morning sickness.

"Kyle, you've known about this for a while. What do you want me to do, back out?"

"Can you?"

"No, Kyle. You've gone on trips while I was pregnant. Women deal with this daily. It's only a week, and you're not alone. You have your mother and Dr. Lawson to keep you company."

"I haven't talked to my mother in over four months."

"Well, maybe you should reach out to her. She feels bad."

"I'd rather be alone than talk to her."

"You haven't talked to Donna about any of this have you?"

"No, I couldn't risk her telling her husband and him telling someone in the military. That would be a nightmare. I'm just glad she's on a mission trip for a year and doesn't have to see me like this. I'm just going to wait until they come back."

"I think that's a good idea; you don't want to worry her."

As Pamela bustles about getting ready for the trip, I head to the bathroom. I step onto the scale, holding my breath as the numbers flicker. When they finally settle, my eyes widen in disbelief.

"What?!" I yell, my voice echoing off the tiled walls. In a fit of frustration, I pick up the scale and slam it against the floor.

Pamela rushes into the bathroom, alarmed. "What's wrong?" she asks, taking in the scene.

"I've gained 20 pounds in a week!" I exclaim, continuing to abuse the scale. "This is ridiculous! Sixty pounds in 28 weeks—that's a little over 2.1 pounds a week!"

"Honey, it's okay," Pamela says soothingly, reaching out to take the battered scale from my hands. "Put down the scale." I relent, letting the mangled device clatter to the floor. I run a hand through my hair, frustration evident in every line of my body.

"Kyle, you knew weight gain would happen. It's not a big deal. You can work it off once you have the baby."

"What do you mean it's not a big deal? Look at me!"

Pamela eyes me up and down. "Well, you have let yourself go. I told you to lay off the rocky road and French vanilla coffee creamer shakes," Pamela says, a hint of exasperation in her voice.

I shoot her a withering look. If anyone should understand pregnancy cravings, it's her. I bite back a retort, remembering her odd peanut butter and pickle phase during her pregnancies. *Why is she being so insensitive? I was never this mean toward her. Was I?*

As if on cue, my stomach growls loudly. Without a word, I brush past Pamela and head for the kitchen, my mind focused on one thing: rocky road ice cream. Pamela, sensing my intentions, darts in front of me, blocking the freezer.

"Kyle," she says sternly, "you don't need any ice cream."

My eyes narrow, a primal hunger glinting in them. "Pamela," I say, my voice low and dangerous, "if you don't give me that rocky road, I'm going to scream so loud it'll wake the neighbors. Now give me my rocky road." Pamela stands her ground, calling my bluff. She opens the freezer, takes out the rocky road, and starts moving toward the trash. I feel something snap inside me. I let out a scream so loud and sudden that Pamela jumps, nearly dropping the ice cream container.

"Really, Kyle?" Pamela says. "Is it that serious?"

In response, I snatch the ice cream from her hands and grab the largest spoon I can find. I then retrieve the French vanilla creamer from the fridge, pouring a generous amount into the ice cream container. As Pamela watches, horrified and fascinated, I stir the concoction vigorously.

But I'm not done yet. My eyes scan the kitchen until they land on what I'm looking for—chocolate chips. I grab the bag, tear it open, and shove a handful into my mouth.

The first bite is pure bliss. I close my eyes, savoring the mix of flavors and textures. The crunch of the chocolate chips, the creamy sweetness of the ice cream, the rich vanilla notes of the creamer—it's a symphony of flavors that makes every taste bud sing.

As I continue to devour my unconventional breakfast, lost in a world of sugary ecstasy, a small voice breaks through my thoughts.

"Daddy?"

I freeze, the spoon halfway to my mouth. I turn slowly to see Marissa standing in the doorway, her eyes wide as she takes in the scene.

"Ice cream isn't one of the four major food groups," Marissa says, her voice a perfect imitation of my usual lecture tone. Irritation flares. I want to tell my little smart aleck to go read a book and leave me alone, but I know she's just parroting back what I've preached for years.

Marissa walks over to the cabinet, pulls out a bowl

and spoon, and approaches me with an expectant look. I instinctively hug the ice cream container closer, turning away from her.

"Pretty please?" Marissa asks, pushing her bowl closer. Her pigtails swing as she tilts her head, unleashing the full power of her puppy-dog eyes. I remain unmoved.

"What about 'sharing is caring'?" Marissa tries again. "Or 'it's better to give than receive'?"

Pamela and Marissa stand with their arms folded, waiting for my response. I look from one to the other, then back at my precious ice cream.

"I do not care to share my ice cream," I declare. "And I am giving myself ice cream and receiving pleasure from it."

"That's why your tummy is getting bigger," Marissa observes innocently. My head snaps up.

"What did you say, little girl?"

"I said that's why—" Marissa begins, but Pamela quickly intervenes, ushering her out of the kitchen. As Marissa grabs her backpack, I hear her muttering under her breath.

"He's telling us to eat healthy, and he's over here eating ice cream for breakfast."

"Little girl, what did you say?!" I call out sharply.

"She didn't say anything," Pamela interjects quickly. "Our chauffeur is here. We'll see you in a week."

"What am I going to eat for breakfast?" Marissa asks, her voice tinged with complaint.

"I'll pick you up something on the way," Pamela promises.

"Yes!" Marissa's face lights up. But as she looks back at me, her expression turns serious. "You need to work on that, Dad," she says, gesturing to my stomach. "It's getting out of control. Please don't come to career day looking that fat."

I look at Pamela, feeling a lump form in my throat. Pamela, seeing the hurt in my eyes, quickly steps in. "No body shaming, Marissa," she says firmly. "It's not nice."

"But he does it all the time," Marissa protests.

"Yes, but that doesn't make it right," Pamela counters.

Marissa folds her arms and rolls her eyes, knowing what she must do but clearly not wanting to. "I'm sorry, Dad," she mumbles.

She gives me a quick hug before heading out. I do my best to keep my emotions in check, feeling a confusing mix of shame and pride. Pamela kisses me on the cheek, promising to call later. As the front door closes behind them, I'm left alone in the suddenly quiet house.

With a heavy sigh, I grab my ice cream, make my way to the living room, and turn on Golden Girls. As the familiar theme song fills the room, I feel the first tears begin to fall. I'm overweight, unemployed, pregnant, and utterly alone in my experience. No one can truly understand what I'm going through.

As I sit here, spoon in hand, ice cream melting in my lap, I wonder for the thousandth time how my life has taken such an unexpected turn. But as I feel another flutter in my stomach—my child moving within me—I realize that despite all the challenges, despite the fear and uncertainty, a part of me is starting to embrace this bizarre miracle.

I'm going to be the world's first "Momdy," and while that thought terrifies me, it also fills me with a strange sense of pride. Whatever comes next, I know one thing for certain—it's going to be one hell of a ride.

CHAPTER 38
KYLE

THE CRUNCH of gravel outside makes my heart race. I'm not expecting anyone. I haven't expected anyone for months especially since I changed my number and stopped responding to everyone's text.

A knock at the door startles me. I consider ignoring it, but then a familiar voice calls out,

"Kyle, it's Mike and Jake. We're just stopping by to make sure you're okay, man. You haven't been at work or returned our phone calls, and we're worried about you."

My stomach churns with anxiety. I haven't seen anyone in months—haven't wanted to. But something in Mike's voice—concern, genuine worry—makes me hesitate. I've been dodging calls, ignoring texts. I should have told everyone I was going to be out of town for a while, but the stress clouded my thinking.

"I'm fine," I call out, my voice strained even to my own ears. "I quit my job. Just leave me alone, okay?"

There's a pause before Mike responds, his voice gentle but insistent. "Come on, Kyle. The boss said you quit, but there was confusion when we came over a few months back. We just want to make sure you're alright. Can you open the door? Please?" *It's important that we keep this a secret.* Those are the words that Pamela has repeated to me over and over and that tug at the front of my psyche.

I stand frozen, hand on the doorknob. Part of me wants to stay hidden, keep my secret safe. But another part—a part I've tried to ignore—desperately wants someone to talk to.

With a deep breath, I unlock the door and open it a crack. Mike and Jake's concerned faces come into view, and I see shock register in their eyes as they take in my appearance. I know I look terrible—haven't taken care of myself, haven't had the energy or will to do much of anything lately.

"Jesus, Kyle," Mike breathes. "What happened, bro? What's going on?"

Shame washes over me as I step back, opening the door wider. "You might as well come in," I mutter, turning and shuffling back into the house.

As Mike and Jake enter, I collapse into my armchair, watching as they gingerly take seats on my cluttered couch. I can see them taking in the mess around us—the takeout containers, empty bottles, dirty laundry. I should feel embarrassed, but I'm too tired to care.

"Kyle," Mike begins gently, leaning forward. "Talk to us, man. What's going on? Why haven't you been at work?"

I stare at the floor, unable to meet their eyes. "I'm sick," I whisper.

Jake's voice is filled with concern. "Sick? What kind of sickness? Have you seen a doctor?"

I shake my head, still not looking up. "It's... it's complicated. I'd rather not get into it."

Mike's voice is soft, encouraging. "Come on, Kyle. We're your friends. Whatever it is, you can tell us. We want to help."

Tears prick at the corners of my eyes. How can I explain this to them? How can I make them understand something I barely understand myself?

Taking a deep, shuddering breath, I finally raise my eyes to meet Mike's. "I... I found out something about myself. Something I never knew before."

The room falls silent. I can feel the tension, the anticipation. Mike shifts uncomfortably on the couch while Jake leans in closer.

"What is it, Kyle?" Jake asks softly. "You can trust us."

My voice is barely above a whisper. "I'm...I'm intersex."

I see confusion on their faces, the struggle to understand. Mike blinks, caught off guard. "Intersex? You mean, like, you have both male and female characteristics?"

I nod, my cheeks flushing with embarrassment. "Yeah. I just found out recently. It's been... overwhelming, to say the least."

Jake clears his throat, uncomfortable but trying to be supportive. "That must have been a huge shock, man. But... is that why you quit your job? Why you've been hiding out here?"

I shake my head, tears welling up again. "No, it's... there's more." I pause, gathering what little courage I have left. "I'm... I'm pregnant."

The silence that follows is deafening. Mike and Jake stare at me in disbelief. I can practically see the gears turning in their heads as they try to process what I've just told them.

Jake lets out a nervous chuckle. "Come on, Kyle. Men can't get pregnant. That's not possible."

Anger and hurt surge through me. "It is possible, Jake," I snap, my voice harder than I intended. "Look at me! You think I gained over 60 pounds in seven months by just overeating? There have been cases of intersex individuals who identify as male and impregnate themselves. It's rare, but it happens. The baby normally doesn't survive, but I guess I'm the exception."

Mike holds up his hands, apologetic. "Okay, okay. I'm sorry. I didn't mean to... It's just... This is a lot to take in, you know?"

Jake, who's been uncharacteristically quiet, finally speaks up. "Kyle, man... that's... that's pretty heavy stuff. Have you seen a doctor about this? Are you sure?"

I nod, feeling utterly drained. "Yeah, I'm sure. My family doctor is treating me. She confirmed it."

Mike runs a hand through his hair, overwhelmed. "Jesus, Kyle. Why didn't you tell us sooner? We could have been here for you, man."

"I was scared," I admit, my voice barely audible. "I didn't know how to tell anyone. I was afraid of how people would react, what they might say or do. And then there's the whole media circus that could happen if this got out. I mean, can you imagine the headlines? 'Man Pregnant!' It would be a freak show."

Jake nods sympathetically. "I get it, man. That's a lot to deal with on your own. But you know we've got your back, right? No matter what."

I manage a weak smile, the first in what feels like forever. "Thanks, guys. That... that means a lot."

Mike, however, still looks troubled. "Kyle, I hear what you're saying, but... don't you think you should get a second opinion? I mean, this is serious stuff. Maybe there's been some kind of mistake?"

My expression darkens. "You think I haven't thought about that? I'm terrified, Mike. What if getting a second opinion means more people find out? What if word gets out and my life becomes a media circus? I can't... I can't handle that."

As the conversation lulls, Jake glances around the room. "Hey, where's Pamela? How's she dealing with all this?"

My heart constricts at the mention of her name. "She's gone for the week," I mumble, unable to keep the bitterness out of my voice. "But even when she's here... she's treating me like shit. She's either at the gym or at the club, having bottle service with the girls."

Mike and Jake exchange concerned glances. "What do you mean, 'treating you like shit'?" Mike asks gently.

I sigh heavily, slumping further into my chair. "Ever since I told her about being intersex and the pregnancy, she's been pulling away. At first, I thought she was just shocked, you know? But now...it's like she can't even look at me. When she is home, she barely speaks to me. And she's been going out more and more, staying out late with her friends."

Jake frowns, anger flashing in his eyes. "That's not okay, man. You need support right now, not...whatever the hell that is."

I shrug, feeling utterly defeated. "I know. I've tried talking to her, but she just shuts down or finds an excuse to leave. I don't know what to do anymore. We haven't had sex in months, she complains about my weight, and even tries to control what I eat."

Mike leans forward, his voice gentle but firm. "Kyle, I know you're dealing with a lot, but you deserve better than that. Have you talked to your therapist about what's going on with Pamela?"

I nod, a flicker of relief at the mention of my therapist. "Yeah, we've discussed it. My therapist thinks Pamela might be struggling to process everything too, but that doesn't excuse her behavior. We're supposed to have a couple's session next week, but... I don't know if she'll even show up."

Jake stands, determination written across his face. "Alright, here's what we're going to do. First, we're cleaning up this place. It's not good for you to be living like this—pregnant or not."

Mike nods, already starting to gather empty takeout containers. "Yeah, and we'll stock your fridge with actual food. No more living on pizza and Coke."

I feel a rush of emotion—gratitude, relief, and a touch of embarrassment. "Guys, you don't have to—"

Mike cuts me off. "No arguments. We're here to help, whether you like it or not. And while we're cleaning, we can brainstorm about next steps. Maybe we can find a doctor who specializes in intersex health—someone who can give you a thorough checkup without judgment."

As Mike and Jake bustle around, tidying up and making plans, I watch them with a mixture of gratitude and lingering anxiety. Part of me wants to believe that everything will be okay—that with their support, I can face whatever challenges lie ahead. But another part of me can't shake the feeling that there's more to my condition than meets the eye—that the truth, whatever it might be, is still lurking just out of reach.

As the afternoon wears on into evening, I find myself joining the cleaning efforts. My movements are tentative at first, but as I work alongside my friends, I feel a spark of something I haven't felt in weeks—hope.

By the time the sun sets, the three of us sit around the kitchen table, a spread of sandwiches and fruit before us. The conversation flows more easily now, punctuated by moments of laughter as Jake cracks jokes to lighten the mood. We discuss potential doctors, strategies for my physical and mental health, and ways to approach the situation with Pamela.

As Mike and Jake prepare to leave, promising to return the next day with groceries and more information, I feel a weight lift from my shoulders. The road ahead is still uncertain, full of challenges I can't even begin to imagine. But for the first time in weeks, I don't feel alone.

The house feels different now—cleaner, lighter somehow. As I get ready for bed, I catch a glimpse of myself in the bathroom mirror. I still look tired, still heavier than I used to be, but there's something different in my eyes—a spark that wasn't there this morning.

As I lie in bed, one hand resting on my swollen belly, I think about the future. It's still terrifying, still full of unknowns. But for the first time in months, I feel a glimmer of hope. Whatever happens, whatever challenges I face, I know I'm not alone anymore.

And that, I realize as I drift off to sleep, might just be enough to get me through this.

CHAPTER 39
KYLE

ONE WEEK **Later**

The sound of a key sliding into the lock jolts me from an uneasy slumber. I've become a light sleeper lately, always on edge. The lock turns with a soft click, and my eyes dart to the glowing numbers on the digital clock. It's late—or early, depending on how you look at it.

I try to heave myself off the couch, but my swollen body betrays me. Each attempt ends with me sinking back into the worn cushions, my muscles trembling. I feel like a turtle flipped on its shell—helpless and exposed.

Pamela walks in, her eyes immediately locking onto my pathetic struggle. Irritation flashes across her face, quickly masked by a forced smile. She's upset that I'm exactly where she left me a few days ago, as if I'm some piece of furniture that hasn't been moved.

She approaches, extending her hand to help me up. I reach for it, grateful for the assistance but burning with shame. As I continue to fail in my attempts to stand, familiar anger bubbles up inside me—my constant companion these past months.

Pamela tries to stifle a giggle, but it escapes anyway. The sound grates on my nerves like nails on a chalkboard. Finally, with one last effort, I manage to heave myself to my feet. But my anger has reached its boiling point.

"Why are you laughing at me?" I snap, my voice harsh in the quiet room.

My words only seem to fuel her amusement. Her giggles transform into full-blown laughter, echoing off the walls. I stand there, one hand pressed against my aching back, watching my wife laugh at my misery. The scene feels surreal, like I'm trapped in some bizarre nightmare.

A tear slides down my cheek. Horrified, I turn away, furiously wiping at my eyes. But it's as if a dam has broken. Tears stream down my face, and I'm powerless to stop them. Pamela's laughter dies away, replaced by an awkward silence.

After what feels like an eternity, I feel her hand gently grasping mine. She doesn't speak, just holds on, allowing me this moment of vulnerability. But her touch, once so comforting, now feels like sandpaper against my skin.

"Why do you keep laughing at me?" I choke out between sobs. "You of all people should know what I'm going through."

"Women all over the world have done this since Adam and Eve," Pamela responds, her tone matter-of-fact.

My temper flares again. "Yes, but you knew about this upfront. You knew the risks, the changes. You were prepared."

I watch as something shifts in Pamela's eyes. The gentle, understanding wife disappears, replaced by a stranger with fire in her gaze. "Prepared?" Her voice rises, sharp and cutting. "No woman is prepared the first time they get pregnant. You act like we grew up with babies in our bellies."

"You know what I mean," I mutter, but even as the words leave my mouth, I know I've made a mistake.

"No, I know what you said."

Pamela's tirade continues, each word a dagger to my heart. She talks about the loneliness, the unkindness, the physical changes—all things I'd been blind to during her pregnancies. As she speaks, she moves around the room, picking up discarded items, her movements sharp and angry.

I listen—really listen—for what feels like the first time in years. The weight of my own selfishness settles on my shoulders, heavier than the child growing within me. Pamela, realizing how heated things have become, starts to leave the room.

"Pamela, Pamela," I call, desperate to continue our conversation, to make things right.

Suddenly, a sharp pain lances through my abdomen. I look down in horror as I pee on myself unable to control my bladder. Another wave of pain hits, stronger this time, forcing a loud moan from my lips.

Pamela turns back, her eyes widening as she takes in the scene. "Oh my God," she breathes, rushing to my side. "Your water broke. The babies coming early. I'm calling Dr. Lawson."

I collapse to the floor, my heart pounding so fast I can barely breathe. Pamela reappears with a warm towel, pressing it gently against my face. "It's going to be okay, Kyle," she soothes.

"Dr. Lawson is on the way."

Confusion floods my mind, battling with the pain

wracking my body. My vision blurs, darkness creeping in at the edges.

Terror grips me as I realize something is very wrong. As consciousness slips away, one thought echoes through my mind: God, please don't take my baby. Then darkness claims me, leaving me adrift in a sea of uncertainty and fear.

CHAPTER 40
KYLE

THE OPERATING ROOM is a flurry of activity, the air thick with the smell of medicine. But this isn't the hospital where we had our regular visits. It looks like a huge basement or warehouse. I lie on the table, trembling with fear and anticipation, my hands handcuffed to the bed. The blue surgical drape across my chest creates a barrier between me and the surreal scene unfolding beyond.

"Kyle," Dr. Lawson's voice comes from behind the drape, steady and reassuring. "This is Dr. Newman she will be preforming your caesarean. We're about to begin the incision. You'll feel some pressure but no pain. Are you ready?"

"Where am I? And why am I chained up?" I ask, panic rising in my chest.

Pamela's hand squeezes mine, and I turn to meet her eyes. The worry I see there frightens me. Water fills her eyes.

"It's going to be okay," Pamela whispers, but there's a tremor in her voice that betrays her own uncertainty. My mom, Beatrice, stands on my other side, her usual composure cracking as she watches me prepare to give birth. It's the first time I've seen her in months, but if I'm honest, I'm glad she's here.

"What the hell is happening? It's only been about seven months. Why are we here?"

"If we wait any longer, it could jeopardize your health, Kyle. You could die," Dr. Lawson says, her voice firm.

"I'm here, sweetheart," my mom murmurs, stroking my hair. "Momma's right here."

As Dr. Newman begins the procedure, I close my eyes, my mind racing with thoughts of the baby I'm about to meet. As they continue the procedure, I lose all sense of time as I imagine tiny fingers and toes, a button nose, wisps of dark hair. I think of all the dreams I have for this child—teaching her to ride a bike, cheering at her graduations, dancing at her wedding. My heart swells with a love so profound it takes my breath away. I don't know if it's a girl or not because I wanted it to be a surprise, but I feel like it's a girl. If it is, I've decided on the name Kayla—the name Pamela was going to give the child she lost. I know it doesn't make up for what we did, but I hope this helps us heal. The erratic beeping on a nearby machine pulls me out of my daydream.

Suddenly, the atmosphere in the room changes. My eyes fly open, sensing the shift. The bustling activity has ceased, replaced by an eerie stillness.

"What's happening?" I ask, my voice cracking with fear. "Is the baby okay?"

Dr. Lawson's voice, when it comes, is heavy with sorrow. "I'm so sorry, Kyle. The baby... there's no heartbeat."

"What do you mean, no heartbeat?" I feel as if I'm falling, spiraling into an abyss of grief and disbelief. "No,"

I whisper, shaking my head in denial. "No, that can't be right. Check again!"

Pamela's grip on my hand loosens as she stumbles backward, her free hand flying to her mouth to stifle a sob. Beatrice lets out a small, choked sound, her eyes wide with shock.

"Let me see my baby," I demand, my voice rising with hysteria. "I need to hold my child!" I yank my arms repeatedly and try desperately to break free from the handcuffed that are secured against the bed.

Dr. Lawson's face appears above the drape, her eyes filled with compassion and regret. "I'm sorry, Kyle. We can't risk any further complications. We need to finish the procedure."

My anguished cry echoes through the room. I try to sit up, desperate to see my baby, but the restraints and the effects of the anesthesia keep me immobile. Two other doctors come inside the room and restrain my legs with leg cuffs. "Please," I beg, tears streaming down my face. "Please, just let me hold her once."

Pamela, her own face wet with tears, moves to the other side of the drape. I watch, heart breaking, as Dr. Lawson hands her a small bundle wrapped in a soft blanket. Even from a distance, I can see that the baby is perfect—tiny, beautiful, and utterly still.

"Pamela!" I call out, my voice raw with emotion. "Bring the baby here! Let me see!"

But Pamela, her face a mask of grief—and something else, is it guilt?—shakes her head.

"I can't let you hold this child," she whispers. "I'm sorry, Kyle. You took my baby and so many other women's children, so now I am taking yours."

And then she's gone, rushing out of the operating room with our silent child cradled in her arms.

"No!" I scream, thrashing against the restraints. "Pamela! Bring the baby back! Please!"

Beatrice tries to calm me, her hands gentle on my shoulders, but I'm beyond consolation. My cries of anguish fill the room, a sound of such raw pain that it brings tears to even the most seasoned medical staff.

As Dr. Lawson and her team work to complete the cesarean, my mind is consumed with thoughts of the child I will never hold. I imagine the weight of the baby in my arms, the soft skin against my chest, the tiny hand wrapped around my finger. Each sensation is a knife to my heart—a cruel reminder of what I have lost.

"I'm so sorry, little one," I whisper between sobs. "Daddy loves you so much. I had so many plans for us. I was going to protect you, watch you grow, love you every day of your life. I'm sorry I couldn't keep you safe."

The physical pain of the surgery is nothing compared to the agony that tears through my soul. I had carried this child for months, felt every kick and movement, dreamed of the future we would have together. And now, in the span of a heartbeat, all those dreams have been shattered.

As the procedure ends, I feel hollowed out—empty in a way that goes beyond the physical. The room fades into a blur of muted sounds and indistinct shapes. I'm vaguely aware of being moved to a recovery room, of Beatrice's constant soothing presence, of doctors and nurses speaking in hushed tones.

But all I can focus on is the absence. The silence where there should be a baby's cry. The emptiness in my arms where my child should be. The vast, echoing void in my heart that I know will never truly be filled.

As the first light of dawn creeps through the windows, I lie in my hospital bed, tears silently tracking down my face. I have experienced a love so profound, so all-encompassing, that its loss leaves me shattered—adrift in a sea of grief that seems endless.

The world outside continues, impossibly unchanged, while my entire existence has been altered forever. I mourn for the child I have loved and lost, for the future that will never be, and for the part of myself that died in that operating room. The journey of healing will be long and painful, but for now, in this moment, I allow myself to be consumed by the raw, devastating power of my grief.

CHAPTER 41
KYLE

24 HOURS **Later**

The room is shrouded in darkness, save for the pale moonlight filtering through the half-drawn curtains. I sit on the edge of my bed, a silhouette of despair against the dim backdrop. My hands tremble as I reach for my second phone, the screen's harsh glow illuminating the anguish etched across my face.

For the thousandth time, I dial Pamela's number, each unanswered ring driving a nail deeper into my already fractured psyche. "Pick up the phone, Pam," I whisper, my voice cracking. "I fucking need you, Pam." The silence on the other end is deafening. With a guttural cry of frustration, I hurl the phone across the room. It shatters against the wall, the sound of breaking glass a fitting metaphor for my shattered world.

I bury my face in my hands, my body wracked with uncontrollable sobs. The weight of loss presses down on me, threatening to crush what remains of my sanity. In that moment of utter desolation, I feel a hand on my back —gentle, comforting.

I look up, my vision blurred by tears, to see my mother standing beside me.

"How are you feeling, baby?" Beatrice asks, her voice soft and soothing.

I struggle to find words, my throat constricting around the emotions threatening to choke me. "I don't think there's a word in the English language that can describe how I feel," I manage.

"But if I had to try, it feels like a truck is parked on my chest, and it doesn't want to move."

Beatrice's lips curve into a sad smile. "Welcome to motherhood—or as you say, 'momdyhood.' I felt the same way after my first two miscarriages." The words hang in the air, heavy with implication. I turn to my mother, shock momentarily overriding my grief.

"You had two miscarriages?" I ask, grasping her hand. "Why didn't you tell me? I'm so sorry that happened to you, Mom."

"It's not something mothers want to talk about." Beatrice's gaze grows distant, as if looking back through the years at ghosts long buried. "Actually, I had an abortion first, and then after that, two miscarriages."

My brow furrows in confusion. "But, Mom, why would you get an abortion? That doesn't seem like you. I know you believe women should have the right to choose, but you always said you wouldn't have one."

A shadow passes over Beatrice's face, her grip on my hand tightening imperceptibly. "I'm against abortion, and if it were up to me, I wouldn't have had it," she says, her voice hardening. "But it wasn't up to me. Your father made me get an abortion, just like you manipulated those women to get abortions."

"Mom, I never manipulated women to get abortions, I just watched the live ones you and Dr. Lawson set up."

"You're such a good liar Kyle. You really think I wasn't going to find out about the twenty plus women you paid off in the last seven years to watch them have abortions in person. Some you impregnated, some you didn't."

The room seems to grow colder as mother and son lock eyes, the unspoken truth hanging between us like a guillotine blade.

"Yes, I know about Cindy and Chloe. I know you got them pregnant because you wanted them to be your next victims. What boggles my mind—was that you didn't want Pamela pregnant. You fell in love with her. When I saw that, I thought there was hope for you."

"Mom, I can explain," I begin, but Beatrice cuts me off with a sharp gesture.

"I don't want an explanation," she says, her voice eerily calm. "I know why you did it. You're a killer, Kyle. You get joy from forcing women to kill their babies at the last minute. I thought I was helping you by letting you watch those abortions. I thought it was working."

"Mom it was working, but when Pamela started talking about children again it triggered me and yes, I did start watching live abortions again, but I couldn't help it. But I never forced a woman to get an abortion. I asked but never forced."

Beatrice's laugh is cold and brittle. "But you didn't tell me about it, your biggest advocate. I would have done anything to protect you, but you started killing again and hiding it. You put our family name in jeopardy. It's the green eyes and the handsome face. The girls can't tell you no. You've been blessed with the recessive genes that girls can't resist." Her voice drops to a near whisper. "I thought the first girl, Penny, was lying when she told me what you did. But when six other girls repeated the same stories over the years, I had to awaken from my delusion and realize that you were just like your father. You are your father's son, and it's in your blood. You wanted to maintain your 'good boy' image to hide the darkness in you."

I feel as if the floor is tilting beneath me. "What do you mean I'm just like my father?" I ask, dreading the answer.

Beatrice's eyes glitter in the dim light, a mix of sorrow and something darker—something I've never seen in her before. "Your father was just like you, and if it wasn't for me, you wouldn't even be alive."

The words spill out of Beatrice now, a torrent of long-buried truths. "Like I said, I had two miscarriages before you. The last one happened when your father pushed me down the stairs when I refused to let him see the fetus pulled from my body. He enjoyed it. He got me pregnant just to see the baby die. He liked to play God."

Bile rises in my throat as the horror of my mother's words sinks in. "Why are you trying to ruin the memory of my father. He would never harm you. He accepted me. He didn't try to change me like you did."

"Your father was a liar. He lied to you. He lied to me. He lied to everybody." Beatrice continues, her voice taking on an almost manic edge. "When he killed himself, I told myself I wouldn't let you be like him. But it was too late. He already had his claws in you, and if it wasn't for me, you would be dead! The sick fucker. The only reason you're alive is because I left him until I gave birth to you."

She goes on, her words growing more frantic. "I realized you were just like your father when you started killing animals and dumping their bodies in the ocean behind our house. He said he was teaching you to drive a boat, but I knew when the neighborhood dogs and cats went missing, he was teaching you how to end life."

"You knew about that?"

"Of course; I knew he was training you, so you could exist like him and not get caught."

"But if Dad was like me, why didn't he tell me?"

"You worshipped the ground your father walked on; he wasn't going to ruin that and have you see him how I saw him, as a monster. So, I came up with a plan. After all the previous attempts to cure you failed, I decided to see if watching live abortions and viewing the tapes of the abortions would work, and it looked like it was curbing your appetite. Then you fell in love with Pamela and didn't want her to have your child. I thought I had found the cure for you. A cure that wouldn't take you through so much pain. It worked for a while and then women came to me crying, saying you forced them to have abortions, that you'd chain them in the basement and watch the procedure. I paid them off and decided it was time to teach you a lesson—a lesson that would cure you of your sickness, no matter the cost."

My mind races, trying to piece together the fragments of this new, terrifying reality. "What do you mean, 'teach me a lesson?'"

"Kyle, have you watched a tape or had the urge to kill since your first trimester?"

I think back and realize that for the first time in my life, I haven't had the urge. "No, I haven't. Now that I think about it, how is this possible?"

Beatrice's next words fall like hammer blows, shattering the last vestiges of my understanding of my life. There is a reason for that Kyle. She leans in close and whispers in my ear, "You were never pregnant. Men can't get pregnant. We used pregnancy to cure you."

The silence that follows is deafening. I stare at my mother, my mouth opening and closing like a fish out of water, unable to form words. The weight of her revelation crashes over me in waves, each one threatening to drag me under.

"But...but the symptoms," I finally stammer. "The tests, Dr. Lawson..."

Beatrice's smile is sad, tinged with a mixture of pity and something else—satisfaction, perhaps? "All part of the plan, my dear. We needed you to believe it, to feel it. To understand, even for a moment, what it's like to have that choice taken away from you."

My mind reels, memories flooding back—the nausea, the weight gain, the tender breasts. Had it all been a lie? An elaborate ruse designed to... what? Punish me? Teach me empathy?

"How?" I whisper, my voice hoarse. "How did you do this?"

Beatrice settles herself on the edge of the bed, smoothing her skirt with an eerily calm gesture.

"The prenatal vitamins you took daily gave you the symptoms of pregnancy and if you missed a day Pamela made sure to put them in your coffee or food. The tapes you watched not only suppressed your appetite to kill but slowly hypnotized you into believing you were intersex. That hypnotic message has been slowly seeping into your subconscious for over twenty years. The human mind is remarkably susceptible to suggestion, especially when it's primed by guilt."

As she speaks, I feel a shift within myself. The grief that consumed me moments ago transmutes into something else—a cold, hard anger that seems to crystallize in my chest.

"You...... you made me believe I'd lost a child," I say, my voice low and dangerous. "You hypnotized me? You let me grieve, let me suffer......" Beatrice meets my gaze unflinchingly. "Yes. Just like you've done to so many others. How does it feel, Kyle? To have that hope, that potential for life, ripped away from you?"

"You're insane," I snarl. "All of you – you, Dr. Lawson, Pamela...you're all fucking insane!"

Beatrice remains seated, seemingly unperturbed by my outburst. "Are we? Or are we simply holding up a mirror to your own insanity, Kyle? To the monster you've become?"

As I stand there, trembling with rage and confusion, a terrible clarity begins to descend upon me. The secrets, the lies, the manipulations—they stretch back further than I had ever imagined, tendrils of deceit woven through the very fabric of my existence.

"What am I?" I whisper, more to myself than to Beatrice. "If everything's been a lie, then what am I really?"

Beatrice rises, reaching out to cup my face in her hands. Her touch is gentle, almost loving, but her eyes are hard as diamonds. "You're my son. You're not intersex," she says softly. "I started setting this plan into motion when you were a child. Those pills you take daily weren't hormones. They were placebos. When you were a child, I told you they were to suppress your urges and to help you with depression and anxiety. When you were supposedly pregnant, I told you they were hormones and that they were suppressing your estrogen, but they were nothing but sugar pills, placebos. I made you wear shirts in the pool to cover your man boobs that I helped develop by feeding you fattening snacks, I allowed your hair to grow and didn't let you cut it so that you would look more like a girl. I paid children to call you fat and girly. I did all this so that you would have memories to draw on when we started to enact our plan. After you drowned that girl in the pool and showed no signs of empathy, I knew I was going to have to go to extreme measure to make you feel. You're your father's son. You're a product of violence and manipulation. But you're also something else, Kyle. You're a chance for redemption. You are no longer a killer."

I jerk away from her touch. The room seems to spin around me, reality blurring at the edges. I fall to my knees. I feel the last pieces of my identity crumbling away. The pregnancy, the loss, the grief—it had all been a fabrication. Beatrice stands over me, her shadow stretching across the floor like a dark omen.

I look up at my mother, at the woman who has both created and destroyed me. In that moment, I realize that the abyss I had always feared isn't some external darkness—it's inside me, a void created by lies and manipulation, by secrets kept and truths revealed.

CHAPTER 42
KYLE

MY BARE FEET slap against the cold linoleum as I stumble forward, one hand clutching my abdomen, the other braced against the wall for support. The world sways around me, a funhouse mirror version of reality that threatens to shatter at any moment.

Kayla!" I scream, my voice hoarse and desperate. "Where's my baby? Somebody help me!"

Nurses and orderlies turn to stare, their faces blurring into a sea of confusion and concern. I ignore them, my eyes wild and searching, focused solely on reaching the nursery at the end of the hall.

Behind me, I hear my mother's voice, calm and measured, explaining to the startled staff. "He's having an episode. We're working with his doctors..."

Her words fade into the background as I finally reach the front of the building. I press my face against what appears to be the nursery window, my breath fogging the glass as I scan the rows of bassinets.

I see her bassinet with her name, but she's not there. "She has to be here," I mutter, my fingers clawing at the glass. "Kayla! Daddy's here!" A firm hand grips my shoulder, and I whirl around to find a security guard towering over me.

"Sir, I need you to calm down," the man says, his voice a mixture of authority and caution. I shake my head violently, backing away until I hit the nursery window.

"You don't understand," I plead. "They're trying to take my baby. My mother... she says I was never pregnant, but I felt her. I carried a baby in my body."

"You were pregnant?" The security guard's expression shifts from concern to confusion, but his grip remains firm. "Sir, there's no record of a baby named Kayla being born here recently. Why don't we go somewhere quiet and talk about this?"

My mind races, fragments of memories flashing before my eyes: the first ultrasound, the feeling of life growing inside me... But with each image comes a whisper of doubt, a shadow of uncertainty that grows longer with each passing second.

"No," I whisper, more to myself than to the guard. "No, it can't be true. I remember..."

But what exactly do I remember? The C-section is a blur of pain and drugs. Did I see the incision, feel the moment Kayla was lifted from my body? Or had I simply been shown a baby, my mind filling in the blanks with what I expected to see?

Beatrice appears at my side, her face a mask of motherly concern. "Kyle, let's go back to your room. We can talk about this, try to make sense of it all."

I turn to her, my eyes brimming with tears and confusion. "Mom," I choke out, "Please tell me it's not true. Tell me Kayla was real." For a moment, something flickers in

Beatrice's eyes—regret? Pity? But it's gone as quickly as it appears, replaced by a steely resolve.

"Oh, Kyle," she sighs, reaching out to cup my face. "I wish I could. But it's time for you to face the truth."

The security guard, sensing the delicacy of the situation, steps back slightly. "Ma'am, does he need psychiatric attention?"

Beatrice shakes her head. "No, thank you. We have a team of doctors working with him. If you could just help me, get him to his room..."

I feel the fight draining out of me, replaced by a bone-deep weariness. I allow myself to be led back down the corridor, Beatrice's arm around my waist, the security guard following close behind.

As we enter my private room, my eyes fall on the empty bassinet in the corner. Just hours ago—or was it days?—I had seen my daughter. I can still see the back of her head, imprinted on my mind.

"Sit down, Kyle," Beatrice says gently, guiding me to the bed. "We need to talk about what's happening."

I sink onto the mattress, my body feeling impossibly heavy. "What's happening is that you're trying to convince me my child never existed."

Beatrice pulls up a chair, sitting so close that her knees nearly touch mine. "Kyle, I know this is difficult to hear, but you need to understand. The pregnancy, the birth... It was all an illusion. A carefully crafted scenario designed to make you experience what you've put others through. Every morning you wake up and keep going through the same routine. You've been here for over a week."

I shake my head, a humorless laugh escaping my lips.

"An illusion? Mom, I felt her kick. I saw her on the ultrasound. How can you explain that?"

Beatrice's voice takes on a clinical tone, as if she were explaining a complex medical procedure. "It's called Seahorse Syndrome. Seahorses are the only species where the male delivers the baby, and that's how we came up with the name." She turns my right-hand palm up, revealing a tattoo of a bloody seahorse. "The blood represents life leaving you, and the seahorse symbolizes you."

"When did I get this?" I ask, bewildered.

"You got it while you were sedated. Seahorse Syndrome is a formula we developed years ago that can induce pregnancy symptoms. You were our first subject. We combined creative storytelling, hypnosis, theatrical staging and paired it with our formula and it created a very convincing illusion of pregnancy and birth."

Beatrice's eyes harden. "You needed to understand, Kyle. The pain, the hope, the loss... all of it. You've spent years playing God, forcing women to terminate pregnancies for your own twisted pleasure. It was time you felt what that's like."

"No," I whisper, shaking my head. "No, that's not... I never forced anyone. They chose..."

"Did they, Kyle?" Beatrice's voice is sharp now, cutting through my denials. "Or did you manipulate them, pressure them, use your charm and your money to make them do what you wanted?"

Beatrice nods, her expression grim. "This was the only way to make you see, to make you feel..."

"Feel what?" I roar, whirling to face her. "The loss of a child that never existed? The grief over a life that was nothing but a lie?"

"Exactly," Beatrice says softly. "Now imagine that

grief, that loss, but knowing the child was real. That's what you've done, Kyle. Over and over again."

"I remember," I whisper, my voice cracking. "How can she not be real?"

"We changed the mirrors in the house so that you looked bigger than you were. We had your clothes taken in so that they barely fit, and we altered the scale so that it showed you an exaggerated weight. I even hung pictures of seahorses to subconsciously anchor the intersex and pregnancy thought into your psyche. I put one in the doctor's office, above my mantel, and we even bought that property on the beach and planted them along your jogging trail. She points to the ruby seahorse pendant around her neck. "I bought this just for you. To help cure you."

Beatrice moves to kneel beside me, her voice gentle but firm. "The mind is a powerful thing, Kyle. Given the right circumstances, the right suggestions, it can create experiences that feel entirely real."

I look up at her, my eyes searching her face for any sign of deceit. "But the physical symptoms... the weight gain, the morning sickness..."

All induced by the Seahorse Syndrome formula," Beatrice explains. "Combined with your belief in the pregnancy, your body responded as if it were real."

A terrible thought strikes me, and I feel my blood run cold. "The other women," I say slowly. "The ones I... convinced to have abortions. Did they know? About this... experiment?"

"This was a secret experiment." I feel a wave of nausea that has nothing to do with phantom pregnancies.

"Oh God," I moan. "What have I done? What have we all done?"

Beatrice reaches out to touch my shoulder, but I flinch away. "We did what we had to do," she says, her voice hard. "To make you understand, to make you stop."

I look at her, really look at her, perhaps for the first time in my life. I see not just my mother, but a woman capable of incredible manipulation and cruelty—all in the name of what she believes is right.

"Who are you?" I whisper.

"Who am I?" Beatrice's smile is sad, tinged with a mixture of love and something darker. "I'm a mother. A mother willing to do anything to save her son."

"Where is Pamela?" I ask.

"She's long gone. I told her once this experiment was done, I would release her. I gave her a nice settlement, and she left." Beatrice throws a stack of papers on the hospital bed. "Those are the divorce papers you handed her a few months ago. I changed some of the language so that she got more money because I felt she deserved it. She helped heal my son."

My mom reaches over and hugs me, and it's the first time I feel genuine affection from her. Although a part of me wants to push her off, another part of me wants—no, needs—to feel her embrace. I return her hug, and for the first time, I feel truly loved.

CHAPTER 43
KYLE

EPILOGUE

Three Months Later

The cemetery sprawls before me, a patchwork of granite and marble stretching as far as the eye can see. A chill wind whispers through the trees, carrying the scent of freshly turned earth and wilting flowers. I stand before a small, unassuming headstone, its polished surface gleaming in the weak fall sunlight.

Kayla Witherspoon
Beloved Daughter
Forever in Our Hearts
5/26/2024 – 5/26/2024

My fingers trace the engraved letters, a lump forming in my throat. The rational part of me knows the truth—Kayla never existed, a phantom child conjured by drugs, hypnosis and manipulation. Yet the ache in my chest, the hollow feeling of loss, feels as real as anything I've ever experienced.

My gaze drifts down to my midsection, the slight paunch and stich scars remaining as a testament to the physical toll of my imaginary pregnancy. Strangely, I feel no revulsion at the softness that has replaced my once-chiseled abs. Pride washes over me. These changes, this perceived imperfection, are a badge of honor—a reminder of the love I felt for a child who never drew breath.

I wonder, now for the first time, how real pregnant women feel after giving birth. *Do they wear their stretch marks and cesarean scars like battle wounds, proud symbols of the life they nurtured and brought into the world?* The thought brings a sad smile to my face. How little I understood, how callously I treated the women in my past.

With reverence, I place a small bouquet of white roses at the base of the headstone. A single tear escapes, tracing a path down my cheek.

"I know you weren't real, Kayla," I whisper, my voice barely audible above the rustling leaves. "But the love I felt for you... that was real. I'll always acknowledge you, always remember you."

As I straighten, preparing to leave, a sound catches my attention. Harsh, guttural sobs echo across the cemetery, filled with a pain so raw it tightens my chest. My eyes scan the rows of graves until I spot the source—a man, perhaps in his early thirties, hunched over a headstone several yards away.

Without conscious thought, I move toward the grieving stranger. As I draw closer, I see the man's body shaking with sobs, his arms wrapped around the cold stone as if trying to embrace the person buried beneath.

"It's going to be okay, man," I say softly, placing a comforting hand on the stranger's shoulder.

The man turns, his face a mask of anguish, and throws himself into my arms. I stagger slightly under the unexpected weight but manage to keep my balance, awkwardly patting his back as he continues to sob.

"I can't believe she's gone," the stranger chokes out between heaving breaths. "I can't believe my little girl is gone."

I feel as if I've been punched in the gut, his words striking a chord so deep it resonates through my entire being.

"What happened to your little girl?" I ask, dreading the answer.

The man pulls back slightly, his red-rimmed eyes darting around the cemetery as if checking for eavesdroppers. When he speaks again, his voice is low, tinged with grief and paranoia.

"No one believes me, but..." He pauses, swallowing hard. "I was pregnant with a baby girl, and when I went to give birth, they told me she died. But they never showed me a body."

The world tilts around me, my mind reeling as the implications of his words sink in. *It can't be possible. Can it?*

The stranger continues, his words tumbling out in a frantic rush.

"Then my wife left me, and now I'm dealing with the death of our daughter all alone. The doctor told me I had this rare disorder called Seahorse Syndrome and that less than one percent of men experience it."

My mouth goes dry, my heart pounding so loudly I'm sure he can hear it. Seahorse Syndrome. The same term my mother used to explain my phantom pregnancy. But she said it was fabricated—a cruel experiment designed to teach me empathy. I thought I was the only subject.

With trembling fingers, I grab his hand and turn over his wrist. I nearly scream when I see that he has the same Seahorse tattoo that I have. We lock eyes and I show him my wrist.

"What the fuck man; did they do this to you too?"

"Hold on, I'm going to get some answers." I reach for my phone, scrolling to my mother's number. I need answers. But as I hit the call button, I'm met with voicemail. In that moment, the full weight of the deception crashes down on me. I haven't been the only one. This isn't an isolated incident, a twisted lesson meant solely for me. This is something much larger, much more insidious.

"How long ago did this happen to you?" I ask, trying to keep my voice steady.

The man wipes his eyes, sniffling.

"About a year ago. Why?"

My mind races, calculating. My own "pregnancy" ended just three months ago. Which means...

"Have you ever heard of a woman named Beatrice Witherspoon?" I ask, dreading the answer. The stranger furrows his brow in confusion.

"No, I don't think so. My doctor was Dr. Lawson. Why? Do you know her?"

I feel as if I'm standing on the edge of a precipice, teetering between the world I thought I knew and a vast deception I can scarcely comprehend. How many other men have been subjected to this experiment? *How long has it been going on? And most chillingly, what is the true purpose?*

"I think," I say slowly, my voice barely above a whisper, "that we've both been part of something much bigger than we realized. And I think it's time we found out exactly what that is."

The stranger's eyes widen, a mixture of hope and fear flickering across his face.

"What do you mean? Do you know something about my daughter?"

I hesitate, weighing the impact of my next words. *To shatter his grief and tell him his child never existed... Is that mercy or cruelty?* But as I open my mouth to respond, my phone buzzes in my pocket. With trembling fingers, I pull it out, half-expecting Pamela's number, but the number is unfamiliar.

For a moment, I hesitate, my thumb hovering over the answer button. Every instinct scream at me to ignore it, to focus on pursuing Dr. Lawson. But something—curiosity, desperation, or perhaps deeper intuition—compels me to accept the call.

"Hello?" I say cautiously, still moving through the rows of graves.

There's a moment of silence on the other end, broken only by the sound of a deep, shaky breath. Then, a voice—familiar yet distorted, as if speaking through a voice changer.

"Kyle Witherspoon," the voice says, each word deliberate and charged with meaning. "If you want to know the truth about Seahorse Syndrome, about your daughter, about everything... meet me at the old Westview Hospital in one hour. Come alone."

The line goes dead before I can respond. I stare at the phone in disbelief, my mind whirling with possibilities. *Who is the mysterious caller? What do they know? And most importantly, can I trust them?*

As I look up, the stranger stares at me, confusion and hope mingling on his tear-stained face.

"What's going on?" he asks. "Who was that on the phone?"

I take a deep breath, weighing my options. I could tell him everything, putting him in danger. I could lie, send him away, and face whatever is coming alone. Or...

"I think," I say slowly, a plan forming in my mind, "that we're about to uncover the truth about what happened to us. To our children. But I need to know—are you ready to face whatever we might find? Because I have a feeling that once we start down this path, there's no turning back."

The stranger's face hardens, a steely resolve replacing the grief that consumed him moments ago.

"If it means finding out what really happened to my daughter, I'm in. Whatever it takes."

I nod, realizing I'll have to tell him that his daughter didn't exist.

"Alright then. We've got one hour to get to Westview Hospital. And something tells me

that what we find there is going to change everything."

As we hurry out of the cemetery, I cast one last glance at Kayla's headstone. The flowers I placed there flutter in the breeze, a reminder of the love I felt for a child who never existed. But now, faced with the possibility of uncovering a truth far vaster and more terrifying than I imagined, I realize my phantom pregnancy might have been just the beginning.

Whatever awaits us at Westview Hospital, whatever dark secrets lie behind Seahorse Syndrome and the manipulation of men's bodies and minds, I'm determined to uncover it all. For Kayla. For the stranger's phantom daughter. And for every other victim of this twisted experiment.

As we reach the car, the sun dips below the horizon. I can't shake the feeling that we're being watched, that unseen eyes are following our every move. But there's no turning back now.

The game is afoot, and the stakes are higher than I ever imagined.

The End

Go to the next page to get a SNEAK PEAK into Book 2

BOOK 2: SNEAK PEAK

The Husband's Revenge

The cruel metal restraints bite deeper into my raw, chafed wrists with every feeble attempt to break free. A brutal reminder that I'm rendered powerless, a prisoner in the terrifying depths of this godforsaken basement.

My eyes keep darting back to the woman 'whose loving embrace I would have once given anything to feel again. But now, her face is contorted into a cold, remorseless mask that bores into me with an almost sadistic triumph. This twisted shell is all that remains of the sweet, caring soul I was certain I knew better than myself.

A thick droplet of blood traces a burning path down the side of my throbbing head before splattering onto the filthy concrete. The metallic stench invades my nostrils. As more drops follow in a slow but steady stream, the pounding behind my eyes intensifies viciously.

The harsh realities of our dire situation distort and elongate like a fun-house mirror as the corners of my vision gradually consume the hazy image of this nightmare. The coppery taste of my own blood coats my mouth, and panic claws at my insides with growing urgency.

I know that if I allow the vertigo to drag me under completely, we'll be at her cruel mercy. With my last ounce of waning strength, I suck in one final, ragged breath and let out a guttural, primordial scream that bounces off the damp walls.

"Help! Somebody, please!" My voice cracks and trails off as I fight for consciousness with every fiber of my being. I feel a needle piercing the side of my neck. This can't be how it ends—not here, not like this. Not without one last chance to understand how my safe harbor and my perfect life were demolished by a violent tornado whose wrath I can no longer contain.

"Calm down my child. Everything is going to be okay, Donna," Beatrice says.

Order The: **The Husband's Revenge**

SIGN UP TO MY EMAIL LIST

SIGN up to my email list to get free stories and information on upcoming releases.

My Website

PLEASE LEAVE A REVIEW OR RATING

Thank you for taking the time to read this story. I am forever grateful for you.

If you loved the story, please leave a review or rating. I enjoy reading and hearing what readers think and reviews help authors in more ways than you can imagine!

They help us sell more books and give great feedback to readers!

Thank you to all the Beta Readers: Jeanetta, Jessica, Katrina and Rebecca and all the ARC Readers. This story would not have been as good without you!

Follow me on Facebook@ Franklin Christopher's Fans

Follow me on TikTok @ franklinchristopher_

ALSO BY FRANKLIN CHRISTOPHER

Psychological Thrillers

The Husband's Revenge

The Reflection

The Perfect Vow

Made in United States
Orlando, FL
29 March 2025

59949243R00176